DATE DUE

BB		

GAYLORD   #3523PI   Printed in USA

A TIME TO MEND

This Large Print Book carries the
Seal of Approval of N.A.V.H.

A Time to Mend

Angela Hunt

THORNDIKE PRESS

An imprint of Thomson Gale, a part of The Thomson Corporation

THOMSON
━━★━━ ™
GALE

Detroit • New York • San Francisco • New Haven, Conn. • Waterville, Maine • London

THOMSON
★ TM
GALE

LIBRARY OF CONGRESS CATALOGING-IN-PUBLICATION DATA

Hunt, Angela Elwell, 1957–
[Gentle touch]
A time to mend / Angela Hunt.
p. cm. — (Thorndike Press large print romance)
"Refreshed version of Gentle Touch, newly revised by author."
ISBN 0-7862-9160-5 (hardcover : alk. paper) 1. Breast — Cancer — Patients — Fiction. 2. Nurses — Fiction. 3. Physicians — Fiction. 4. Winter Haven (Fla.) — Fiction. 5. Large type books. I. Title.
PS3558.U46747G46 2006b
813'.54—dc22   2006026746

U.S. Hardcover:
ISBN 13: 978-0-7862-9160-1
ISBN 10: 0-7862-9160-5

Published in 2006 by arrangement with Harlequin Books S.A.

Printed in the United States of America on permanent paper
10 9 8 7 6 5 4 3 2 1

In memory of Jean Hunt,
whose bright spirit lives on in her son.

When we walk to the edge of all the
light we have
and step out into the darkness of the
unknown,
we must believe there will be something
solid to stand on
or that we will be taught how to fly . . .

Author Unknown

CHAPTER ONE

A dazzling white blur of sun stood fixed on the easternhorizon, bathing the enormous Chambers-Wyatt Hospital complex in a sterile light. Jacquelyn Wilkes stepped from her car, adjusted her spotless uniform, then drew a deep, contented breath. Before her stood the concrete and glass cancer clinic, the hospital's facility for outpatient therapy. Her home away from home. The spot she'd been longing for through two eternal weeks of what was supposed to be a solitary and restful vacation on a Bahamas beach.

"No problem, mon, I'm happy to change gears," she whispered. "Back to work. Let the rich and famous keep the beaches, I'll take my job any day." She lifted her chin, easily slipping back into the disciplined frame of mind through which she had captured the title of "Nurse of the Year" at the hospital's last two awards banquets. At twenty-seven, she had been the youngest nurse ever to win that coveted honor, and she intended to keep it.

Gaynel Morrow, the receptionist, flashed a warm smile as Jacquelyn entered the building. "Ah, look who's back! But where's your tan?"

"Hiding beneath a layer of sunblock, where it belongs." Jacquelyn paused to sign in. "Skin cancer, remember?"

Gaynel rolled her eyes. "You're no fun at all, Jackie. You're the only person I know who could go to the beach for two weeks and come back without a tan — or a man."

"Red hair and sun don't mix." Jacquelyn snapped the pen to the desk. "And I wasn't looking for romance, I'm perfectly happy with Craig. I wanted to rest!"

In truth, she'd wanted rest about as much as a dog wants fleas, but what else could you do on a solitary vacation?

She sighed in feigned despair as she looked around the reception area. The same old magazines littered the tables, the same morning talk shows droned from the television in the corner. "I see nothing around here has changed."

"That's what you think." Gaynel leaned forward and lowered her voice. "There's a new doctor in your office. Dr. Kastner finally found someone to replace Dr. Winston."

"Another one of his old medical school buddies?"

"Hardly." Gaynel let out a low, throaty laugh. "Jonah Martin is anything but old. He's —" She grinned. "Well, you'll have to see him for yourself."

Jacquelyn felt a disturbing quake in her serenity. She was glad to be back, but she wasn't sure she wanted to deal with a new doctor. The recently retired Dr. Winston had worked at the clinic for years, and she had grown so used to him she could practically read his mind. But a new doctor would have his own way of doing things, and she'd have to learn to deal with an entirely different set of idiosyncrasies. He might even be one of those bossy types that ordered nurses about with impunity and flung blame on everyone from interns to orderlies when something went wrong. . . .

Jacquelyn leaned against Gaynel's desk. "What do you know about this new guy?"

"I have his bio right here." The receptionist pulled a brochure from the papers scattered over her desk. "Dr. Jonah Martin graduated from University of Virginia Medical School with honors seven years ago. He served at UVA Hospital, then transferred to

Tidewater General, then to Roanoke Community, followed by the Thomas Morris Cancer Institute in Seattle. Last year he worked at Jackson Memorial in Tallahassee." She dropped the brochure and lifted an eyebrow. "Now he's here."

"So many places." Jacquelyn frowned. "Don't you think that's strange? So many hospitals in how long — seven years? I can't imagine a doctor moving his family around so much."

"He's not married." Amusement twinkled in the receptionist's eyes. "And his résumé is impressive — Dr. Kastner says the guy just keeps moving up to bigger and better things. He says we're lucky Dr. Martin is willing to come here."

Jacquelyn drummed her fingers on the desk, bracing herself for the day ahead. Not only was she going to have to shift her mental focus from vacation to work, she was also going to have to shift from Dr. Winston mode to Dr. Martin mode, whatever *that* was. . . .

"Do you like him?" Jacquelyn's brows lifted at the question.

"What's not to like?" The phone buzzed on Gaynel's desk, so the receptionist gave Jacquelyn a parting wave as she answered the call. Jacquelyn's mind bulged with

10

unasked questions as she crossed the reception area. Gaynel liked the new doctor, and that was a good sign. But receptionists and doctors didn't work together as closely as doctors and nurses.

A breath of cool morning air blew past her as the wide glass entry doors slid open. Jacquelyn turned and flashed a quick smile at Mrs. Johnson, who led her five-year-old daughter, Megan, by the hand. Megan had gone completely bald from the effects of her treatment, but she gazed up at Jacquelyn with a bright smile and waved enthusiastically.

Jacquelyn gave a quick wave in response, then turned and quickened her pace, sighing in relief when she entered the hallway that led to the nurses' station. She'd make sure Lauren or Stacy worked with little Megan this morning. The darling kid had been in treatment for two years and the prognosis was not good.

Jacquelyn moved toward the chattering voices at the end of the hall. She could claim to be so exhausted from all the fun she'd had on vacation that she couldn't handle a squirming child as her first patient of the week. . . .

"Dr. Martin, extension 210. Dr. Martin,

please pick up."

An unusual thread of exasperation echoed in the receptionist's voice, Jacquelyn noticed as she checked her watch and pressed her fingertips to her patient's pulse. "Pick up, Mystery Doctor, wherever you are," she murmured. She paused to look up and smile at the woman seated in the chair beside her. "You'll have to excuse my little wisecracks, Mrs. Baldovino," she said, loosening the blood pressure cuff around her patient's upper arm. "But Dr. Martin is new around here, and I'm beginning to think he's the invisible man. I haven't even seen him yet, but that's the third time I've heard him paged this morning."

"I like him," the woman answered, her eyes darting nervously to the chart where Jacquelyn recorded the sphygmomanometer's reading. Thin wisps of dark hair escaped from under the hat she wore and framed her pale face. "I saw him last week, and he's the first doctor I've met who makes me feel like I'm not taking up too much of his time. How is it today — the blood pressure, I mean?"

"Pretty good." Jacquelyn folded the cuff. "But a little on the low side. Of course that could be a reflection of the weight you've been losing."

Mrs. Baldovino lifted her hands in apology. "It's the chemo. I can't eat after my visits here. I've tried everything from soup to crackers, but nothing will stay down." She released a nervous little laugh. "I guess it's to be expected, but sometimes I wonder if starvation will kill me before the cancer does —"

"We won't let you starve, Mrs. Baldovino, I promise." Jacquelyn turned away and studied the patient's chart. "I see that you were given Adriamycin and Cytoxan on your last visit. Well, the antinausea medicines I'll give you today should help. Emend and Kytril usually do the trick, and the doctor can prescribe a form of Compazine for you to take at home."

The woman lifted one shoulder in a helpless shrug. "I know the drugs should help, but they don't."

"If you're feeling sick, you should try not eating or drinking anything four to six hours before your chemo treatment. And when you eat, think of yourself as a grazing cow, not a hog at the trough." Jacquelyn gave her patient a stern smile and took a deep breath for what felt like her ten thousandth speech about how to avoid nausea. She'd pestered her supervising nurse, Lauren Oakes, to put this and other standard lectures on videotape, but Lauren had insisted that personal instruction was more important than saving her nurses time and effort.

Jacquelyn pitched her voice to the tone she would use with a stubborn child. "Eat lightly, take in five or six small snacks a day instead of three traditional large meals. And if you experience uncontrolled nausea, vomiting, or diarrhea, you should pick up the phone immediately and call us. Ask for me, Lauren or Stacy, not the doctor. If you let the condition continue all day, you will become dehydrated and we'll have to put you in the hospital. And I don't think you want that, do you?"

Blushing, the woman shook her head.

"I thought not. Call us right away, and we'll be able to get an antiemetic to help control your nausea." She smiled to cover her annoyance. "So if you're feeling sick, what will you do?"

"I'll call you, Nurse Jacquelyn." Mrs. Baldovino opened her mouth as if she would say something else, but Jacquelyn stood and snapped the chart shut. Unlike Lauren and Stacy, she never encouraged her patients to talk about anything but routine matters. Cancer patients tended to want assurances and answers and Jacquelyn had none to give. She was a medical professional, not a counselor or preacher. How many times had that been hammered into her head during nursing school? She could still hear the echo of her professor's mantra: *Let a patient into your heart, and you won't last ten days in oncology.*

"Let's get you ready for Dr. Martin. I'm sure he'll want to hear about this nausea." Jacquelyn lifted her hand and gestured toward the examination room. "If the invisible doctor materializes, that is."

Without waiting for her patient, she moved down the hall to the freshly prepped exam room. She slid the woman's chart into the holder on the door and smiled at the efficient thunking sound the file made. Mrs. Baldovino was now Dr. Martin's concern.

"Will he be long, do you think?" Mrs. Baldovino asked, one hand lightly gliding over the wallpaper as she moved with glacial slowness down the hall. "I'm feeling a bit nauseous now. I don't know why, but I don't know how long I can wait without having to —"

"I'll get you a basin." Leaving her patient, Jacquelyn hurried to the supply closet. She flung the door open, then blinked in surprise.

Stacy Derry, another nurse, stood with her back against the shelves, a wad of tissues in her hand. Her nose was red, her face blotchy, and a hint of tears still glistened in the wells of her dark eyes.

"Stacy! Are you all right?"

The nurse nodded, her dark curls bobbing. "I'll be okay." She dabbed at her eyes. "It's just that Hospice called a few minutes ago. Alicia Hubbard passed away last night. Her husband wanted us to know about the funeral."

"Oh." Jacquelyn pressed her lips together in a sign of respect. "Wasn't she one of Dr. Kastner's patients?"

"Yes." Stacy gave Jacquelyn a teary smile. "She was such a sweet lady. Always smiling, she never once complained. I know she was in pain, especially at the end, yet she never said a harsh word to anybody."

As Stacy broke into fresh tears, Jacquelyn folded her arms and took a deep breath. She was used to the sight of tears; she'd cried more than her share of them when her own mother died from complications stemming from breast cancer. At sixteen, Jacquelyn had been a lot like Stacy — frightened, unsure and heartbroken. But broken hearts could mend . . . if you learned how to bury the pain.

"Listen," Jacquelyn spoke with calm detachment, "I know it hurts to lose someone. But you've got to get past the pain. Trust me, I know. I lost my mother and then became an oncology nurse because I want to help people get better. And as a nurse, I've learned to detach myself from the hurt."

The tissues muffled Stacy's words. "That sounds impossible."

"No, it's not." Jacquelyn placed her hand on Stacy's arm. "You can't help your patients if you allow yourself to be paralyzed by sorrow or worry. They need someone who can be objective, who can stay cool in a crisis. They aren't asking for our pity. If you go out there looking like this, you'll only upset the patients who are still fighting to survive. If you're going to be a good nurse, a professional nurse, you've got to stop blubbering every time something goes wrong."

Do whatever you have to, but don't let the pain into your heart.

A cloud of guilt crossed Stacy's face. "I suppose you're right."

"Of course I am." Jacquelyn sighed. She'd never get that emesis basin for Mrs. Baldovino if Stacy didn't surrender the supply closet. "Listen, I know you haven't been here as long as I have —" she reached past Stacy for the stack of aluminum basins on the shelf "— but this is an oncology practice, and many of our patients die. Some of them live for years after treatment, some for months, but death is a part of life. We've all got to die sometime, and some of our patients die sooner than the others. But you can't let it get to you."

There. She'd just given Stacy the standard speech on how to successfully work in an oncology practice. It was good, practical advice, if Stacy could make it work.

"I can't help it," Stacy whispered. She wiped her nose again. "I don't think I'll ever be able to stop missing people like Mrs. Hubbard. She wasn't just a patient, she was a friend. She brought me a pot of home-made chicken soup last winter when she heard I was out with the flu. She said her children always liked chicken soup when they were sick —"

"That's where you made your mistake," Jacquelyn interrupted, tucking the basin under her arm. "Rule number one — don't accept gifts from patients, don't tell them about your love life, and never, *ever* go to their homes. They can call rent-a-nurse if they need home care. Don't get tangled up in their personal lives and don't let them into yours. Don't go to funerals. If you were close to a patient, you can send a card to the family. Trust me, I've been here five years, and I know what I'm talking about."

Leaving Stacy in the closet, she tossed a final bit of advice over her shoulder as she moved away. "Don't grieve for the ones we lose, Stacy, celebrate the ones we manage to save — if even for a little while."

"Concetta Baldovino, if you keep losing weight, I'm going to have to submit your picture to the Ford Modeling Agency."

Jacquelyn paused outside the open door of the examination room, the emesis basin in her hand. The tall stranger inside the exam room had to be Jonah Martin, but this man looked like no doctor Jacquelyn had ever seen. He was *exquisite* — no other word for him. Muscles rippled under the tailored denim shirt he wore, and the arm under his short sleeve was bare and silky with golden hairs. His hands, beautiful, long-fingered and strong, held the patient's chart with nonchalant grace.

Half-aware that her pulse and breathing had quickened, she stood like a deer caught in a car's headlights when he looked up.

For a moment he studied her intently, then his square jaw tensed visibly. "Nurse Wilkes, I presume?" he said, the blue of his eyes washing over her like a cold wave. "Does it always take ten minutes to retrieve a basin from the supply closet? Mrs. Baldovino was in need of your attention."

Momentarily speechless in surprise, Jacquelyn could only gape at him. She hadn't been gone ten minutes; she had left her patient alone for three minutes at the most. And who was *he,* the invisible man, to judge *her?*

"I — I'm sorry, Doctor," she stammered, the words tripping over her unwilling tongue. She moved into the room and thrust the basin forward onto the table next to Mrs. Baldovino, then moved out of the range of those blue eyes.

The clear-cut lines of his profile softened as he turned again to his patient. "Now, about those photos for the Ford Agency —"

His ridiculous banter brought a smile to his weary patient's face. "I don't think so, Doctor." Mrs. Baldovino shook her head. "My clothes are about to fall off me. And my husband says he's not going to buy me a new wardrobe because as soon as I go into remission I'll start eating again." For an instant, wistfulness stole into her expression. "I think Ernesto prefers me with a little padding on these old bones."

"I'm sure you grow more beautiful to him with each passing day." Dr. Martin leaned back in the rolling chair and slid his hands

20

into the pockets of his khaki trousers. "In fact," he said, the warmth of his smile echoing in his voice, "as soon as you've completed this round of chemo, I'll treat you and your hubby to a lasagna dinner. You name the place and time."

"Ah, Dr. Martin." Mrs. Baldovino's dark eyes gleamed with wicked humor. "You don't know what you are saying. We Italians are very picky about our pasta."

"Of course you are," Dr. Martin answered, leaning forward to pick up her chart. "Why do you think I'm asking *you* to name the place?"

Mrs. Baldovino's smile deepened into laughter.

What happened here? Jacquelyn stared at the back of Dr. Martin's head. A moment ago she had been subjected to a verbal scalding because this patient was supposedly about to vomit, but now the woman was talking about pasta and planning a dinner. . . .

"Excuse me." Jacquelyn stepped forward, crossed her arms and glanced pointedly at the emesis basin on the exam table. "I thought you were feeling nauseous, Mrs. B."

"I was." The woman's smile brightened as she turned to her doctor. "But this man, he makes me laugh."

"Ah, Concetta, now you are going to get me into trouble." Dr. Martin flipped open Mrs. Baldovino's chart. "According to Nurse Wilkes's notes, you've decided to forego a mastectomy so I can give your husband a tummy tuck."

The woman threw back her head and let out a great peal of laughter. "Ah, Doctor Martin, you are naughty! But you are right, my Ernesto could use more than a few tucks!"

Jacquelyn turned toward the row of cabinets along the wall and rolled her eyes. So much for polished and proficient . . .

She turned to him with a let's-be-professional look on her face and flinched slightly when his powerful gaze met hers.

Dr. Martin leaned toward his patient and lightly slapped his hand on his knee. "I know how to really spice up this dinner we're planning," he said, his lowered voice a rough stage whisper. "For entertainment, let's invite Nurse Wilkes. I have the feeling she's a regular barrel of laughs."

Jacquelyn pursed her lips and stared at the ceiling, her embarrassment yielding quickly to raw fury.

"Oh, I don't know if that is a good idea," she heard Mrs. Baldovino answer. "My husband would be happy to have such a pretty young woman along, but since I am not as attractive as I used to be —"

"Ernesto won't even look in her direction," Dr. Martin answered, making a note in the patient's file. "He will be too busy gazing at you, Concetta."

And what am I — dog meat? The prideful thought skittered like a wild rabbit through Jacquelyn's brain. She glared at him, then jerked in alarm when the doctor lifted his gaze and frankly assessed her.

"Oh, my." A mocking light gleamed in his eye. "I'm afraid I've offended Nurse Wilkes and we've only just met. I wouldn't want us to get started on the wrong foot."

"The wrong foot?" Jacquelyn sputtered, bristling with indignation. In an instant she forgot everything she'd ever heard about airing her grievances in front of a patient, about professional manners, about the respect a nurse should show to a doctor. He was new; he hadn't yet earned her respect. He didn't deserve it.

Rancor sharpened her voice. "I'd call sexual harassment the wrong way to start a working relationship." She looked pointedly at Mrs. Baldovino, searching for an ally. "Wouldn't you agree, Mrs. B.?"

"Oh, my." If possible, the woman grew a

shade paler. "Nurse Jacquelyn, the doctor was only joking."

Jonah Martin's jaw clenched as he rejected the patient's softly spoken defense. "Without a doubt, my joke was in bad taste." Like a Boy Scout taking an oath, he lifted his right hand and stared into Jacquelyn's eyes with solemn sincerity. "On my word of honor, Nurse Wilkes, I hereby promise that I did in no case intend to demean you or suggest that your participation in an evening of camaraderie and lasagna would be necessary for you to continue your employment. I hope that my jest did in no way cause you discomfort, humiliation or mental distress."

The biting tone in his voice set Jacquelyn's teeth on edge — was he teasing or just being cynical? Either way, she didn't appreciate his approach to his patients or his co-workers.

She lifted her chin and met his icy gaze straight on. "Doctor," she said, ignoring Mrs. Baldovino's stricken expression, "if you will approve this patient's blood tests, I'm ready to take her to the chemo room. We're behind schedule, and other patients are waiting to see you." Though why, she couldn't imagine.

"Of course." The infuriating man smiled again at his patient, whose nausea had apparently fled with the handsome doctor's approach. "Mrs. Baldovino, I'm afraid we must get down to business. But my offer for that dinner still stands."

"I'll hold you to it, Doctor," the woman answered, her thin lips twitching with amusement as she took the doctor's extended hand and slid from the examination table. "Lasagna it will be. But I'd rather have the tummy tuck for Ernesto."

"That's plastic surgery and not my field, I'm sorry to say," Dr. Martin answered, his voice pleasant as he stepped back to let Jacquelyn follow Mrs. Baldovino from the room. As Jacquelyn passed, she thought she detected a flicker in his intense eyes, but then he lowered his gaze to the patient's chart and offhandedly remarked, "And it's about time you returned from vacation, Nurse Wilkes. I must admit, I was anxious to observe the fabled 'Nurse of the Year' in action." When he looked at her again, the mocking light was back in his eyes. "And now that I have, my life is complete."

No honest sentiment in *that* acknowledgment.

"Good," Jacquelyn countered, her mouth tight with mutiny. "Now you can die a happy man." Without a backward glance, she lifted her chin and followed her patient to the chemo room.

CHAPTER TWO

"So what did you think of him, Jackie?" Stacy applied just enough lipstick to emphasize her perfect mouth, then studied her reflection in the mirror of the ladies' room.

"Honestly?" Jacquelyn ripped a paper towel from the dispenser on the wall, then dramatically scrunched it between her hands. "That's what I wanted to do after my first meeting with him today. I think I really hate him."

"You do?" Stacy lifted a brow. "I'll admit he's no Doctor Delight, but he's been very professional with me." She pouted prettily in the mirror. "*Too* professional, in fact. It's a shame that someone so good-looking has to be so . . . distant. I've been using every fail-proof approach in my little black book, and I can't even get a spark of interest from him."

"Maybe he's too busy for a social life."

"He's only been here two weeks, how busy

could he be? I think he's got a girlfriend somewhere else. Dr. Kastner said he comes from Virginia —"

"I've seen his history. He comes from about everywhere." Jacquelyn cleared her throat, not wanting to appear too interested, but dying to know more. "Strange, isn't it, that he's moved around so much? Has Dr. Kastner said anything about this guy's experience?"

"Not really." Stacy lowered her voice and turned to face Jacquelyn. "But now that you mention it, I have noticed something strange about him. Lauren tried to draw him into our conversation the other day at lunch, and when she mentioned the names of people she knows at the University of Virginia Hospital, he got real quiet and changed the subject. And then Dr. Kastner was asking him about someone in Seattle, and again, he changed the subject. Not too subtly, either."

"At least we know he didn't amputate the wrong leg or something." Jacquelyn folded her arms as she leaned against the sink. "He's not a surgeon. But some strange things have happened in hospitals."

"Dr. Kastner wouldn't have recommended him if he weren't a good doctor," Stacy pointed out. "You know that. So if there is some deep and dark secret in his past, you can be sure it has nothing to do with medicine."

"I hope not." Jacquelyn threw the wadded up paper towel into the trash bin and studied her reflection in the mirror. The receptionist was right, not a single trace of her vacation lingered on her face. Not a freckle or even the flush of sunburn to indicate she'd spent two weeks moping on a Bahamas beach . . .

"So, what about tonight?" Stacy pulled on a stray strand of hair. "Are you coming with me? There are bound to be half a dozen doctors at this party, all available, all up-and-coming and all desperate for a little relaxation and companionship."

"Thanks, but I'm not looking and I'm tired." Jacquelyn lathered her hands carefully, then immersed them into a steady stream of warm water. Nursing school had brought her a healthy appreciation for the secret life of viruses and germs, and thorough hand washing had become somewhat of a ritual for her.

"I'm pretty sure Dr. Jonah Martin *won't* be there," Stacy added helpfully.

"Well, that's something." Jacquelyn lifted her hands out of the basin so that the water dripped down toward her elbows as she moved to the paper-towel dispenser. "But I didn't bring a change of clothes, and I'm not going to a party in my uniform." Stacy had already changed from her white pants and teal smock into a short, beaded cocktail dress. She looked every inch a sizzling girl of summer, and not a whit like a nurse.

"You'll be sorry," Stacy answered in a singsong voice. "Have you met Dr. Fenton, the new guy in the surgical unit? He was asking about you the other day."

"Dr. Who?"

"See, you really do want to come! Dr. Fenton is the tall Adonis with the killer smile. Last week he stopped Lauren in the cafeteria and asked who the gorgeous red-haired oncology nurse was."

"Maybe he wanted to report me for taking too many catsup packets in the lunch line."

"Nope. He told Lauren he saw you observing one of Dr. Wilder's mastectomies. Said he was impressed with your commitment to knowledge, or something like that."

Jacquelyn snorted softly. "Yeah, right. They're all looking for a woman who's *committed* to them. If he wanted a good nurse, he wouldn't care what I looked like, but he's looking for a trophy wife just like the others. A little missus to sit in his elegant home and host his cocktail parties."

"What's wrong with that?" Stacy flashed her bright smile in the mirror. "I'd be thrilled to stay home and organize a doctor's social life. Lunching with the ladies at the country club beats the hospital cafeteria any day." She paused once again to check her reflection in the mirror, then picked up the shopping bag into which she'd tossed her uniform. "After that call about Alicia Hubbard, I need a little cheering up. An evening of inane flirtation and senseless conversation suits me just fine. So are you coming or not?"

"Have fun without me." Jacquelyn tossed the wet paper towels in the trash bin and leaned toward the mirror, pointing at nonexistent bags under her eyes. "See how tired I am? Dr. Blue Eyes kept slowing me down all day."

Stacy grinned. "I didn't think you'd notice what color his eyes were."

"I didn't — I mean, I don't care what color they are." Jacquelyn studied her mussed hair and abruptly pulled the hairpins out of what had once been a neat chignon. "He's all wrong, and he's too familiar with the patients. He's like Baked Alaska — warm and crumbly on the outside, but cold as ice on the inside. With me he was cool and sarcastic, but he was practically flirting with the patients."

"Jealous?" Stacy dimpled.

"Of course not. I just think he's unprofessional and flippant."

"But the patients think he's cute and completely charming." A thoughtful smile curved Stacy's mouth. "I'll admit he's not exactly fun to work with, but patients seem to like him better than Dr. Winston. They often said he was too impatient."

"What do patients know?" Jacquelyn shrugged, then fluffed her hair around her shoulders. "The best doctors have learned to keep a professional distance and stick to a schedule."

"It all depends upon how you define 'best.' " A devilish look filled Stacy's eyes. "Well, you may not have noticed much about Dr. Martin, but he certainly noticed *you.*"

Jacquelyn froze, halted by the teasing tone of Stacy's voice. "He did? How?"

Stacy's brows lifted in accusation. "He asked why you brought Mrs. Baldovino in this morning when little Megan Johnson was the next appointment. He asked me if you had something against kids."

Jacquelyn glared at Stacy's reflection in the mirror. "I hope you set him straight. I like kids, and Megan's one of my favorite patients!"

"That's what I told him." An indulgent glint appeared in Stacy's eyes. "And I told him the truth — you haven't the heart for working with the younger patients when things begin to go downhill. I told him that though you're one of the best nurses in the hospital, that tough act of yours is just that — an act. You carry it off okay around adults, but around kids and animals you melt like a marshmallow on the grill."

"Stacy —" Jacquelyn's lips thinned with anger "— you don't know what you're talking about."

"Don't forget, you dragged me off and made me go see the *Lion King* with you. You were bawling like a baby in the first five minutes of the movie."

"It was the song. Music moves me."

"Yeah, right." Stacy smiled and shook her head. " 'The Circle of Life,' remember? You couldn't take it. Face it, Jacquelyn, you may have the patients fooled, but you can't fool me and Lauren. We know you too well."

"You didn't have to say anything to Dr. Frigidaire. I hope you didn't tell him that I cry in kids' movies —"

"Maybe I did and maybe I didn't." Stacy grinned and moved toward the door. "Well,

I'll miss you at the party. And since you don't want Dr. Fenton, I'll consider him fair game."

"Have at him," Jacquelyn answered, turning to follow her. "I'm going home where my very considerate, always steady Craig has promised to meet me for dinner."

"Craig Bishop?" Stacy made a face as she pulled the heavy restroom door open. "I thought you two broke up."

"No." Jacquelyn caught the door. "After six months, we're as steady as ever — or as steady as a couple can be when one of them is the world's most ambitious entrepreneur. Craig's the one who put the word 'rising' in 'enterprising.' "

"Yeah, he's a regular Mr. Wall Street," Stacy quipped, leading the way out of the ladies' room. "And about as dull as a dog biscuit."

"Hey!" Jacquelyn lifted a brow. "Don't knock dog biscuits — they definitely have a place in the scheme of things." She smiled, thinking of Bailey, her year-old mastiff pup.

"Oh, yeah, I forgot about your drool hound." Stacy's mouth twisted in a wry smile. "Honestly, Jackie, if you spent as much time and attention on men as you do that mutt —"

"My mastiff is no mutt," Jacquelyn answered, waving goodbye to Gaynel at the reception desk. "And he drools only a little more than a salivating young doctor. So good night, Stacy. Have fun keeping the wolves at bay."

A warm wind whipped through Jacquelyn's hair as she zigzagged through the parking lot toward her car. The wide highway outside the hospital hummed with six o'clock traffic, causing her to mutter, "Please, Craig, for once in your life, leave work on time!"

Craig Bishop was extremely devoted to his custom car business and, despite herself, Jacquelyn had to smile at the memory of Stacy's dog biscuit remark. Craig *was* a bit like a lovable, cuddly golden retriever. Solid, strong and responsible. Good husband material.

A blur of movement caught her eye and she looked up to see Dr. Jonah Martin standing next to a red Mustang convertible parked near her own car. With one hand he carried a battered briefcase, with the other he dug uselessly in his pocket for his car keys. Jacquelyn felt her frown deepen. She should have known Dr. Baked Alaska would drive a *modest* sports car — it fit the casual, nice-guy image he tried to project for his patients.

She wanted to ignore him, but if she walked by without speaking he'd realize she'd deliberately been rude — and would probably say something about it tomorrow. "Having trouble?" she called, reluctantly pausing as she passed. "Did you lose your keys?"

"No," he answered, looking over at her. Like Stacy, he'd changed clothes, too. His gold hair moved freely now in the wind, blowing over the collar of a casual knit shirt. In baggy pants and loafers, he looked more like a *GQ* model than a doctor. He was probably trying to look like a friendly, easygoing kind of guy for some party at the country club.

Nice try, Dr. Martin. But it won't work.

"I know they're here somewhere." His gaze dropped quickly from her eyes to the pavement at his feet. "Unless I've grown a hole in my pocket. Ah — there."

With a flourish he produced his keys and held them up for her to see. She nodded and began to move away. "Wait a moment, Nurse Wilkes," he said, unlocking the car door. "I'd like a word with you." His words sent alarm bells ringing within her. Was this about Megan? Mrs. Baldovino? Against her

36

will, she stopped while he opened the door, tossed his briefcase into the backseat, then came around the car to stand beside her.

Instinctively, she turned to face him head-on, ready for whatever attack he might launch. This could not be good. In five years of nursing she had learned that doctors did not request "a word" unless they had a complaint.

Great job, Jacquelyn. First day back at work and the new guy already despises you.

"Yes, Doctor?" She folded her arms and tried to steady her voice. "Have I done something that doesn't meet with your approval?"

He stepped closer, thrust his hands in his pockets, and for an instant a thoughtful smile ruffled his mouth. "That's funny. I was about to ask you the same thing."

His nearness was so *male,* so bracing, that for a moment her mind refused to function. She could only stare blankly at him, struggling with the sense of confusion his presence elicited. The other doctors never affected her like this — and neither did Craig. Why should this man?

He didn't seem to notice that bewilderment had stolen her voice. "You see, Nurse Jacquelyn," he went on, his eyes raking boldly over her, "though men are decidedly less intuitive and sometimes blind to the others around them, in the few hours of our acquaintance I have sensed that you harbor a profound dislike for me. And since we really have no choice but to continue working together, I need to know if this dislike will impede our working relationship. If you don't like me personally, well, I suppose we can rise above our personality differences and concentrate on the work ahead. But if you have a problem with my professional conduct, my evaluations, or my practice, perhaps we should make arrangements for you to work solely with Dr. Kastner's patients."

All traces of amusement faded from his blue eyes as he regarded her. Jacquelyn had been ready to protest whatever he said, but his words were so unexpected she snapped her mouth shut, stunned by his insight and bluntness. He had just voiced her exact complaint about *him.*

She took a half step back, giving herself a stern mental shake. His complaint, if she could call it that, had nothing to do with her conduct, her evaluations, or her work. For an instant, relief flooded her heart, then her smoldering resentment flared. Why did he care what she thought of him? If this was just a ploy to help him appear generous and understanding, some trick to win friends and influence patients . . .

"If you've gathered the impression that I don't like you, I must apologize," she answered, calling on reserves of grace and tact she didn't know she possessed. "I'm sure that you're a wonderful doctor. The patients seem to adore you, and the other nurses respect your judgment. Dr. Kastner seems to think you're the best oncologist in the country."

"But not you." His twisted smile sent her pulse racing.

"I don't share your sense of humor, Doctor. Mrs. Baldovino was very ill this afternoon, yet you joked with her, making light of her condition."

His expression stilled and grew serious. "I assure you, I am never more serious than when I am with a patient. I don't make jokes about cancer. What I did, if you had cared to see, was lift the cloud of gloom that surrounded that woman. She was worried sick that her husband no longer found her attractive. And she may have to undergo a mastectomy if this protocol fails to achieve remission —"

"We have a video to cover the self-esteem issue. We have videos to cover everything from hair loss to mastectomy scars. We'd have even more videos if I had my way, because it is inefficient for us to give the same speech twenty times a day —"

"A video." Temper flared in his eyes. "I'm afraid a video would not help Mrs. Baldovino. She needed assurance — calm, competent, *masculine* assurance —"

"Which is not your place to give," Jacquelyn interrupted,setting her chin in a stubborn line. "What gives you the right to interfere in your patients' personal lives? You are a doctor, a professional. One thing I learned from Dr. Winston is that a physician shouldn't worry about trying to make his patients like him. There's something seriously wrong with the personality of a doctor who cares too much about seeking his patients' approval. A good doctor should only care about doing the right thing for his patient. If you do the right thing, your patients will like you. And if they don't, well, at least you've done what's right."

"Are you saying —" a silken thread of warning vibrated in his voice "— that my personality is seriously skewed?"

A pair of doctors walking through the parking lot glanced curiously in their direction. Jacquelyn closed her eyes, horrified to think she might be overheard arguing with a doctor.

Jonah Martin hadn't finished. "You've worked *eight* hours with me — how can you know I'm only seeking my patients' approval?" His voice was low, like velvet, but edged with biting steel. "It must be wonderful to have such insight into other people's characters."

"I only wish I had your flair for sarcasm." Jacquelyn's face burned with humiliation and she looked abruptly away, unable to face the blue flame of cynicism in his eyes. "I don't know you well, but I know doctors."

"You should spend more time learning to know patients." His accusing gaze remained riveted on her. "You forget, Nurse Wilkes —" he stepped closer and lowered his voice "— that unlike any other medical condition, to patients like Mrs. Baldovino, breast cancer is an intensely personal affair."

"You don't have to tell me —"

"Apparently I do. A refresher course in basic patient relations is obviously in order. Let's say, for the moment, that Mrs. Baldovino had come to me with appendicitis. That course of treatment would be pretty straightforward once she found a competent surgeon. She wouldn't have to concern herself with her surgeon's philosophy of appendectomy. She wouldn't have to worry about which type of surgery he'll perform. Her chances for survival after the operation would be excellent. And she would have little or no concern about the small scar on the side of her abdomen. The loss of her appendix would have virtually no impact on her physical or social well-being, nor would it pose much of a threat to her self-image."

Jacquelyn bit down hard on her lower lip, recognizing the point of his illustration.

"But Mrs. Baldovino came to me because she has *breast cancer,*" Jonah Martin finished, his straight glance seeming to accuse her of unspeakable ignorance. "And if you have a brain in that pretty little head of yours, I should not have to say anything more."

Choking on the words she wanted to fling at him, her lower lip trembled as she returned his glare. A black veil moved painfully at the back of her mind, stirring memories of herself as a sixteen-year-old girl who had just learned that her mother would never get well; that the surgeries, radiation and chemotherapy had failed. . . .

She turned away, her thoughts racing. He didn't know about her mother or about the careful camouflage she had placed over her own pain. For an instant she was tempted to fling the knowledge in his face — *I know about cancer, you arrogant imbecile* — but then he'd want to know how she could know about cancer and not be more sympathetic toward her own patients.

Calm down, Jacquelyn. It's your first day to work with him. This is just a misunderstanding; he's on some macho kick or trying to prove something. This showdown isn't worth risking your job. . . .

Like a drowning swimmer, she mentally kicked toward the surface dispute and took a deep breath of reality. "I suppose I'm just not used to your approach," she finally said, sheathing her anger. She looked up to face his scrutiny. "I've been working in the oncology department for five years, and you've only just arrived. Dr. Kastner and Dr. Winston are objective professionals, more detached with the patients —"

"I know hundreds of doctors like Winston and Kastner, and I respect them," Dr. Martin said, shifting his weight as he raised his hands in a gesture of assurance. "But their attitude is impartial. They are like judges. They see the patient and the cancer standing before them as equals. They are happy if the patient wins, but they are not particularly on one side or the other.

"On the other hand, Nurse Wilkes —" his eyes darkened with emotion "— I am a defense attorney. The tougher the case, the bigger my challenge. I will fight for my client. I will not be intimidated by an aggressive cancer, but will fight it with all the vigor, skills and techniques that I can muster. A happy, confident patient is a stronger client, and a strong client increases our chances of winning the case." The eyes he turned toward her smoldered now. Taking a step forward, he rested his hands on his hips and inclined his head toward her. "Can you understand that?"

Jacquelyn had to resist the urge to step away, so unnerved was she by the staggering challenge of his nearness. His burning eyes held her motionless, and she felt herself slowly nodding. "I can try," she answered, suddenly anxious to be away. The pull of those blue eyes was hard to resist when he chose to be sincere — no wonder his desperate patients adored him!

"Good." He hesitated for a moment, then quirked his eyebrow in a question. "I'm assuming you'll want to continue working for me? I haven't proven myself too much of an ogre?"

"Not too much," she answered, amused by the almost vulnerable look on his face. For the briefest instant she thought she had somehow disarmed him, but then the chilly

44

mask of professionalism fell over his features again.

"Good. I want you to know I was joking about the Baldovinos and the victory dinner. I fully expect to attend, but I wouldn't think of pressuring you to join us. I'm sure you have a full and satisfying personal life of your own."

The chilly nature of the man reveals itself again.

"Now that I understand you," she said, deliberately injecting a light note into her voice, "please be assured that I wouldn't think of accepting any invitation you might ever extend." She moved toward her car door, calling to him over her shoulder. "I realize now that your theatrics are performed solely for the sake of your patients."

"I'm sorry if I offended you," he answered, his face as implacable as stone as he watched her open the door. "You're a good nurse. Today I saw you pull organization out of turmoil and instill calm in chaos. You might even manage to keep me on schedule. Nurses with that kind of ability are hard to find."

"Thanks." She rested her arms on the open car door, then gave him a tight smile. "And I wish you the best with Mrs. Baldovino. I hope you are able to have that lasagna dinner."

He nodded formally, then turned and moved toward his car.

Jacquelyn felt her smile fade as she slid into the driver's seat. Given Mrs. Baldovino's current condition, she wasn't likely to be making those dinner reservations any time soon.

If Jonah Martin could overturn the death sentence looming over Mrs. Baldovino's chart, perhaps he was a miracle worker.

"Of course, I understand, Craig," Jacquelyn mumbled. With one hand she held the phone to her ear, the other hand lay imprisoned beneath Bailey's massive head. "State legislators don't come around every day."

Craig droned on about the lucrative deal he was about to sign, and Jacquelyn yawned. Stretching out on her wide antique bed for a nap had seemed like a good alternative to wasting the evening in front of the television, so she and Bailey had fallen asleep waiting for Craig to come by. Her day with Dr. Baked Alaska had totally worn her out.

"Call me tomorrow and let me know how things turned out," she murmured, slowly sliding her hand from under Bailey's velvety jowls. "Yeah, I know you're sorry. But you can make it up to me Friday night. Dinner out or something."

"Where do you want to go?" Craig seemed sincerely apologetic.

"I don't know." Jacquelyn tried to smother another yawn. "Italian maybe. I've got a sudden yen for lasagna."

Craig laughed and said goodbye, and Jacquelyn rolled onto her stomach to replace the telephone receiver. As she reached for the bedside table, she felt an unexpected twinge in her chest.

"Oh, brother," she groaned, flipping onto her back. Bailey's eyes opened and blinked, then the dog lifted his huge head and looked at Jacquelyn with a curious expression. "No big deal, sweetie," she said, pillowing her head on her left hand. She slipped her right hand beneath the T-shirt she wore and slowly probed her left breast. There. On the side, at about two o'clock. A small lump, probably a cyst, nothing serious. The twinge was pain, and that usually meant there was nothing to worry about.

"Nurse, heal thyself," she murmured, rolling onto her side. "No caffeine for a long time, and vitamin E at breakfast. The doctor's recipe to counter fibrocystic disease."

As her drowsiness thickened, she curled around a pillow and fell asleep to the sound of Bailey's gentle snoring.

CHAPTER THREE

Jacquelyn was delighted when Labor Day dawned in a glorious burst of blue. Craig had suggested they spend the traditional last day of summer by the lake. "I'd love a picnic," she had told him when he called Saturday to tell her he wouldn't be over because he was entertaining a prospective client. "I can't think of a better way to spend a day away from the clinic."

She'd now put in an exhausting two and a half months with Dr. Jonah Martin. Though they had managed to be civil toward one another, she had to continually bite her tongue in his presence. With the patients he was unlike any doctor she'd ever met — boundlessly optimistic, encouraging, patient and attentive to every complaint. And yet with the nurses he was aloof, distant and rigidly controlled. In one moment he would be laughing with a patient in the exam room, in the next he would be impatiently thrusting a chart toward Jacquelyn with a mocking, exasperated look in his eye. The buzz around the nurses' station was that Dr. Martin held a special contempt for nurses, orderlies and office workers. And for the first time in Jacquelyn's memory, Stacy didn't rise to defend a handsome man.

"He's an angel," Jacquelyn heard one patient gush enthusiastically. "With those blue eyes and that golden hair — just like a halo!"

"A fallen angel, maybe," Jacqueline muttered as she cleared her breakfast dishes off the iron table in her backyard and headed into the kitchen with Bailey padding along behind.

Dr. Martin was difficult to work with, and yet part of Jacquelyn was glad that he had joined the clinic staff. He lightened the workload considerably, even accepting several of Dr. Kastner's difficult terminal cases. In the course of a month, Jacquelyn noticed remarkable improvements in their attitudes, and happier patients generally meant healthier, longer-living patients.

She learned that an encyclopedic mind lay behind the doctor's charming facade. He knew dosages, drugs and protocols — medical treatment plans — by heart; contraindications and advisability results rolled off his tongue as smoothly as the alphabet. The receptionist was constantly paging him; doctors from across the country regularly called to ask his advice about one protocol or another. By slyly peeking at his telephone messages, Jacquelyn learned that Jonah Martin was involved in an ongoing study at Johns Hopkins and another at the Fred Hutchinson Cancer Research Center in Seattle. In the mornings when Jacquelyn arrived at the clinic, he was already on the phone in his office, and he remained busy when she left in the evening, long after the clinic had closed to patients.

A masculine force enveloped him, a great presence fostered by his striking good looks and enthralling blue eyes. Jacquelyn could not deny that he was intelligent, powerful and charismatic — when he chose to be. But he was also enigmatic, quick-tempered and, she suspected, more than a little dangerous. He generated awe wherever he went, but in the beginning, she reasoned, so had a lot of people. . . .

Jacquelyn shook the thought away as she started her dishwasher and tried to concentrate on getting ready for a day at the lake.

She wanted to dislike him, but she couldn't. He was too good a doctor. She would have settled for a decided feeling of apathy toward him, but her heart quickened every time his gaze met hers. She told herself her body was only reacting to residual anger from their first confrontation, but why did her heart hammer foolishly on the occasions he called specifically for her? He radiated a vitality that drew her like a magnet, but she told herself the attraction sprang from his unusual commitment to excellence and his uncommon caring for his patients. He *was* a good doctor, even if his behavior sometimes seemed as erratic and threatening as a summer storm.

For the first time in five years she had begun to see oncology as an exciting and rewarding field. Medicine, as seen through the eyes of Jonah Martin, involved more than cutting, burning and rebuilding. It involved *healing.*

Patients who had given up hope began to go into remission under his protocols, and every time good news came back from the lab, Dr. Martin's eyes gleamed as if each patient were the first he'd successfully treated. He held impromptu celebrations for happy patients in the employee lunchroom and had the nurses send congratulatory cards to those whose cancer had entered remission. Not only did he congratulate the "winners," but he also sent cards of encouragement to patients who were still struggling through chemo or the prospect of more surgery.

At first, Jacquelyn rebelled at the thought of hand-addressing cards. "Doesn't he know we have these names and addresses in the computer?" she griped to Gaynel at the front desk. "And that long ago someone invented a wonderful thing called a mailing label?" But then patients began to show up in the office with his cards clutched in their hands and stuffed into their purses, and Jacquelyn realized that the patients appreciated Dr. Martin's unconventional beyond-the-office attention. Personal greeting cards were silly, senseless and totally inefficient in light of the other paperwork the nurses had to maintain, but the patients loved them. And since something so simple apparently meant so much, Jacquelyn decided the extra effort wasn't too much to ask.

She sighed and gazed out her kitchen window. At least she could go home at the end of the day. And in her cozy little house she could forget about Jonah Martin and enter the world of Craig Bishop. Compared to the unsettling Dr. Martin, Craig was as comfortable as an old slipper. And before saying goodbye when he called on Saturday night, Craig had promised that absolutely

53

nothing would stand in the way of their Monday picnic. Jacquelyn looked forward to a lazy, sunlit day by the lake.

True to his word, Craig pulled into her driveway at 9:00 a.m. Though his mouth puckered in annoyance when Jacquelyn picked up Bailey's leash and snapped it to the dog's collar, he said nothing. Jacquelyn had adopted the dog from a mastiff rescue organization six months before, and she'd already grown closer to the animal than she would have ever dreamed possible. Sometimes, she told Craig as she picked up a water bowl from the kitchen sink, she felt like the huge puppy was almost human. He seemed to sense her moods, her feelings, and he was always there . . . which was, Jacquelyn reminded Craig, more than she could say about *him.*

"You know I have to work odd hours," Craig said, throwing up a hand in defense.

"I understand, and I don't mind," Jacquelyn answered, winding the long leash into her palm. "But I like having someone around. And it's not fair that we should go out while Bailey stays cooped up in the house all day." Jacquelyn led the gentle giant out onto the front porch. "He won't be a bit of trouble, Craig. He'll probably just run around in the sun and then lie down for a nice, long nap."

"Just bring a blanket to protect the car's upholstery," Craig said, sighing heavily as he followed her down the front porch steps. "I was hoping to sell this car tomorrow morning, but if you bring that dog, I'll have to vacuum it tonight."

"I know you well enough to know you'd vacuum it anyway, dog or no dog," Jacquelyn said, opening the door of the sporty convertible. Bailey took one look at the small space that passed for a backseat, then turned questioning eyes toward his mistress. "It's okay, puppy," Jacquelyn murmured in soothing tones. She cast a devilish look toward Craig. "Uncle Craig won't mind if you rest your chin on his shoulder."

Craig shook his head, then turned back into the house. "Where do you keep those little hand towels?" he asked, taking the front steps two at a time. "I'm not wearing dog drool to my meeting tonight. Honestly, Jacquelyn, the things I endure for you . . ."

Jacquelyn reached in to pull the front seat forward, then urged Bailey into the car. When the huge dog had gingerly seated himself, Jacquelyn slid into the front passenger seat and made a face. "Well, this *is* cozy," she murmured, noticing that she would be riding a scant five inches above the pavement. "I'll never understand why men are so crazy about sports cars."

Immediately, the image of Jonah Martin and his Mustang focused in her memory. His car wasn't as sporty as this one, but the same macho tendency toward fast speeds and sleek lines must reside somewhere in his psyche. Thank goodness Craig's personal car was a nice, safe, boxy something-or-other.

Craig appeared a moment later, a small towel draped neatly over his right shoulder. For an instant he looked like one of the harried fathers Jacquelyn used to see coming from the nursery at her church — babies on their arms, spit-up rags on their shoulders. The image suited Craig so poorly that she nearly laughed aloud. Craig Bishop wasn't ready for children. He kept insisting he wasn't ready for marriage, but Jacquelyn knew she could make him change his mind. After all, nine months ago when they met he had assured her that he had no time for a steady girlfriend, and within two dates he'd been calling her every night and sending flowers every weekend. The next steps — marriage and children — well, she'd sway him toward those things as easily as she'd persuaded him to allow Bailey to come along on the picnic.

Jacquelyn was in no hurry. At twenty-eight, she had already battled and defeated the "always a bridesmaid, never a bride" disappointment. She would marry when and if it pleased her, and she'd marry Craig or someone like him. Someone logical, efficient and charming. Someone who wouldn't mind her career, her dog, or her aversion to cooking.

"All right, I think that takes care of everything." Craig slipped into the driver's seat and paused a moment to glare at Bailey, then shook his head again. "Jacquelyn, I'll never understand how a rational woman can lose every shred of sanity when it comes to a dog —"

"The same way a man can lose all his reason when he adores a woman," she answered sweetly. She placed a protective hand on Bailey's collar. "And Bailey is not just any dog. He's a mastiff. I researched the breed, I knew what I wanted, and then I adopted a dog that needed rescuing. I've waited four years to own a mastiff, and I haven't regretted my decision for one instant."

"Okay." Craig held up his hands in a sign of truce, then put the keys into the ignition. "If he's as good a dog as you say he is, I guess I can learn to live with him. But he's your dog, Jacquelyn, not mine."

The engine roared to life, and under the noise Jacquelyn's heart hummed happily. Craig could *learn to live with Bailey.* So he'd actually thought about marriage. Jacquelyn had made it clear that she would never live with a man without being married and Craig seemed to respect her views. He knew her belief in God's commands about sexual purity would not allow her to consider surrendering her body before vowing her life and love at the altar.

Maybe, she thought, relishing the feel of the wind in her hair as the car pulled out into the street, he's planning to propose today. They had packed a romantic picnic for two, complete with flowers and a blanket. The CD player in the trunk was loaded with lush, romantic music. . . .

She turned her face toward the street so Craig wouldn't see the light of hope in her eyes. Her unfulfilled dreams were simple: she wanted a loving man to live in her house, children to fill the empty bedrooms, a promotion to supervising nurse at the clinic. All in good time, of course, but now was as good a time as any to begin.

Jacquelyn wrapped her hand in Bailey's collar, loving the warmth of his fur against her skin and the solid dependability of the man at her side.

The future looked suddenly brighter than it had only a few hours before.

Craig drove with deft skill, slanting from one lane to the next, dodging the slow-moving holiday drivers. Winter Haven, the central Florida city where Jacquelyn had been born and raised, retained many of its small town qualities even as other neighboring communities mushroomed into tourist meccas under the influence of DisneyWorld. Disney's irresistible lure had brought quick money and rows of ticky-tacky motels to towns like St. Cloud and Kissimmee, but Winter Haven remained largely untouched and Jacquelyn was grateful for the city's slower pace.

Over one hundred lakes lay within the area surrounding Winter Haven. She and Craig drove to Lake Silver, one of the larger lakes with a clean public beach. As Jacquelyn staked Bailey's long lead into the ground, Craig dutifully spread the blanket over a shady spot beneath a sprawling oak. The dog's chain was at least twenty-five feet long, long enough for the pup to play freely while keeping him safely within calling distance. Though Jacquelyn knew Bailey had the gentle temperament of a sleepy kitten, but the dog's sheer size might intimidate anyone who passed by.

"Here you go, Bailey," Jacquelyn said, setting a huge bowl of fresh water in a shaded spot. Bailey obediently trotted over, slurped up a drink and then looked at his mistress as if awaiting instructions.

Jacquelyn laughed. "Go on, check things out, have fun," she said, waving the dog away. "It's a holiday."

Craig came toward her, his biceps bulging under the weight of the picnic basket. "He's only a dog, Jacquelyn. He hears everything you're saying as 'blah blah blah.' "

"I disagree," Jacquelyn said lightly, not willing to spoil the beautiful day with an argument. "He understands more than you can imagine." She turned to give Craig a hand with the basket. "And he's smarter than the average dog."

"Yeah, right," Craig answered, but there was no malice in his tone as he lowered the basket to the blanket.

"What on earth did you pack in here?" Jacquelyn asked. She knelt and lifted the lid. "It weighs enough to hold food for ten people!"

"Just a little something to get us through the afternoon." Craig slipped to the blanket beside her. His strong hand closed over her wrist and his brown eyes sought hers. "I wanted this to be a special day. Something we would always remember."

A blush of pleasure rose to her cheeks. *A special day!* Abruptly she looked away, afraid he would read her eyes and know how desperately she wanted to hear that he was ready to marry her. She was more ready than she'd ever been. The past weeks with unpredictable Jonah Martin had convinced her that she wanted safety, logic, dependability in her life . . . and if she were married to Craig, maybe her heart wouldn't jolt and her pulse pound every time Jonah Martin's voice rang through the clinic corridor.

"This looks like fried chicken," she said, lifting out one of the neat containers he'd packed into the basket. "Umm, it smells good. But I can't believe this came from the grocer's deli."

"It didn't. I got everything from Just Desserts." He lifted one shoulder in a casual shrug. "They do more than great cheesecake."

"Potato salad —" she pulled another container from the basket "— and fresh-baked croissants?"

"With honey butter."

"And what's this?" She lifted out a plate-sized blue tin and shook it. Something

61

rattled inside. "Cookies?"

"No, we have cheesecake for dessert." His dark eyes glowed with a secret. "Open it."

She grinned and pried the lid off, half eager, half afraid to discover Craig's surprise. A cry of relief broke from her lips when she opened the tin and found four giant-size dog biscuits.

"They say the way to a man's heart is through his stomach," Craig remarked dryly, watching her. "I suppose the way to a woman's heart is through her dog."

"You are too much." She leaned forward and lightly planted a kiss on his cheek. Though this wasn't the surprise she'd been expecting, at least he was showing some interest in one of her guiding passions. Sometimes, especially when he canceled a date or forgot to show up for dinner, she wondered if he cared about anything other than his business. But he was an entrepreneur, a hard worker, a man who marched to his own drummer . . .

He helped her unpack the rest of the basket, then they arranged the feast on the blanket and began to eat. Though Bailey came over and looked at the food with frank longing in his velvet eyes, he seemed content to take one of his dog biscuits and retreat to a shaded spot under some bushes.

As Bailey delicately nibbled at his treat, Craig explained his latest ambition — an expansion of his custom car lot. "I see us opening a high-end, quality division for pre-owned vehicles," he said, using his fork to chase a slippery cube of potato around his plastic plate. "Nothing but Mercedes, Cadillacs, BMW's, upscale cars. They hold their resale value, and a lot of corporations surrender them at the end of a one-or two-year lease. The companies have no personal stake in the vehicles, so they don't quibble over trade-in value. There's a fortune to be made in that market, and I think I may know how to make it."

"That's great, Craig." Jacquelyn nodded automatically and let her eyes roam over the lake. A half-dozen boats were crisscrossing the crushed diamond water, each dragging a skier or two. The whooping and hollering of the boats' occupants reached even the shore where they sat. Several other families and couples had decided to picnic at this beach, too, though most had spread their blankets and opened umbrellas nearly at the water's edge. Occasionally a small child splashed into the water or walked through the sand with a bucket in hand, an anxious mother not far behind.

Inexplicably, tears welled in Jacquelyn's

eyes. Her own memories of early childhood were sketchy, all but obliterated by the heavy, dark memories of her mother's five-year battle with cancer. More recent memories were painfully clear: the long hours of waiting in the nondescript hospital lobby during her mother's surgeries, the painful sounds of retching, the smell of disinfectant.

But she and her mother had run along a beach like this one; she had faded photographs to prove it. Surely there had been a living warmth in the sun, a delicious joy as mother and daughter laughed and splashed together under a sudsy blue sky. But the memory, the reality of it, had been buried far beneath all those other alive, unspeakable agonies.

Her father had managed to shelve the past and get on with his life. After five years of quietly mourning his wife, he began to date. And after Jacquelyn graduated from college and returned to Winter Haven, her father had presented her with the keys and deed to the house. While she stammered in surprise, he announced his forthcoming marriage to Helen, a quiet, serene woman who'd been his steady companion for several months. He would move to Helen's condo, he told Jacquelyn, and she should keep the house. The neighborhood was settled and safe, the perfect place for a young, single career woman.

How could he walk away to begin a new life and leave her with the old one? Jacquelyn wondered. He had given her a house haunted not by spirits or ghosts, but by memories that had wrapped themselves like an invasive tumor around every piece of furniture, every dish towel, every picture on the wall.

For a fleeting instant Jacquelyn wondered if her father thought the memories would bother her less than they did him, but the place seemed strangely sterile when Jacquelyn returned. During her four years away at college her dad had repainted, sold a lot of the old furniture and installed new carpet throughout the house. The place was tidy, functional and sorely in need of a feminine touch.

And so Jacquelyn thanked her father and moved into the house which had belonged to her parents. During the five years she had lived there, she stenciled and upholstered and wallpapered until the old house now resembled an English cottage. A sloping bed of colorful perennials lined the narrow sidewalk that led to the street, and a white iron fence provided a safe boundary for

Bailey. All in all, the place became a haven. Hers.

But even the safest and most pleasant of havens grew dull after a while. Jacquelyn was not so insecure to think that she *needed* a man, but she knew her life had definitely been fuller since meeting Craig. He did not thrill or challenge her — except to occasionally tax her patience — but she found him a pleasant friend. He understood her ambition; she appreciated his. And if her dad could marry for companionship, why couldn't she? Love was for teenagers and romance novelists. After working all day with emaciated, weak, disease-damaged bodies, Jacquelyn found the idea of passion strangely wearying.

"So what do you think?" Craig's direct question brought her thoughts abruptly rushing back. She flushed miserably, knowing she'd have to confess that she hadn't been listening.

"What do I think?" She made a face. "I think you should tell me —"

A sudden yowling interrupted her. *Bailey.* Fear knotted inside her as Jacquelyn jerked toward the source of the sound, just in time to see the huge puppy clambering out of a stand of brush. He was shaking his head in abrupt, jerky movements while trying to lunge toward Jacquelyn, but his chain had caught on something. In one desperate effort, the dog threw himself into the air with a pitiful yelp, then fell limply to the ground.

"Craig, help!" Jacquelyn leapt up and ran toward the dog. The animal lay on his side, his chest heaving, the velvety folds of skin around his mouth covered with snow-white foam. Terror twisted around her heart. "We've got to do something, Craig! What could be wrong?"

"How am I supposed to know?" Standing beside her, Craig lifted his hands in a helpless gesture. "I'm not a vet, Jacquelyn, I don't know anything about dogs."

"Help me. Let me untangle his lead, then we'll lift him." Jacquelyn scrambled frantically into the brush, then found the chain wrapped around the base of a shrub. As her fingers trembled, she jerked the tangled lead around again and again, until the chain was finally clear of the obstructing branches. Within another moment she had unsnapped the lead from the stake and darted forward to free it from Bailey's collar.

"Now, Craig, help me," she said, tossing the lead onto the ground. She straddled the unconscious animal and bent to slip her arms under the dog's chest.

Unbelievably, Craig stood with his hands

on his hips and calmly shook his head. "You can't carry him. That dog weighs more than you do."

Jacquelyn was in no mood for debate. "Help me!" she yelled, her voice ringing with command.

Responding at last, Craig slipped behind her and struggled to lift the dog's hips. Somehow they half carried, half dragged Bailey to the blanket. Jacquelyn hurriedly tossed the containers of picnic food onto the grass, then wrapped the blanket around the puppy. When the big animal was covered, she knelt and pressed her ear to the dog's chest. The heartbeat was slow and steady, but the skin felt burning hot. What had happened? Heatstroke? The weather was warm, but Bailey had access to water and shade. Snakebite? Certainly possible. And puncture wounds could be tiny, or hidden in the folds of that precious wrinkled skin. . . .

"He's going into shock," she said, forcing a note of calm into her voice. "We've got to get him to the car and to the vet."

"The vet won't be open on a holiday, Jacquelyn."

Something in his infinitely reasonable tone infuriated her beyond all common sense. "Craig, I'm *not* going to sit here and argue with you. Help me lift him! Now!"

Stunned into compliance, he knelt by Jacquelyn's side.

"Hang on, Bailey. Mama's going to help you," she whispered, wrapping the animal in the lightweight blanket. She pulled the fabric over the dog's head to keep the sun out of his eyes. "If we can just get him to the road —"

"Honey, let me do this," Craig said, finally rising to the occasion. He did not question or argue now, but gathered the animal in his arms. "On three, we'll lift together, okay? Just help me get a good grip on him."

Jacquelyn nodded, tears filling her eyes. In a pinch, Craig always came through.

"One, two, three!"

Together they hoisted the animal. Jacquelyn caught her breath and breathed a prayer as she ran before Craig to the parking lot. "Dear God, please let Bailey be okay!"

CHAPTER FOUR

An eagle rode hot updrafts rising from the lake and Jonah Martin put down the medical journal he'd been studying and looked up at the sky. Insects whirred from the trees above him, and the distant sound of food being scraped from a picnic plate dulled the cutting edge of his loneliness. Somewhere overhead a jet whispered through the cloudless sky, reminding him for the briefest of moments that he hadn't been home . . . in a long time.

A sudden scream chilled him to the marrow. Out on the lake, a young woman on skis had fallen and was now splashing and screaming for help. For an instant his pulse quickened and his hands tingled in the old adrenaline rush he remembered from his stint in the E.R., then the woman's scream turned to laughter and Jonah saw that her head and shoulders were safely above water. She wore a buoyant life vest, a skier's best friend. Her boyfriend fussed loudly as he turned the boat to pick her up.

"Yeah, hurry back," Jonah murmured as he lowered his eyes again to the reports he had intended to study on his day off. "Don't keep her waiting, buddy, or you'll be sorry."

He reached under his sunglasses and pinched the bridge of his nose, consoling himself with the reminder that he'd learned his lesson. He'd been sorry every single time he'd ever become involved with a woman. Christine, the love of his high school and college years, had been more eager for a ring on her finger than for him. Marriage during medical school and internship wouldn't be practical or fair to either of them, he had warned her; he'd be under tremendous pressure and working long shifts at the hospital. And if their love was real, it could stand the test of time. . . .

But Christine didn't want to put love to the test. He'd received her letter the week after his arrival at medical school; she'd found someone else, an aspiring lawyer from Georgia, a boy willing to marry her right away. "He doesn't mind that we'll be married during his law school years," she had written, and Jonah idly wondered if she realized she'd be financially supporting her new husband as he finished his education. He

71

hadn't wanted to place that kind of burden on her. He was a doctor; he had years of schooling and hard work before he could seriously consider establishing a home. And so, after receiving Christine's letter, he had guarded his heart against romantic entanglements.

He should have learned his lesson then, but he was a normal red-blooded male, and women, for some unaccountable reason, were drawn to him. He'd once heard a professor warn about the tendency for female patients to fall in love with their doctors, but Jonah had always found that his patients — mostly older women — thought of him more like a son than a love interest. His patients were no threat.

But other women worried him. Ever since the incident at the University of Virginia Hospital, he'd been careful to keep younger women at arm's length. He had been naive and completely innocent in his UVA days, but one nurse he dated told a different — and totally fabricated — story. He'd smelled mischief on her as strong as the cheap scent she wore, so after one disastrous date he ignored her advances. Later, he tried to ignore her threats . . . and found that he could not.

And so began his troubles. His running.

Now he was an expert at recognizing the lazily seductive glance that signaled trouble, and it always seemed easier to remove himself from a situation than to call for someone else's job.

Besides, people always believed the woman.

So now he found himself sitting by a lake in Central Florida, one county away from Mickey Mouse, blocks from the southern belles who wore hoop skirts and talked with accents as thick and sweet as honey. Now he was the doctor he'd always dreamed of becoming, and the work here was fulfilling, even if it was lonely. From day one, he'd established a strong rapport with his patients and a frigid enmity with the women at the clinic — especially Jacquelyn Wilkes, whom he found particularly unsettling. He'd been harder on her than the others, though he couldn't say what drove him to alienate her so ruthlessly. Perhaps it was her skill, her quiet competence . . . then again, maybe it was those green eyes.

"Hurry, Craig! I can't hear him breathing!"

A familiar voice jangled across his nerves, nudging him out of his musings. Jonah dropped his magazine and stood. Jacquelyn Wilkes and a man were coming from the picnic area; the man staggered under the weight of a blanket-wrapped body in his arms. From the look of the sagging form in the blanket, the patient was a heavy adult, possibly a drowning victim. . . .

Without hesitating, Jonah unclipped his cell phone and dialed 911. "We need an ambulance sent to the picnic area at Lake Silver, stat," he told the dispatcher, then he disconnected and sprinted to intersect Jacquelyn's path.

"Nurse Wilkes!" he called, falling into step beside her. "What's the problem?"

For the first time he could recall, she looked at him with honest appreciation in her eyes. "Dr. Martin, thank goodness! I don't know what the problem is." Her eyes were wide with fear as she continued jogging toward the parking lot. "Heatstroke, I think, or maybe snakebite."

Jonah nodded. "Pulse? Breath sounds?"

"Pulse is strong, but slowing," Jacquelyn answered, huffing. "Breath sounds are erratic."

"Puncture wounds?"

"None that I could see. But I didn't look closely, there wasn't time. His breathing was so erratic —"

The wail of sirens cut through the summer afternoon as an ambulance screeched to a halt in the parking lot.

The thimble-shaped man carrying the victim stopped abruptly and sent Jonah a crooked smile. "You called an ambulance?"

"Of course." Jonah frowned, unable to understand the man's expression, but there was no time to consider the quirks of Jacquelyn Wilkes's friends. The emergency medical technicians were spilling out of the vehicle, and a curious crowd had begun to gather.

"Possible heatstroke or snakebite," Jonah called, hurrying forward. He pulled the back doors of the truck open himself. "I'm a doctor, and I'd be happy to ride with the patient to the E.R."

"Is this the victim?" one of the rescuers asked, pointing down the path.

Jonah turned and followed the man's gaze. Jacquelyn and her friend were approaching, the blanket-wrapped body still in the man's arms. "Yes," Jonah answered, reaching for the stretcher. "Let me give you a hand."

"Jacquelyn," the burly man panted, halting with his burden. His flush deepened to crimson before the eyes of the curious crowd. "You've got to tell them."

Jacquelyn lifted the blanket. "Tell them what?"

Jonah's nerves tensed as the blanket fell

away. The face resting on the man's shoulder was black and furry; a velvet ear trailed over his arm. Long, lanky limbs pointed toward the sky, and a limp tail drooped out the side of the blanket. Jacquelyn Wilkes's boyfriend was cradling the most massive dog Jonah had ever seen.

Someone in the crowd of onlookers snickered and one of the paramedics turned away to hide a smile. The other EMT's face purpled in sudden anger. "What's this?" He turned to Jonah. "You called us out here to tend to a *mutt?*"

Jonah held up his hand, but couldn't think of a single word to offer in explanation. The red-faced man lowered the dog to the ground, then stood back, his arms folded tight across his chest. From the expression on his sweaty face, Jonah knew the man was wishing he could melt into the growing crowd and disappear.

At that moment Jonah could have walked happily into the crowd himself and wished the day away. But his traitorous eyes moved to the place where *she* stood, clenching and unclenching her hands, copper curls clinging damply to her forehead and the nape of her neck, her eyes welling like a stormy sea.

A jolt of sudden and unexpected desire forced him to look away. Jacquelyn Wilkes was a beautiful and desirable woman, reason enough for him to avoid her. She thoroughly disliked him, of that he was certain. Her dislike he could handle, he could even welcome it. He could work with her frigidity, aversion, even disgust . . .

But she'd honestly hate him if he didn't help her now. One look in her eyes had convinced him that the dog, mutt or not, was precious to her. And if she hated Jonah, she'd want to destroy him. It'd be only a few months before he was adding yet another hospital to his résumé.

"Please, Doctor. Will you help him?" If Jonah had any doubts, they vanished when Jacquelyn spoke in the fragile and shaking voice he'd heard a thousand times from his patients.

Ignoring the flustered paramedics, he knelt to examine the animal.

"What happened?" he asked, lifting one of the dog's eyelids. The jowls at the sides of the animal's mouth had swollen, and the dog seemed to have difficulty drawing breath. Jonah abruptly brought his hand through the dog's line of vision and noted that the animal's blink reflex had slowed to almost nothing.

"I can't see any puncture wounds," Jacquelyn said, her voice choked with urgency

77

and rising panic.

Jonah gently lifted the swollen jowls and peered into the dog's mouth. A layer of white foam covered the teeth and gums, but after wiping the substance away he observed tiny red blisters flaring angrily along the pink flesh.

"I'd say the dog got into a nest," he said, gently lowering the animal's head. "Wasps or bees. This is probably an allergic re-action."

"Allergies?" Jacquelyn looked at him with blank eyes. "But . . . that can be fatal! If his esophagus closes up —"

Jonah looked up at the red-faced ambu-lance driver. "Take us to the E.R.," he said, pulling his wallet and ID from the pocket of his shorts. "I'm Dr. Jonah Martin. I'll be responsible."

"No way." The driver planted his feet and crossed his arms, well aware that at least a hundred curious potential letter writers had gathered to watch the spectacle. "I am not running a canine to the hospital. Call a vet."

"Look, you have to return to the hospital anyway," Jonah pointed out. "Why not take us along for the ride? I'll take full responsi-bility."

"I am not —" the man paused for empha-sis "— pulling up into *my* parking lot before *my* boss with a canine on *my* gurney. No way."

"If you don't take this dog somewhere," Jonah lowered his voice, "it may die. Do you want that on your conscience?"

He had spoken quietly, but the crowd heard. "Give the dog a break, man!" someone called.

"Have a heart!"

"Ain't you got a dog of your own?"

The driver fidgeted uncomfortably. "It still isn't right. I'll be in major trouble if I take a canine anywhere near the E.R."

"You can take him to my office." Jonah bent to help Jacquelyn lift the dog onto the gurney. "I'll tend him there. And I'll cover the bill for this run."

Bowing to Jonah's logic and public pressure, the driver threw his hands up and went to the front of the vehicle. The second paramedic helped Jacquelyn and Jonah load the gurney into the truck, then he waved to the crowd and went to the front of the ambulance. Obviously neither paramedic was going to risk his job by taking care of a sick animal.

Jonah turned to Jacquelyn. "I'll have to ride along to let them in the building," he said, watching the play of emotions on her lovely face. He'd never seen such a depth of caring in her eyes — not even with her most troubled patients. "I suppose you'll want to follow later with your friend."

"I won't leave Bailey," Jacquelyn said, hopping up into the ambulance beside the gurney.

"I'll follow in the car after I gather our things," the boyfriend called, backing away from the ambulance. Before Jonah could climb in and pull the double doors closed, he had disappeared.

But he'd said *our* things.

As the ambulance pulled out, Jacquelyn leaned forward and crooned to the animal on the stretcher. "It's okay, baby dog. Mama's right here." Surprisingly, the dog whimpered and struggled to nuzzle her hand. Something in the tender exchange caught at Jonah's heart.

Enough. Fix the dog up and send them home. And he'd have done his part to keep peace in the office.

Jonah settled into the rhythm of the swaying ambulance, then motioned to Jacquelyn. "If you hand me that bottle of saline solution behind you, we can start cleaning out his mouth." He reached for a pair of sterile gloves and snapped them on. "I don't know how many regulations we're breaking here today —" He looked up at her and paused, struck by the fine shape of her mouth and the slender column of her throat. When he could speak again, his voice was more subdued. "But I trust this is for a good cause."

Jacquelyn did not look up. The fringe of her lashes cast shadows on her cheeks as she monitored the dog's breathing and reached for the saline. "Yes, Doctor, it is. If you have a dog, I'm sure you understand."

Jonah leaned over the animal, his jaw tightening. "I don't have a dog. I live alone."

She did look at him then, and in her expressive eyes he saw mingled tenderness and pity. "Well, I'm sure you've loved a dog sometime. And you know we dog people would do just about anything for our animals."

He lifted a brow and looked back down at his patient, gingerly running a gloved finger around the inside of the dog's jowl to check for any abrasions or lumps. "He won't bite me, will he?"

"No," Jacquelyn answered, taking the animal's massive head into her hands. She cast Jonah an inquisitive look. "For some reason, I thought you'd have a dog. I kinda figured you were the Chow type. Or maybe a Rottweiler."

"No dog, no cat, not even a gerbil," Jonah

answered, absently reaching for her hand. She inhaled sharply at his touch and he ignored her reaction, though the slight contact sent a giddy sense of pleasure through his own senses.

"If you please, Nurse," he said, keeping his eyes upon the dog as he moved her hand toward the animal's muzzle, "would you retract this flap of skin? I need a clear look inside that mouth."

"Of course." Her strong, sure fingers left his and pulled back on the loose jowls. Jonah flipped on the overhead dome lights and peered into the animal's mouth. A series of red, angry welts glared through a thin layer of whitish foam. His hunch was right. Jacquelyn's dog had disturbed a nest of insects, probably yellow jackets from the vicious look of things. During his E.R. rotation Jonah had treated a little boy with similar welts.

"No pets at all?" Jacquelyn made a soft clucking sound as she handed him a square of sterile gauze to wipe the inflamed area. "How do you live? No shoes chewed, no vet bills to pay, no snores waking you in the middle of the night." Grateful green eyes slanted toward him. "How can you come home to an empty house when you could have unlimited hugs and snuggles?"

His inner antennae picked up what could have been a not-so-subtle flirtation and he stiffened, instantly on his guard. But she was studying the dog, concentrating on the animal, and after an instant Jonah decided that she meant nothing by the remark. After all, she had been at the park with a man. And if Jonah's luck was running true to form, he was the last man on earth an intelligent woman like Jacquelyn would ever be drawn to. The women he attracted were like radio stations — anyone could pick them up, especially at night.

He gently wiped the swollen area, then tossed the soiled gauze toward a trash bin. "I hope my house won't always be empty." Now who's dropping hints? He took pains to keep his eyes on the patient; it wouldn't be wise to lose himself in Jacquelyn's emerald gaze.

"Oh?" Her voice was cool and impersonal. "Planning on getting a pet — or a wife?"

He lowered the animal's lip and motioned for her to turn the dog's head so he could check the other side. He couldn't bring himself to risk touching her hand again.

"I don't know." He reached for another square of gauze. Funny, he should have been annoyed at this interruption of his holiday, yet he was enjoying every minute of this chance encounter. "Maybe I can find a wife who will give lots of snuggles and not chew shoes."

It was the most pleasant, teasing thing he had ever said to her, and he didn't dare lift his gaze to see how she'd respond. She remained silent for a moment, almost as if she were holding her breath. When she spoke again, her voice was light. "If you're very lucky," she said, one hand beginning to stroke the dog's sweaty side, "you'll find a wife with a dog."

Enough. Stop now. Why in the world was he flirting with a nurse? He scarcely knew Jacquelyn Wilkes, and he had no idea how she was reading his comments. If he wasn't careful, tomorrow she'd be telling the entire office that he'd asked her to marry him, and when he denied it she'd sue for sexual harassment or breach of promise or something.

He frowned. "You animal lovers are the strangest people." He wiped the inflamed gums with the sterile square. "You're totally illogical. People like you are the happiest when they are the most inconvenienced."

He looked up, expecting to see her usual stern expression, but she only smiled and took the dirty gauze from his gloved hand.

"Isn't that what love is all about?" she

asked, looking at the dog with a tenderness he'd never seen in her eyes before.

The ambulance engine slowed and died, and a moment later the surly paramedic opened the rear doors. "End of the road for the mutt, Doc," he said, gesturing to the clinic outside. "Your office, just like you ordered."

Jonah smiled his thanks and grabbed the end of the stretcher. "Just give me a hand getting the dog in, and I'll see you get a commendation for going above and beyond the call of duty."

After injections of steroids and antihistamines to treat shock and counter the insect venom, Jonah measured out a ten-day supply of amoxicillin from pharmaceutical samples, then labeled a prescription bottle for "Bailey Wilkes."

"I'd say give him two and a half of these twice a day, but you'll want to double-check the dosage with your vet." He made a note on a chart he'd improvised from the supplies on hand, then looked up to find Jacquelyn studying him, a glint of wonder in her eyes. He frowned. "Something wrong?"

"No," she said, a smile trembling over her lips as she soothed the recovering animal. "It's just that — well, you've surprised me,

Doctor. Dr. Kastner would have let Bailey die right there at the lake. Probably ninety percent of the doctors in this hospital wouldn't want to be bothered with an animal, especially on a holiday."

"Ninety percent of the doctors in this hospital don't have my seriously skewed personality." He snapped the file shut and slid it toward her. "They don't care if their patients like them."

A blush ran like a shadow over her cheeks. "I'm sorry. I was wrong to say that."

She looked so vulnerable, so guilty, that he had to stifle an urge to walk forward and pull her into his arms.

"No, you were right." He looked away, pretending to search for something on the desk. "A doctor must be careful not to get so involved that he can't see things clearly. But I've always found it's far easier to get involved with the patients than with —"

Attractive nurses. He stiffened, embarrassed at what he'd almost said. Fortunately, Jacquelyn's attention seemed focused on the animal.

"I guess you could say I'm just a sucker for eyes that color," he whispered, keenly feeling the great gulf between what he was and what he suddenly wanted to be.

"They're coffee-brown," she said, casting

him a fleeting smile. "I'm a sucker for Bailey's eyes, too."

He turned away to clean up the counter, allowing her to misunderstand what he'd meant. Don't even think about it, he warned himself. She's your nurse. She has a boyfriend, that's plain enough. Remember the past, stay aloof. Romance and medicine don't mix.

As if she'd read his thoughts about the boyfriend, Jacquelyn quietly left the room and walked out to the reception area. When she came back a few moments later, she carried a yellow sticky note. "A message from Craig," she said, a frown settling between her delicate brows. "He says he came, he waited, he had to leave. He had an important appointment at four o'clock."

Jonah glanced up. "Is that a problem?"

"A little one." She smiled tentatively. "I hate to bother you, Doctor, especially after all you've done today for me and Bailey. But we're stuck." She tucked her hands into the belt at her waist. "Without a car, I mean. I guess I could call a cab, but I don't know how I'll get Bailey into the backseat."

"There's no way you can carry this dog by yourself," Jonah pointed out. "And Bailey still doesn't look very steady on his feet. I'll call a taxi and take you both home.

I jogged over to the lake, so I'll need a cab to get home, anyway."

Her face was firmly set in deep thought. "That's asking too much. I need to stay here and clean up the mess we've made. I should move Bailey to the waiting area so I can sterilize and prep this room, and then I have to make a list of all the meds you gave him so I can submit and pay the bill."

She suddenly smiled and tilted her sleepy-cat eyes toward him. "And since I can't afford your hourly rate, Doctor, just forget about doing anything else for me. Bailey and I can hang out here until Craig is done with his appointment. I'll call him at five or so. He'll come and pick us up when he can."

He laughed, honestly amused by her detailed sense of integrity. "Forget it. Don't bill yourself for anything," he insisted, turning toward the sink. "Practically everything I used was a free sample. Don't worry about it."

His gaze came to rest on her questioning eyes, then his instinct for self-preservation forced him to turn away.

What was he *doing?* Acting like a fool, again. He ought to leave her and take a cab back to his apartment. He could spend the night surfing the Internet, and he needed to check out some recent stats from a Johns

Hopkins project . . . but it was a holiday and he *did* need to relax.

Maybe, just this once, nothing bad would happen.

He cleared his throat. "I've never walked out on a patient without making sure that he or she was resting comfortably, and I don't intend to start now. Really, I'd love to see you home . . . unless you'd really rather wait for — what's his name? Craig."

A spark of some indefinable emotion lit her eyes at the mention of the boyfriend's name. She smiled to herself, then crossed her arms and leaned against the door frame. "There is no way of knowing how long Craig will be. Are you sure you wouldn't mind taking us?"

He turned the faucet and began to scrub his hands. "Absolutely sure, that is if Craig won't mind. I wouldn't want him to get the wrong idea."

There. In one statement he'd told her that he meant nothing by his offer and given her the perfect opportunity to laugh and say that Craig was her brother, her cousin, or some casual friend she barely knew . . . but she didn't.

"Craig would understand," she said, her smile fading a little. "A ride home is . . . no big deal."

Jonah forced a smile as he shut off the water and allowed his hands to drip into the sink. "Well, you're going to need help carrying the beast to the waiting room so we can clean up in here. By tomorrow morning, not even the county health department will be able to tell that we've treated anything other than Homo sapiens in this clinic."

Her pensive expression softened into one of fond gratitude as she moved toward the cabinet containing the cleaning supplies. "I will never be able to thank you enough, Dr. Martin. What you did today . . . well, I wouldn't have expected it from any doctor. You really surprised me."

"Nurse Wilkes," he said, smiling wryly as he reached for a paper towel, "sometimes I surprise myself."

CHAPTER FIVE

The cab pulled up in front of one of the older, dignified homes Jonah had often admired along the lakefront. Wide stuccoed pillars lined the edge of a gleaming wooden porch where a swing for two drifted lazily in the afternoon breeze. Jonah paid the taxi driver and together the two men hoisted the huge mastiff from the vehicle's backseat.

Bailey, still a bit wobbly on his feet, had to be half urged, half carried up the front steps, but as soon as Jacquelyn and Jonah got him into the house the dog perked up and trotted gratefully to an old blanket by the fireplace.

"He knows he's home," Jonah observed, watching as the dog curled up for a nap. "And I have to admit, it's nice to see a dog by the fireplace."

"Even if we hardly ever have a fire," Jacquelyn answered, dropping her keys on a small desk as she passed through the foyer

91

into a cheery kitchen. "Let me get you a cold drink, Doctor Martin. It's still as hot as blazes outside and carrying Bailey is no easy job."

He paused, weighing the heaviness of his past experience against the unwelcome prospect of another night alone in his apartment. Why shouldn't he stay for a few minutes? He had planned to walk back to his apartment from here, and it would be nice to enjoy a cold drink before setting out. This meant nothing. Jacquelyn Wilkes had a boyfriend; she certainly wasn't interested in him. In fact, as soon as her gratitude for his help wore off, she'd probably pick up her quiet crusade of aversion right where she left off.

"I'll take a Coke, if you have one," Jonah answered, following her into the kitchen. "Thanks for the offer, Nurse Wilkes."

"Nurse Wilkes?" She wrinkled her nose as she gracefully stepped to a cupboard. "After the day we've had, don't you think you can call me Jacquelyn? Dr. Kastner does."

He pressed his lips together, uncomfortable with this new level of intimacy. "If that's what you'd prefer."

"I prefer. I don't want to hear any more of this 'Nurse Wilkes' stuff. It's Jacquelyn. Or Jackie. Whichever you like better."

"Which do you prefer?"

She paused. "Funny," she said, slowly opening the cupboard door. "No one's ever asked me that. My father calls me Jacquelyn, pronounced the French way — you know, Zhock-leen. My brother calls me Jack, and Craig calls me Jacquelyn."

The boyfriend. He was someone significant, or she wouldn't have mentioned him. Jonah felt his reserve begin to thaw. He forced a smile. "And what does Bailey call you?"

Amusement flickered in her eyes. "Mom."

She pulled two glasses from the cupboard, then stole a glance at his face. "It's okay to smile, you know, neither Bailey nor I will bite you. Why so formal, Doc?"

He crossed his arms and leaned against the wall. "I'm not always. You yourself said I was too informal with the patients."

"But not with your nurses." She held the glasses for an instant, watching him, then smiled and pointed toward the refrigerator. "Ice would be a good idea, don't you think? Why don't you get it while I dig some Cokes out of the pantry?"

He came forward and took the glasses from her, feeling a bit like an alien in hostile territory. Since entering the house her spirit had unfurled like a blooming rose, while at the threshold his courage had begun to shrivel. Soon there'd be nothing left of him but a Cheshire cat smile . . . unless he got out of here. Fast.

"Don't go to any trouble for me," he called, looking toward the pantry into which she had disappeared. "I just remembered that I really need to go over some figures for a research study. I promised some colleagues out in California that I'd send my analysis —"

"Drat." She stepped out of the pantry, wiping her hands on her shorts. From the concentrated look on her face he doubted she'd heard a word he'd said. "I thought I had some Cokes. Hold on a minute, will you, while I look outside in the garage?"

"Jacquelyn, I —"

She didn't stop, but sprinted out the back, the screen door slamming behind her like an exclamation point. Sighing, Jonah moved toward the refrigerator and held the glasses to the ice dispenser. He *was* thirsty. Maybe he could stay a few minutes and then beat a quick retreat.

The screen door creaked and slammed again, and she stood in the kitchen, her face flushed. "I forgot! I don't have any Coke, nothing with caffeine at all. But I've got Sprite and ginger ale."

"Anything will do." He placed the ice-filled glasses on the table. "I'd even take water, anything convenient." *And fast.*

"Okay." She moved to the pantry and pulled out a two-liter bottle of clear soda, then began to pour. In the silence, Jonah took a seat at her small table and looked around. He had expected his capable nurse's kitchen to be spotless and efficient, but the room was more charming and homey than he would have imagined. Blue-and-white gingham curtains fluttered from the open windows, and the cheerful pattern was repeated on the seat cushions, place mats and even on dishes in the wooden plate rack. The decor reminded Jonah of his mother's comfortable kitchen, a memory he resisted with all his might.

"Drinking healthy, are you?" he asked, searching for a way to make safe conversation. "Avoiding caffeine and all that?"

"Yes." She lowered the soda bottle and waited for the bubbles to settle. One of her slim shoulders lifted in a shrug. "A few weeks ago I felt a cyst in my breast and decided to cut out caffeine and take vitamin E. You know, the standard deal."

"Are you certain," he said, watching her pour again, "the lump is a cyst? Did you have it aspirated?"

She flashed him a confident smile. "Now, Doctor, don't start recruiting me as a patient. I'm twenty-eight years old and I don't have breast cancer. I mean, what are the odds?"

He accepted the drink she offered and debated whether to continue or let the matter drop. "The odds?" He casually sipped from his glass. "Perhaps you should tell me. Have you ever borne a child?"

Her hand flew to her throat in an expression of mock horror. "That's a bit personal, don't you think?"

He leaned forward. "I'm not joking, Jacquelyn. And you ask our patients questions like these all the time. You asked about the odds, so let's figure them out. So tell me — have you ever given birth to a child?"

She sank into a chair opposite him and smiled in tolerant exasperation. "No."

"Fine. Did you begin your menstrual periods before age twelve?"

She rolled her eyes. "No."

"Good. Have you ever had an abortion?"

Her eyes narrowed and grew serious. "This *is* personal."

"I'm a doctor."

"You're not *my* doctor."

"Answer the question. An abortion before age eighteen increases a woman's risk for breast cancer — so have you had an abortion?"

"No."

"Fine." He sank back in his chair. "So far, so good. Just one more thing — have you a female relative with breast cancer?"

A cold, hard-pinched expression settled on her face. "Yes."

"Your mother?"

She nodded.

He inhaled a deep breath. "Was your mother's breast cancer pre-or post-menopausal?"

"Pre. She died at thirty-six." Jacquelyn's voice fell to a whisper. "I was sixteen."

A flicker of apprehension coursed through him. This was not terribly serious; women whose mothers developed pre-menopausal breast cancer in one breast stood only one and a half times the risk of the general population.

"Your mother's cancer —" he forced himself to maintain his professional tone "— unilateral or bilateral?"

"Both breasts were involved," she said, uncertainty creeping into her expression. "She had a double mastectomy, but too late. The cancer had spread into her bones. It was hopeless."

Jonah's hand clenched beneath the table.

First-degree relatives of bilateral, pre-menopausal breast cancer patients were at a nine-fold risk of developing the same disease. And daughters of women with breast cancer tended to develop their cancer at younger ages than did their mothers.

But Jacquelyn should know this.

"Jacquelyn," he said, deliberately pressing his palm to the table for emphasis, "you must have that lump checked. Don't delay. Don't mess around with vitamin E and caffeine-free diets."

"I will," she said, casually reaching for her glass. But her smile, when her eyes met his, trembled with repressed emotion. "But you know what they say. Doctors and nurses make the worst patients."

"Promise me you'll do it. Soon."

"We're so busy at work. Maybe next month, when things slow down a bit."

"Now. You need to call your physician tomorrow and take the first available opening. Promise me you will, or I'll not let you work tomorrow."

She sighed heavily, then pasted on a nonchalant smile. "All right, but only because I owe you a favor. I'm quite certain there's nothing to worry about. I'm a health professional, too, you know."

"And about the best nurse I've ever had

the pleasure of working with," Jonah answered, lifting his glass in salute before the careful, cautious doctor inside him could stomp his feet in frustration. He'd said too much. Without meaning to, he'd shown particular, deliberate attention to a specific nurse — a gorgeous creature who had brought another, quite different, man inside him to life.

"Make that appointment, Nurse Jacquelyn," he repeated, forcing his face to remain set in grim lines. "I'd hate to lose a good nurse."

"My, my." A sardonic smile lit her face. "I had no idea you were so fond of the help. I had the feeling that on your scale of significance, nurses were about as low as a beetle's bellybutton."

For some reason, her jibe stung him, but Jonah pushed back his chair and gave her a humorless smile. "I've spent over two months training you," he said, standing. "I can't afford to waste time training someone else."

He walked out of the room, but paused in the hallway that led to the foyer, darkened now by the setting sun. Still sitting at the kitchen table, she was eyeing him as if he were a bad smell.

"Don't bother getting up," he said, knowing she wouldn't. "I know the way out."

September laid a warm shoulder of sun against the clinic windows the next morning, and Jacquelyn found herself wishing she were out at the lake again with Bailey and — whom? Craig or Jonah Martin?

Jonah had come through when Craig failed, but only because they'd experienced a medical emergency. If she'd been out at the mall and come up twenty dollars short, Craig would have heroically jumped to her defense. If her car broke down, he'd bring someone to repair it within ten minutes. If the roof was leaking, he'd know just who to call and how to wheel and deal for the best price to fix it.

Why was she defending Craig? He was the man she respected, the one she hoped would share her house, her life, her love. He was certainly nothing like Jonah Martin. Craig was an executive, Dr. Martin an enigma. Craig was logical, Jonah practically schizophrenic. Craig was hers; Jonah Martin was as independent and aloof as the moon.

Last night in her kitchen there had been one moment when those freezing blue eyes had warmed and she thought they might become friends, but later she decided that the setting sun had been playing tricks on her eyes. Dr. Baked Alaska just wasn't the friendly type.

So why was she thinking so much about Jonah Martin?

This little fascination will wear off, she told herself as she picked up the file on a new patient who waited for her in the reception area. Jonah Martin was adorable and she was only infatuated because he'd been nice enough to help Bailey. But she was a grown woman, old enough to know that infatuation was a childish, passing thing. Besides, after you scraped away the nice veneer, Jonah Martin was just another egotistical, smart-aleck doctor.

She paused at the doorway leading into the waiting room. Three patients waited there: an older man impatiently leafing through an issue of *Good Housekeeping,* a middle-aged woman with a bright orange scarf tied around her head and another woman with striking strawberry-blond hair.

"Daphne Redfield?" Jacquelyn asked the room.

The tall strawberry-blonde stood and came toward her, smiling.

"Hello, Mrs. Redfield," Jacquelyn said, automatically extending her hand. "I'm Jacquelyn Wilkes and it's my pleasure to welcome you to our clinic."

"I'm so glad to be here," the woman answered, and from the look of gratitude in her eyes, Jacquelyn thought she honestly meant it. "We've just moved here from Ohio, and the hospitals there are so drab — nothing at all like this! My family and I are thrilled that I'll be able to take my chemo in this gorgeous place."

Jacquelyn smiled and gestured down the hall, intent on her routine. She weighed her patient, took blood pressure readings, pricked the woman's index finger. While the blood sample went to the lab, she escorted Mrs. Redfield to the small sofa in the interview room and pulled several photo-copied sheets from the nurses' desk drawer.

"Make yourself comfortable, Mrs. Redfield," she began. "We'll just be talking today — we won't be administering any drugs."

"Please, call me Daphne," the woman insisted, her bright blue eyes meeting Jacquelyn's as she gracefully draped herself over the sofa cushions. "We'll probably be seeing a lot of each other."

"All right, Daphne," Jacquelyn agreed. "We're glad you're with us. Now I'm going to give you several booklets, and you're to take them home and read them carefully. We understand that many of our patients are fearful of the unknown when they come to us, but —"

"Oh, I'm not," Daphne interrupted.

"You're not what?" Jacquelyn paused, confused. She'd been so intent on getting through her standard lecture that she couldn't remember what she'd just said.

"I'm not afraid of the unknown." Daphne smiled with warm spontaneity. "The Lord is with me, you see, and He knows what lies ahead. I trust Him completely."

Jacquelyn smiled indulgently. "Good. Now, where was I? Oh, yes. Whatever reports you have heard from some other cancer patients, well, forget them. We are all individuals, and we respond individually to treatment. If and when you have any unpleasant side effects from the chemo drugs, you are to call us immediately. Don't wait a day, don't wait an hour. Call us right away, and we'll be able to help you. Lauren is our nursing supervisor, and Stacy and I are the other nurses here five days a week. Please call if you need anything."

Mrs. Redfield nodded.

"Now let's see what protocol Dr. Martin has designed for you." Jacquelyn opened the folder and skimmed the patient's chart. Daphne Redfield had stage IV cancer; the disease had spread beyond the breast and the axillary lymph nodes to the bones, liver and lungs. Over the past three years she had undergone a biopsy, a modified radical mastectomy and a course of chemotherapy. Dr. Martin wished to keep her on long-term chemotherapy.

The chart had *hopeless* written all over it. Jacquelyn's mother had been an aggressive stage IV cancer case. Her heart swelled with sympathy toward the woman sitting beside her, then she determinedly beat the emotion down. She couldn't open her heart to this one, no matter how much she wanted to. Daphne Redfield would need her faith in God, probably soon.

Jacquelyn looked up and managed a tentative smile. "It looks like you're going to be with us awhile," she said, trying to keep her voice light. "Dr. Martin wants you to receive Adriamycin and Cytoxan. Before you receive these drugs, you'll receive Kytril, Decadron and Emend, antinausea medicines, through an IV drip. If, after treatment, you develop uncontrolled nausea, vomiting, or diarrhea, a fever of 101 degrees or higher, unusual bleeding or bruising, shortness of breath, burning or frequency with urination, or pain, redness, or swelling at the IV site, call us immediately. Avoid aspirin and products containing aspirin. If diarrhea

develops, take Kaopectate or Imodium AD
—"

"What's wrong, honey?"

The woman's blunt question caught Jacquelyn by surprise. Most first-time patients were so afraid and overwhelmed by the rush of information that they said little and rarely met Jacquelyn's eyes. But this woman had listened carefully to every word, her bright gaze roving over Jacquelyn's face like a searchlight.

Jacquelyn stiffened. "I beg your pardon?"

"Something is bothering you, dear. Would you like to tell me about it?"

Tell her about what? Jacquelyn took a deep breath and adjusted her smile. "I'm sure I don't know what you mean."

The woman's long, elegant hand came to rest on Jacquelyn's arm. "Honey, even if I didn't have the gift of discernment I couldn't help but see the shadows behind those lovely eyes of yours. Something is lying heavy on your mind, and it has nothing to do with my pitiful case. So tell me — what's troubling you?"

"Nothing," Jacquelyn stammered, stumbling for words. "And even if there was something, my personal life has no place in the office."

"Dear heart, I've yet to meet a woman

who can split herself like an amoebae and leave her heart in one place and her brain in another. So tell me what's troubling you."

Jacquelyn had one sudden, lucid thought: She knows. But *what* did she know? What concern had bled over into Jacquelyn's expression? Her infatuation and recent attraction to Dr. Martin was sheerly superficial, not nearly serious enough to merit discussion. She had been greatly distressed over Bailey's accident and unhappy when Craig vanished when she needed him most. And yes, there was that bothersome cyst, that small, sinister unknown entity that had lodged itself near her heart. . . .

Maybe she was more worried than she wanted to admit. It was all Jonah Martin's fault, of course. He'd raised all sorts of doubts and worries in her mind. So she'd tell this woman about the cyst, and next week they'd laugh about it.

"It's nothing, I'm sure," Jacquelyn said, lowering her voice. "But I found a lump in my breast a few weeks ago. I'm sure it's a cyst, but I've been doing all the right things and it won't go away. And I can't seem to put it out of my mind, because someone's always bringing up something to remind me of it."

Daphne nodded. "Tell me this, please —

are you a follower of Christ?"

This question surprised Jacquelyn even more than the first one. "Why, yes," she said, nodding. "I accepted the Lord when I was a child."

Daphne closed her eyes and slowly smiled. "Then that nagging doubt is the voice of the Spirit. Heed it, my dear. Have that lump checked. Don't make the Lord have to take desperate measures to get your attention."

Desperate measures? Jacquelyn looked away, thinking. Had Bailey's accident been God's attempt to get her attention? She went to church occasionally and read her Bible when there was nothing on television, but it had been a long time since she and God had had a heart-to-heart talk.

Maybe God had sent Jonah to remind her of the risks she was taking as well as to help Bailey. He *had* made her promise to call and make a doctor's appointment to have the cyst checked — something she hadn't yet done. And now God had sent Daphne Redfield as reinforcement.

People said God worked in mysterious ways. Jacquelyn looked again at her patient, almost expecting to see that the golden-haired woman had disappeared in a flurry of angel's wings. But she sat there still, a smile of concern on her refined face.

"Thank you." Jacquelyn nodded. "I will call my gynecologist as soon as we're finished here."

Three days later, Jacquelyn sat in the exam room of her gynecologist's office. Wrapped in a soft cotton gown, she fidgeted with the tie ends of the open garment and fretted about the lump that had brought her to this place. It was only a cyst. She'd felt pain one night as she rolled over onto her breast, and cysts were usually painful.

An abrupt knock rattled the door, then Dr. Rita Shaw stepped into the room. "Well, Miss Jacquelyn, what seems to be bothering you today?" she asked in a cheerful voice, her eyes intent upon the nurse's notes on the chart. "A breast lump?"

"Left breast, two o'clock." Jacquelyn shrugged. "A cyst, I'm sure, but I've been doing the vitamin E, no-caffeine regimen and the lump seems to be unaffected."

"Lie back, will you?" The doctor placed the file on a tray and began to gently palpate the suspicious area. "How long have you been avoiding caffeine?"

With her left hand pillowing her head, Jacquelyn stared at the ceiling and counted backward. "About ten weeks."

"Do you give yourself monthly breast self-exams?"

Jacquelyn rolled her eyes. "I know I should. But sometimes I forget, and other times when I do it, my breasts feel so lumpy and bumpy that I can't tell what's what."

Dr. Shaw made gentle tsking sounds. "Jacquelyn Wilkes, you should know better. We're always telling women to take charge of their own health —"

"Spare me the lecture, Doc, I could give it in my sleep." Jacquelyn closed her eyes and winced as the doctor probed the tender spot. "Bull's-eye, that's it. So what do we do about it?"

The doctor said nothing for a moment, then stepped back and consulted Jacquelyn's file again. "Your mother died of breast cancer, right?"

"Yes. Pre-menopausal, bilateral cancer."

Dr. Shaw lifted an eyebrow. "Then we order an ultrasound and a mammogram, if necessary, stat. Get yourself over to the Women's Medical Center. If it's a cyst, it'll show up on the ultrasound. If we still can't tell what it is, perhaps the mammogram will help. In any case, they'll send me the films. I'll take a look and call you."

Jacquelyn breathed a sigh of relief and sat up. "I'm sure it's a cyst. Or only a fibroadenoma. Young women often have benign lumps."

"I certainly hope that's what it is," Dr. Shaw said, opening the door. "Get dressed and come on out to the appointment desk. I'm sending you over to the medical center today."

CHAPTER SIX

Arms resting on the back of her living room sofa, Jacquelyn turned and fixed her gaze on the churning lake across the street. Rain thrummed on the roof of the house; sheets of water streamed over her car, the yard, the porch awnings. It was a typical Florida afternoon thunderstorm, but Jacquelyn stared at the power of the water, fascinated.

How many storms had blown over this house in the years of her life? Hundreds, maybe thousands. Her family had even endured a hurricane or two beneath the tile roof. It was a sturdy structure, built to withstand the toughest weather Florida could offer, and yet today she felt as though the house and her entire world were about to come crashing down.

Surely she had no real reason to be afraid. The girl who performed the ultrasound hadn't been able to identify the lump as a cyst because it was hidden behind dense breast tissue. Jacquelyn had even sat up from the exam table and searched the monitor herself, hoping desperately for some sign of a fluid-filled sac, but there were none. And so she had proceeded to the mammography room.

The female technician was quick and efficient. In fact, her pleasant "this won't take but a moment" patter reminded Jacquelyn of her own little speeches. She stood before the huge machine with her breast resting on a cold sheet of glass, then felt pressure as the machine pressed her breast into a mass thin enough to clearly X-ray. "Don't breathe," the technician ordered, smiling cheerfully as she ducked behind the screen. "It will all be over in a moment."

When the mammogram was done, Jacquelyn slipped back into her own clothes and sat in the waiting room with several other women, one with a whining preschool daughter. The attendant had taken Jacquelyn's X-rays to the radiologist on duty; he would give a preliminary report immediately.

The doctor's door was ajar, and Jacquelyn tilted her head, straining to hear the conversation between the attendant and the radiologist. "I don't see . . ." she heard him say, then the little girl wailed so loudly Jacquelyn couldn't hear the doctor. She closed her eyes and resisted the impulse to shush the child.

"Miss Wilkes?" The attendant, draped in a smile of professional concern, stood outside the radiologist's office. "The doctor will call Dr. Shaw this afternoon, and we'll messenger these films to her office."

"What did he see?" Jacquelyn whispered, the words scraping her throat.

The woman smiled again. "A small growth, probably benign, given your age. He's recommending a fine needle aspiration. Your doctor will review the films and call you with her opinion."

Four hours had passed since Jacquelyn heard those words. She had taken the rest of the day off, the first sick day she had requested in over two years. The clock on the mantel chimed five times, and Jacquelyn sighed, realizing that her coworkers were now finishing up their patient charts and preparing to head home. Dr. Shaw's staff would be doing the same thing, so if she were going to call —

The phone rang, startling her. After a moment of paralysis, she dashed into the kitchen and lifted the receiver. "Hello?"

"Hi, honey." Craig's voice.

"Hi, yourself." She failed miserably in her

attempt to sound lighthearted.

"I called your office and they said you were sick. What's wrong?"

"Nothing really, I just needed to see a doctor. It's no big deal."

"Are you okay?"

Bless him for asking. She hadn't realized how desperately she wanted to talk to someone, to share her burden.

"I don't know." She gulped as hot tears spilled from her eyes. "I found a breast lump, Craig, and the doctor recommended a mammogram. So I went to the hospital, and now I'm waiting for the results."

Her news was met with silence.

"Craig? Are you still there?"

"Sure, honey. Well, what do they think it is?"

What do you think they think? She wanted to scream. Instead, she forced her voice to remain steady. "I thought it was a cyst, but now I think it's probably a fibroadenoma — a kind of benign lump common in women my age."

"Well, then." Craig's voice boomed with confidence. "That's nothing to worry about."

"Right." She smiled at her reflection in the polished oven door. "Nothing at all."

"Good." His voice took on a familiar let's-get-down-to-business tone. "I'm sorry, hon, but I won't be able to make it over tonight. I'm meeting with that guy from Haines City who wants to sell his dealership."

"That's okay." Her eyes lifted to the rain-streaked windows. "I probably wouldn't be very good company anyway. I'm really tired."

"Well, I hope you feel better." His tone was distant, as if he were already making notes on his calendar or something.

"Thanks."

The phone clicked in her ear, and she replaced it slowly. Craig knew her mother had died of breast cancer, but he didn't know about the high-risk factors for daughters of women with cancer. If he had known, would he have remained on the line to comfort her? Somehow she didn't think so. Craig wasn't big on nurturing.

The rain, sharp as a lance against her wide kitchen windows, blurred the world outside as tears blurred the room around her. She sank into a chair at the kitchen table and pillowed her head on her arms, releasing in a flood the frustration and fear that had been building for days. She would cry now, she told herself, and get it out of her system. Later, she'd laugh at the thought that a mere fibroadenoma could drive her to such a state.

Bailey's soft feet padded across the floor, his nails softly clicking against the hard tile. The dog seated himself at Jacquelyn's side and lifted his muzzle, releasing a long, mournful howl.

Palming away tears, Jacquelyn sat up and placed her arms around the dog's velvety neck. "Sweet thing, you're the only one who can see me like this," she whispered, lowering her cheek to the dog's black ear.

The brilliant ringing of the kitchen phone jarred her again. The doctor. She sniffed, then picked up the receiver.

"Hello?" Her voice, eerily calm and rational, sounded as it if came from another body.

"Nurse Wilkes?" She felt a flush run over her face as she recognized the caller's voice. Why would Jonah Martin call her?

She thumbed tears from her cheeks. "Is something wrong, Dr. Martin?"

"I was going through my charts, and came across Bailey's," he said, only the faintest trace of humor in his voice. "Not wanting the nurses to stumble over this case, I thought I'd place the follow-up call myself. How is the puppy doing today?"

"He's fine." Jacquelyn smiled, relieved to

talk about something other than herself. She hadn't mentioned Bailey's "case" in the office, not wanting to cause any trouble. She didn't think Dr. Kastner would appreciate Jonah's use of the clinic as a canine emergency treatment center.

"Bailey was a little groggy the night after his adventure, but the next morning he was his old self. The swelling's gone down, and his appetite's normal. Apparently he's as good as new."

"That's great." The doctor's soothing words were oddly disconcerting. "Perhaps I should ask how *you* are. I noticed you weren't in the office today. Lauren said you were out sick."

"I went to see my doctor, just like you recommended," she said, twisting in her chair.

"And?"

"She ordered an ultrasound and mammogram, which I had this afternoon. I'm waiting to hear from Dr. Shaw's office."

"I suppose I should let you go, then."

"I suppose."

A long, awkward silence fell between them. Why didn't he say goodbye and hang up?

"If you need anything," he spoke with

staid calmness, "please don't hesitate to let us know."

Jacquelyn closed her eyes, knowing he would say the same thing to any of his patients . . . or the other nurses. Even in his chilliest moments, Jonah Martin was unfailingly polite. "Thank you, Doctor. And thanks for checking on Bailey."

She hung up and replaced the phone, then stared out the window at the driving rain. Surely this miserable weather accounted for her inexplicable feeling of emptiness.

Despite the painful knot of fear inside, Jacquelyn had to smile as she lay back on Dr. Shaw's treatment table four days later. Some sassy nurse had plastered the ceiling above with glossy eight-by-ten photos of Mel Gibson, Brad Pitt and Denzel Washington.

"I like your artwork," she told the attending nurse who was busily arranging tools on the doctor's tray. She pointed toward the ceiling.

"Ah, those." The young nurse grinned. "They're all cute, for sure, but they're so — old. And none of them are my type."

"And who is your type?" Jacquelyn asked lightly, trying to steer her thoughts away from the dark clouds that had lately occupied her mind.

The nurse smiled and leaned forward. "Well," she said, her eyes darting left and right as if she were divulging a great secret, "last week at the main hospital I saw this doctor who was so drop-dead gorgeous I nearly screamed out loud. Blond, blue-eyed, well-built, with a smile as broad as a barn door." She sighed. "But then I found out he works in one of the clinics, so the chances of me meeting up with him again are slim to none."

"Which clinic?" Jacquelyn asked, her eyes drifting up to the picture of Mel Gibson. With blond hair instead of brown, and a few less wrinkles, good ol' Mel might resemble the man the nurse had been describing —

"He's the new doctor at the cancer clinic."

Jacquelyn gave the nurse a sidelong glance of utter disbelief. "About thirty? Probably six feet tall?"

The nurse nodded vigorously. "That's him! You know him?"

"I work for him," Jacquelyn said, returning her eyes to the ceiling. "And yes, Jonah Martin is attractive. But I don't know if he's *anybody's* type. For one thing, he knows he's handsome. He flirts with all his patients, especially the grandmothers. And he's a terror in the office. We can never find him when we need him — he's always sitting down in the chemo room listening to some guy's story about his grandkids or some woman's complaints about her wig. And while he's sweet to the patients, he's like an underfed grizzly with us nurses. We never know how he's going to react."

The door opened, and Jacquelyn fell silent as Dr. Shaw stepped into her line of vision. "Good morning, Jackie," she said, flashing a brief smile before she dove into Jacquelyn's chart. "I'm sure I don't have to tell you about the aspiration procedure. We're going to clean the area with Betadine, then I'll inject a small amount of local anesthetic into the skin where most of the nerves are. You won't feel any serious pain."

"Fine by me," Jacquelyn said, crossing her legs in an attempt to act as though this hadn't upset her in the least. But, lying here awake on the table before the doctor and her assistants, Jacquelyn couldn't help but feel like some sacrifice to an ancient temple deity.

"I'll insert a fine, hollow needle into the lump and draw any fluid into a syringe," the doctor went on, clearly on autopilot. "But since the ultrasound leads us to believe no fluid is present, I'll push the needle back and forth through the tissue to free some cells, aspirate them into the syringe and then smear them on a slide for the lab."

"And if the lab finds no malignancy, I'm clear, right?" Jacquelyn asked.

Dr. Shaw pressed her lips together. "Not entirely. A negative report only means that we didn't find any cancer cells on this aspiration. If we don't find any, I'm going to recommend an excisional biopsy of that lump so we'll know exactly what we're dealing with. But if we do find malignant cells, we'll have a good idea what kind of cancer we're fighting."

Jacquelyn closed her eyes. If they found nothing, she'd be hospitalized just long enough for a biopsy. And if they found cancerous cells —

No!

She pushed the thought from her mind, struggling to maintain her fragile control. She would hope for a negative result, have the thing cut out, and be altogether done with the mess.

"I'm ready," she said, gripping the edges of the exam table.

Nine days later, on a Thursday afternoon, Jacquelyn took a seat on the sofa in Dr. Shaw's beautifully appointed office. The doctor swiveled slowly in her leather chair behind the desk, Jacquelyn's chart open in front of her. The green-lined report from the pathologist's lab lay atop a pile of neatly stacked pages.

"Jacquelyn." Dr. Shaw's voice, though quiet, had an ominous quality. "I'm sorry to report that the pathologist did find malignant cells." She eyed Jacquelyn with a calculating expression. "But since we know cancer is present, we can skip the excisional biopsy. I've studied your history, and I'm recommending that you see a surgeon. A lumpectomy followed by radiation treatments seems feasible. The nodule appears small, and you are young. . . ."

The words faded away into a jumble of sounds as Jacquelyn lowered her eyes and focused on one word: *cancer.* The savage monster that had snatched her mother had sunk its claws into her, too. How would her father handle this news? She couldn't tell him. After losing a beloved wife to cancer, he wouldn't be able to handle the fact that he might lose his only daughter as well. And what about Craig? Craig hadn't been able to handle Bailey's emergency, how would he react to hers?

Breast cancer. Who would have believed it? Aside from the lump, she had no other symptoms. No shortness of breath, no real pain. Her kidneys were fine, her digestion normal, her blood pressure steady as a rock. She had been tired, but not sick, and yet somehow, against her knowledge, she'd been drafted into the breast cancer club, where membership metastasized at a rate of two percent a year and death collected the dues. Her mother paid and she'd pay, too, if the disease had its way. . . .

"Jacquelyn?" The doctor's eyes caught and held hers. "I know this must be a terrible shock, even to someone who works in a cancer clinic. I strongly advise you to find someone to act as your personal advocate. You're going to need a responsible friend to help you remember all you learn, someone to help you evaluate your options, someone to lean on. This person should be available to be with you during these first important medical consultations."

Jacquelyn felt as though the doctor spoke through a wall of cotton; the words were muffled, disjointed, automatic. Surely they could have nothing to do with *her*. She had been healthy and fit when she walked into this office and nothing had changed. She would walk out the same way she came in.

"How are you feeling, Jacquelyn?" Dr. Shaw's voice had softened, and Jacquelyn had to learn forward and strain to hear it. "Can I call someone for you?"

"No." Jacquelyn's hand reached automatically to twist in her hair, a nervous childhood gesture she hadn't resorted to in years. "And I feel —" she held up a strand of hair "— I feel like you've just told me there's a knot at the end of my hair that could kill me."

"Then I suggest," Dr. Shaw said, nodding slowly, "that we get rid of the knot as soon as possible."

Jacquelyn immediately called Craig, who dropped everything just as she'd hoped he would. He met her at Dr. Shaw's office, a twisted smile on his face and lightning bolts of worry in his eyes. Though he tried to be pleasant and relaxed, his false calm evaporated under Dr. Shaw's somber gaze.

"I've already explained to Jacquelyn that I believe a lumpectomy and follow-up radiation is all that will be necessary," Dr. Shaw explained. "But I'll be referring her to one of the oncologists at the Chambers-Wyatt cancer clinic for treatment. One of the surgeons at the affiliated hospital will handle the surgery."

"She'll be a patient in her own clinic?" Craig asked, his bushy brows drawing downward in a frown. "Won't that be a bit . . . awkward?"

"I'm a chemo nurse," Jacquelyn replied woodenly. "I don't work in radiation. The patients wouldn't see me . . . right there beside them."

Dr. Shaw nodded. "I don't think it should matter, but that's true. And, for the record, I think we can be grateful we caught this one as quickly as we did."

Jacquelyn looked over at Craig. He leaned sideways in his chair, one hand supporting his head, the other hanging limp at his side. The light had vanished from his eyes and his face was stiff with fear.

A flash of annoyance jarred Jacquelyn. *She* was the one who had just been given a possible death sentence — why did *he* look so distraught? She needed him to be steady, sensible and sympathetic, but he hadn't been able to meet her eyes since walking into the room.

"I think you two need some time to talk things out," Dr. Shaw said, closing Jacquelyn's file. "I'm going to write a referral for you, Jacquelyn. For years I've been sending all my patients to Dr. Kastner, and since you know him —"

"No," Jacquelyn said, interrupting. "I would prefer to make my own choice.

Please, ask Dr. Martin to take my case."

"Dr. Martin?" For an instant, Craig roared to life. "But you hate him!"

One of Dr. Shaw's brows lifted. "He hasn't been at this hospital very long."

"Long enough," Jacquelyn answered. "He's a fighter, and his patients believe in him. Dr. Kastner is a fine doctor, but I'd prefer Dr. Martin."

Dr. Shaw shrugged. "It's your choice."

She stood, a formal indication that their meeting was finished. "Go home, Jacquelyn," she said, tapping her desk in an emphatic gesture. "Relax. Do the things you enjoy. We're going to take good care of you." Despite her words, the faint smile she gave Jacquelyn held more regret than confidence.

The proverbial cat must have swiped Craig's tongue, for he said nothing as he walked Jacquelyn to her car in the doctor's parking lot.

"Thanks for coming," she said finally, pausing outside her door. She ran her fingers lightly over his silk tie. "I know you had to leave some important client in order to come here."

"What can I do?" he asked, his voice gruff with emotion. "Honestly, Jacquelyn, I don't know what to say. I've never been through

126

anything like this."

"Just hold me," she said, moving into the circle of his arms. He did hold her for a long moment, but she felt no comfort in his embrace, no strength. With one good push, she could have knocked him down; he was reeling from the announcement as much as she was.

"I'd better let you go," she whispered, backing out of his arms. "I'll be at home, if you want to call me later. You know — to talk about being my personal advocate. I'll need to know how much you want to do."

He looked at her with a blank expression. "Sure. I'll call."

"Okay." She turned to unlock the car, then gave him a last smile. "Thanks, Craig. I don't know what I'd do without you."

"Yeah. Talk to you later." He turned and walked away, his shoulders hunched with the burden she'd just placed squarely on his back.

Weakened by Dr. Shaw's news and a pounding headache, Jacquelyn called in sick the next morning. Whether the headache was stress related or not she couldn't tell, but she curled up in her bathrobe on her overstuffed couch and sipped hot tea in front of the television.

127

Bailey didn't mind at all that she had taken the day to stay at home. He lay obediently on the floor at her feet, a three-dimensional bearskin rug sprawled over the living room floor.

Just after noon the doorbell rang. A florist stood outside with a basket of daisies in his arms, and Jacquelyn flushed with bittersweet pleasure when she realized that only Craig could have sent them. "Thank you," she said, tipping the messenger. She brought the flowers into the house, placed them in the center of the kitchen table and unfolded the attached card.

Handwritten on "Get Well" stationery, the note was short and simple:

Dearest Jacquelyn:
You deserve the best life can offer, and I'm not at all what you need. You will have my affection and prayers, but you need to find someone stronger, better and with more experience than I. Know that my thoughts are with you always, but I can't help you now. You deserve more than me.

Always,
Craig

Jacquelyn slipped to the floor beside her

128

anxious dog as a wild flash of grief ripped through her.

CHAPTER SEVEN

"Is that all, Dr. Martin?" Stacy Derry thrust her head through Jonah's office doorway, a concerned smile on her face. "If there's anything else you'd like me to do —"

"No, go on home." He looked up from the charts he'd been studying and waved the dark-eyed nurse away with an abrupt gesture. "It's Friday, the week's over. Get out of here, go home."

Not easily rebuffed, the nurse dimpled. "I am on my way out, but I wanted to make sure everything was covered, you know, since Jacquelyn wasn't here today. But if there's nothing else —"

"Goodbye." He cut her off, eager for her to go, then snapped his glance back toward her. "Stacy, wait a minute. You and Jacquelyn are good friends, right?"

Interested, the nurse stepped out from behind the wall and leaned against the door frame. "Well, I don't know that we're *best* friends," she said, "but we're friends, yes."

Jonah returned his gaze to the charts in his lap and pretended an offhanded interest. "Has she been in touch with you? It's not like her to drop out of sight without a word of explanation, is it?"

Stacy shrugged. "She spoke to Lauren when she called in this morning." Her indifferent expression broke into an open, helpful smile. "But I could check on her this weekend, if you like."

"Don't bother. I'll have Lauren call Monday if Nurse Wilkes hasn't graced us with her presence by eight o'clock." He briskly nodded a farewell, then looked back down at his charts.

"Is there anything else?"

Though her smile had frayed slightly, her eyes still shone with eagerness. Jonah shook his head and waved her away again. "No. Go home. We don't pay overtime."

Undaunted by his gruffness, she tossed a final smile over her shoulder, then moved down the hallway. Jonah sighed as he returned the chart to his desk. His inner warning systems had been clanging ever since he received his first unusually eager smile from Stacy Derry. He'd met dozens of women like her, and knew enough to steer clear of their pathetically girlish

131

behavior. Stacy was sociable and charming, the perfect public relations nurse, but on more than one occasion he'd noticed her low tolerance for routine. Blood pressure readings, taking blood, recording weights and heights — those things bored her, and that was a pity, for routine was a large part of nursing. Why on earth, he wondered, had she become a nurse in the first place? And why, despite his intentionally frosty manner, did she insist on worming her way into his office?

Alarm bells sounded in his brain whenever he and Stacy were alone together. He found himself making excuses to leave the lab when she leaned in close to hand him a chart or a blood sample, and whenever he had the freedom to choose a nurse to help with a procedure, he usually called for Lauren, who eyed him as if he'd been born and bred among the Mafia, or Jacquelyn, whose rapier wit in the last while was nearly as cutting as it had been before he treated her dog.

He closed the chart on his desk, aware that for the last five minutes he'd been staring at his notes without internalizing a single word. Lately his mind had been altogether too occupied with thoughts of his sharp-tongued, copper-haired nurse. Some deep-seated intuition told him that her absence from the office today did not bode well, and the fact that she hadn't spoken to Stacy only reinforced his concern. He knew from the nurses' whispered conversations that she had left early yesterday for an appointment with Dr. Shaw. If she were out today with something as trivial as a cold, surely she would have mentioned it to someone. This silence — so unlike her — was unnerving.

The trilling of the phone broke his concentration, and he glanced at the clock before picking up the receiver. Six o'clock. None of the patients would be calling the clinic at this hour; the answering service automatically picked up all patient calls after five and beeped him for emergencies. The service had transferred this call to his private line.

"Hello?"

The crisp voice on the other end was polite and professional. "Dr. Martin, this is Rita Shaw from the Chambers-Wyatt Women's Center. I have a patient who presents a malignant nodule in the left breast. Although there is a strong family history, I believe lumpectomy and radiation will take care of the problem, though I expect you will make the final recommendations for

133

treatment after your examination."

"I'm not sure I understand, Doctor." Jonah shifted in his chair. He'd heard through the grapevine that he shouldn't expect referrals from Dr. Rita Shaw. She and Robert Kastner were fast friends, and so far, without exception, her patients had chosen to be supervised by Dr. Kastner.

"What part don't you understand? I have a patient with breast cancer, and she specifically asked that I refer her to you," Dr. Shaw answered, her voice even more brisk and businesslike than before. "To be honest, I tried to dissuade her. You are new to this hospital —"

"I will do my best to be certain her faith in me is warranted," Jonah interrupted, his temper flaring. "Now, if you'll give me the patient's name, I'll tell my staff to watch for her file."

"That leads to another of my objections," Dr. Shaw said. "The patient is your nurse — Jacquelyn Wilkes. And I don't think it's wise to complicate the doctor-patient relationship with a working relationship. . . ."

She went on, but Jonah didn't hear. The muscles of his forearm hardened beneath his sleeve; his breath seemed to have solidified in his throat. Jacquelyn Wilkes — cancer? He'd known it was a possibility when she mentioned the breast mass, but he had been nearly as certain as she that the mass would prove to be a cyst or even a fibroadenoma. Breast cancer at her age was unusual; seventy-seven percent of women with diagnoses of breast cancer were fifty or older.

His thoughts whirred and lagged; he came back to reality in time to hear the summation of Dr. Shaw's speech. "So you see why I tried to talk her out of the referral. If you agree, why don't you refer her to Robert?"

Send Jacquelyn to Robert Kastner? He couldn't. Kastner would elect the most liberal treatment possible, probably lumpectomy only. And he'd ignore the fact that cancers of younger women were generally more aggressive and very nasty.

"Jacquelyn works for Dr. Kastner, too," Jonah answered, choosing his words with care. "So I will take her case. Thank you for your call, Dr. Shaw. I'll look forward to receiving her records from your office."

"Good night, then, Doctor," the woman answered, all traces of goodwill gone from her voice.

Jonah heard a click in his ear. He replaced the telephone receiver, then leaned back in his chair and rubbed his chin, momentarily lost in a sea of confusing emotions. His

135

behavior with Dr. Shaw could well be described as cocky, but for years he'd been swatting away comments about his sketchy track record and what others perceived as instability. He'd worked in too many hospitals and made too many enemies for a man of thirty, but it couldn't be helped.

Still, he probably shouldn't have vented his frustrations with Jacquelyn Wilkes's physician. Jacquelyn would need two *cooperative* doctors to see her through the days ahead, and if she would not confide in him — and he sincerely doubted she would — she might open up to Dr. Shaw.

He frowned, suddenly puzzled by a new thought. Despite her obvious contempt for his professional methods and manner, Jacquelyn had asked for *him*. "When the going gets tough, the tough change their minds, right, Jackie?" he murmured, then he flushed in shame at his words. He had won a tiny battle in the war between them, but he couldn't rejoice in his victory.

In the coming days, he and Jacquelyn would face cancer together, and Jonah Martin could not imagine a more formidable enemy.

Jacquelyn was *happy*. She tripped through the house in a contented fog, running her hands over her kitchen table, her sofa, the antique umbrella stand in the foyer. Bailey padded by her side, matching his steps with hers, smiling up at her with soft eyes. She wasn't aware of any special reason for her happiness, but she swam in it, breathed it in, reveled in the sheer childlike simplicity of the feeling. Things were back the way they were before the dark diagnosis led her across an invisible line and into a new phase of life.

In the midst of her slow-motion dance, Bailey began to whine. The soft sound cut through the embracing folds of sleep and her eyes flew open at Bailey's call. Though her mind gripped at the dream with terrible longing, light streamed through the slats in the blinds on her windows as reality and the sunrise conspired to shatter her happiness.

She sat up in bed, instantly and irrevocably awake. With cancer.

Woodenly she swung her legs out of the bed, then slipped into her robe and stumbled toward the bedroom door. The automatic motions came easily enough — whistle for the dog, open the front door, let Bailey out into the yard, pick up the newspaper, check to see that no neighbors were staring. She opened the paper, half expecting to see her name emblazoned in the headlines — Nurse Jacquelyn Wilkes Discovers Cancer! — and briefly marveled that one discovery could profoundly rock her existence and yet go unnoticed by everyone else in the world.

"Come back to reality, Jacquelyn," she told herself, forcing her eyes to skim the front page. "You've got to get through this. Call out the troops, send an SOS. What do you tell your patients? Meet it, beat it, defeat it."

Bailey came trotting up the front sidewalk, a loopy grin on his face, but this morning Jacquelyn found it hard to return the dog's affection. She led him back inside the house, poured his morning meal into a dog bowl as wide as Texas, then sat at the kitchen table, the newspaper spread before her, the phone securely in her peripheral vision.

Surely Craig would call. He just needed time to adjust. After all, he'd been about to propose on Labor Day, and a man who is ready and willing to get married would not walk out on his intended bride. The news of her cancer had rattled him just as it had her, but he would come back. And he always called on Saturday morning, *always*. At nine o'clock sharp, after he'd gotten up and read the business section, after he'd checked his answering machine for any calls he'd missed on Friday night. Saturdays were their sacrosanct time, the only full day they could really spend together.

She automatically opened the paper and tried to read as the digital clock on the microwave soundlessly advanced. Eight-thirty — still too early. She took a deep breath and turned another page. War in the Middle East had erupted again, riots destroyed a remote Sudanese city, and a tragic fire on a ferry in the Baltic Sea had taken ninety-eight lives in the night. Troubles worlds away.

She glanced up. Eight forty-seven. Craig would still be on the phone, checking in with any prospective customers, setting up appointments for Sunday afternoon. She turned to the comics and read her favorites: *Peanuts, For Better or For Worse,* and *Jump Start.* None of them today struck her as the least bit funny.

Eight fifty-nine. She folded the sections of newspaper, stacked them on an empty chair, then linked her fingers together and stared at the phone. Craig had probably passed a restless night, burdened by thoughts of how he'd abandoned her. Maybe he had overslept.

Nine o'clock. She waited a full sixty seconds in silence, then forced a smile to her lips. He must have just landed a really big deal — no, he hadn't, he always told her nobody did business on Saturday morning — or maybe his clock had stopped, or some family emergency had come up.

Her eyes fell upon the bright flowers in the center of the table. Why was she fooling herself? She could wait here until noon and Craig Bishop would not call. In his logical, unyielding way, he had already decided what was best for each of them. He had freed her to look for someone more supportive while allowing himself to keep moving toward his bright ambitions.

She knew she ought to be furious, but she couldn't summon the energy to be angry at someone as dispassionate as Craig. He had been a friend, as solid as a rock and *as dull as a dog biscuit* . . . Stacy's mocking words filtered back through her memory, and despite her misery, Jacquelyn felt her mouth twist in a lopsided smile. She couldn't be angry. She was too afraid.

She lowered her hand to Bailey's warm ears. "It's okay," she whispered, looking into the dog's soulful eyes. "We don't need Craig Bishop, do we? When a girl's in trouble, she needs — family."

Swallowing the despair in her throat, she leaned toward the phone, then hesitated. Was there a standard operating procedure for telling family members about cancer? In her years of nursing she had often been present when doctors gave bad news to patients, but she had no idea how those patients told their families. She couldn't even remember how she'd learned that her mother had cancer. Jacquelyn had been nine or ten when they discovered the first lump, and after that her mother was never well. . . .

She leaned back, her thoughts scampering vaguely around. Maybe the blunt approach was best: "Excuse me, Daddy, but I thought you might like to know that I have cancer." Or "Hi, Dad, having a nice Saturday? I know we haven't spoken in a couple of months, but I just thought you'd like to know that the family genes have corrupted again. I've got cancer, too."

A heaviness centered in her chest. It wasn't fair; children shouldn't have to bring their parents news like this. Something was drastically wrong with the world when a daughter had to tell her father that the disease he feared most had returned to haunt him.

But sooner or later he'd have to know. And

right now Jacquelyn thought he was the only person in the world who would care.

Leaning forward, she punched in her dad's number, then rested her head on her hand as the phone buzzed in her ear. Finally, her father's robust baritone rang over the line. "Hello?"

"Hi, Dad." Her traitorous throat closed suddenly as emotion bubbled up and stopped her words. Why were her emotions erupting now? She'd received the news calmly; she'd had a rational, sane discussion with Dr. Shaw. Why couldn't she, a medical professional, talk to her father about the disease she knew best?

"Jacquelyn? Is that you?"

She heard a trace of panic in his voice, but she could only gasp in response. She waved her hand, a foolish gesture he couldn't see, but it gave her something to do as she struggled to collect her scattered emotions.

"Honey, are you okay? Do you need us to call the police? Triple A? What's wrong?"

"No," she finally whispered in a strangled voice. Pressing her hand over her face, she cleared her throat and took a deep breath. "I'm sorry, Dad, but I'm afraid I have some bad news."

"Merciful heavens. Nothing's happened

to Roger, has it?" Jacquelyn thought of her brother, living far away with his family in Oregon. She hadn't spoken to him in months; how would she know if Roger had problems? But Dad would naturally think about Roger; they had always been close. She had been closer to her mother.

"No, Dad, it's me." She caught sight of her reflection in the polished chrome toaster on the counter. Hurt and longing lay naked in her red-rimmed eyes, and she stared, fascinated, as her lips formed the dreaded words, "I've got breast cancer."

The words seemed to resonate in the air.

"Dad?"

No answer.

"Daddy, are you there? Did you hear me?"

"It's not true. You're too young."

A new anguish seared her heart. Did he think she'd make this up? "It is true. There's a malignant lump. I had it aspirated."

"Impossible."

"Dad, I'm a nurse. I know it's possible. With Mom's history, it was actually *probable* that I'd develop a malignancy —"

"Get a second opinion, Jacquelyn. And then get a third. You're too young to have breast cancer — don't go listening to those knife-happy doctors you work with. Here, talk to Helen. Let her tell you I'm right."

"Daddy?"

He was gone. She heard the clunk of the receiver as he dropped it on the table, then his voice, far away, calling for his wife. Jacquelyn clutched the phone to her chest as a flash of loneliness stabbed at her. He wasn't going to help. He didn't even want to believe her. The knowledge sliced like a knife through her heart.

"Jacquelyn?" Helen's tinny voice echoed from the receiver. "Jackie, are you there?"

Jacquelyn's mouth felt like old paper, dry and dusty, but she lifted the receiver and managed a reply. "I'm here, Helen." Sweet, simple Helen wouldn't want to handle this. She and Jacquelyn had never talked about anything more significant than whether Helen should plant day lilies or coleus at the front of the condo. She wouldn't want to talk about Jacquelyn's cancer — and Dad knew it.

"Jackie, are you okay?"

"I'm fine, Helen. But I have to have . . . an operation, and Dad's a little upset."

"But you'll be okay?"

"Sure. Hey, I work for the best hospital in the state. How could anything go wrong?"

Jacquelyn listened to Helen's sigh of relief, then asked a few questions about their plans for the weekend. When the conversation had

144

run out like sand in an hourglass, Jacquelyn said goodbye and hung up.

She should have known. Her father did not have the stamina or the will to participate in a second bout with breast cancer. As cleanly as a surgeon, he had separated himself from Mom's house, her daughter, even her disease. Jacquelyn knew he loved her, but he didn't have the strength to fight another battle.

Her heart squeezed in anguish as she realized she had no one to turn to. Dr. Shaw had advised finding a personal advocate, but Jacquelyn had no relatives or close friends who could serve in such a role. Stacy was a friend, but highly unsuited for what might be a long-term commitment. Years ago Jacquelyn had close friends at church who would have been willing to help, but she hadn't been to church regularly since before her college days. Jacquelyn's brother, Roger, was far too busy. Roger's wife, Karen, was kind and sympathetic, but she could not function as an advocate or even a confidante living in Oregon. Jacquelyn would need someone to drive her to the hospital, to look after Bailey, to oversee her medications. Someone to talk to. . . .

"God, there's no one but You." She lowered her head into her hands. "Why have

You let this happen to me? Why? I know I haven't been as close to You as I should be, but I've been doing my best to do the work You called me to do. So why did You let me get cancer?"

For a wild, insane moment she wondered if cancer might be contagious after all; perhaps she'd caught it from one of her patients. But such an idea was laughable. Her frantic brain was desperately grasping at straws, looking for someone to blame.

A suffocating sensation tightened her throat, and Jacquelyn lowered her head to the kitchen table and wept.

CHAPTER EIGHT

Jonah shifted to let a few latecomers straggle past him into the church pew, then straightened and tried to concentrate on the responsive reading.

"Save me, O God," the worship leader read from a psalm, "for the floodwaters are up to my neck. Deeper and deeper I sink into the mire — I can't find a foothold to stand on."

"I am in deep water." Jonah pitched his voice a note below those around him in order to hear himself speak the words. "And the floods overwhelm me."

The verse was a familiar one. When the work of the ministry grew too difficult, his father used to quote the old King James Version with weary irreverence. "Hang on, family," he'd say, sitting down at the kitchen table near the end of a trying day. "Today I am come into deep waters, where the floods overflow me."

Isn't Dad the reason you're here now?
Jonah lifted his eyes from the responsive reading and glanced around. Why did he come to church at all, if not out of some misguided allegiance to his father? Old boyhood habits didn't die easily, not even a dozen years after leaving home. Of course he told colleagues who asked — two in seven years, by his last count — that he went to church because he believed a physician ought to be as involved in the community as his patients. "My patients want to know their doctor believes in a power higher than himself," he once explained. "People facing cancer tend to become concerned with getting their own spiritual houses in order. And when their thoughts turn toward the spiritual realm, they want to know their doctor understands."

And Jonah did understand — though he couldn't seem to stir up much personal belief these days. Oh, he still believed that God created the world, and he was even willing to grant God a literal six days instead of six epochs. And Noah and the ark wasn't *too* far-fetched, especially in light of the age-old rumor that gopher wood had been found above the tree line on Mount Ararat. Jonah didn't have trouble believing in either the inspiration of the Bible or the divinity

148

of Jesus Christ. Those truths were as elemental to him as the air he breathed; he'd been taught them since he was a babe in his mother's arms.

It was the personal stuff Jonah couldn't swallow anymore. If God really cared, then why did so many deserving, wonderful patients die prematurely? And if God answered prayer, why hadn't He answered Jonah's cries during those dark days in Virginia? He had nearly witnessed the miscarriage of his entire career; he would have lost everything if he'd insisted upon staying at UVA. That lying witch had convinced everyone from the head of the hospital to Jonah's best friends that she was as chaste as an angel and Jonah practically a criminal. If he hadn't resigned quietly and left, she'd have dragged his name and reputation through the mud, endangering not only his future in medicine, but the fragile confidence of the patients who had placed their faith and hope in him.

He had asked God for deliverance and none came. He had begged God to expose the nurse's lies and manipulation, but in her initial complaint to hospital officials she'd come off as innocent as a cloistered nun. Finally, in desperation, Jonah had asked God to send him someplace where he could be happy and do some good, but eight months after he'd moved and established a practice at Tidewater General, the rumors caught up with him. "If you were innocent, you should have fought the charges," the hospital administrator told him right after Jonah promised to resign. "But you ran. Now you'll be running forever."

How could he have fought? He had taken his accuser out for dinner — once. She was his nurse. They were often alone together in the office. In the end, everything boiled down to his word against hers. A formal investigation would have taken weeks and even if he was cleared, his coworkers would always wonder if he had been guilty. Female patients, the brave, open-minded ones who would still accept him as a physician, would probably shriek in fear or accusation if left alone in an exam room with him even for a moment. . . .

So he'd left Virginia altogether, confident that the truth of his innocence and his skill with patients would lift him above the fracas he'd escaped. And he had immediately changed his work habits. Before the incident at UVA he had worked with both his co-workers and his patients in easygoing cama-raderie. But now he knew better. Nurses were best treated with icy politeness, and he made no effort to curb the residual anger that sometimes spilled over into his words and gestures.

He'd use whatever it took to keep trouble away. He'd found his own recipe for success: equal parts aloofness and adaptability mixed with a willingness to stay above the fray and be ready to move on when necessary.

So far his approach had worked. His reputation as a physician was spotless, his fellow doctors respected him, and despite several interstate moves and a massive student loan, his bank account was finally in the black.

All this he had accomplished with no help from God. So why, he wondered, glancing up at the gold-tinted glass windows across the church aisle, did he still pay lip service to the Almighty? Church attendance didn't do him any good, and he knew God certainly wasn't flattered that Jonah Martin had chosen to show up on a Sunday morning. So why *was* he here?

He stared past the window into his own thoughts, then felt a shiver pass down his spine as an inner voice he'd heard only once or twice before whispered to his heart: *Jacquelyn Wilkes.*

He'd been thinking of Jacquelyn all weekend, ever since the call from Rita Shaw. The nurse had undoubtedly been devastated to learn of her malignancy, sometimes the news knocked patients off their feet for a couple of days. The word "cancer" literally brought about psychosomatic illnesses in some patients — headaches, stomach disorders and the like. Once they moved past the shock of the diagnosis, most found the strength to stand on their feet and fight, but until that point cancer frequently scored the first knockout blow.

But Jacquelyn was a local girl; surely she had family and friends by her side. Several times yesterday Jonah had resisted the impulse to drop by her house, certain that burly Craig Bishop would not appreciate his presence. And how could Jonah explain his visit? She had not yet officially been to see him as a patient, and their professional relationship had always been . . . professional.

Unlike Stacy Derry, who sizzled like a fourth of July sparkler in his presence, Jacquelyn had never given him any sign that his attention would be welcome. She had been grateful for his help with the dog, of course, and had actually smiled at him with warmth and friendliness as they sat in her cozy kitchen and sipped their sodas. But he

152

had nipped that ripening friendship in the bud and she had let him, not calling for help or comfort or solace even though she'd just received what had to be the worst news of her life. . . .

"I am exhausted from crying for help, my throat is parched and dry," the worship leader intoned, the words slicing into Jonah's thoughts like a scalpel. "My eyes are swollen with weeping, waiting for my God to help me."

Jacquelyn.

There it was again. That insistent prodding and quiet nudge.

Was this what his father would call the Voice of God — *WVOG, you'll have to turn up the volume a little, please* — or was he merely feeling a doctor's concern for a future patient? If Jonah wanted to really let the rein out on his thoughts, he'd say Jacquelyn's name galloped so readily into his mind because it had been driven there by pure masculine interest. He'd never seen anything quite so moving as the sight of her emerald eyes, shimmering with love and tears as she knelt beside that overgrown mutt. . . .

The dog was the answer. This afternoon would be the perfect opportunity to visit Jacquelyn. He'd use the dog as an excuse again, and if Craig Bishop was around, Jonah would beat a hasty retreat.

"In your unfailing love, O God, answer my prayer with your sure salvation," he murmured, finishing with the congregation.

The clock on the mantel was softly chiming one o'clock when the doorbell rang. Jacquelyn wrapped her robe more tightly around her waist, cinched the belt and ran her hand through her hair. She looked terrible, but she didn't care. If that was Craig with an apology on his lips, well, he deserved to see her looking like a wreck. A lot of her misery was his fault.

Bailey howled at the door, eager to welcome whoever stood on the other side. "Sit, Bailey," she said, turning the dead bolt. I ought to let him out, just to give Craig a scare. It'd serve him right, the coward. But Bailey, for once, obeyed and sat primly behind her.

Jacquelyn flung the door open wide, then blinked in surprise. Jonah Martin stood there in a suit, his tie loose and slightly askew. In one hand he held a bag from Taco City, and in the other he held a huge rawhide bone jauntily tied with a blue satin ribbon.

"Hi," he said simply, standing there with

nonchalant grace. "I was on my way home from church, and then I realized I hadn't quite finished my rounds. I haven't checked on Bailey in three weeks."

She stood frozen in the doorway. "You go to church?"

"Why, Jacquelyn," he said, his voice deep with mock severity. "Surely you're not surprised that I'm a God-fearing man?"

She shrugged lightly and pulled the edges of her robe closer to her throat. "Nothing surprises me anymore, Doctor."

Without another word, she stepped back and allowed him to enter the foyer. Excited either by his fuzzy memory of Jonah or the smell of the food, Bailey wriggled with joy. Jonah protectively thrust the taco bag toward Jacquelyn, then knelt to embrace the squirming dog. "Ah, good boy! You're as good as new, aren't you? Yes, I see that you are!"

Puzzled, Jacquelyn shook her head, then trudged toward the kitchen. Jonah Martin was as unpredictable as an earthquake; she never knew when or where he'd show up. But she had to admit that she wasn't sorry to see a familiar face at her door after the hellacious weekend she'd endured.

"I'm glad to see that Bailey is himself again," Jonah said, following her into the

155

kitchen. He gestured toward the taco bag in her hand. "And I'm sorry about bringing my lunch with me, but I didn't want to leave it in the car. So I ordered enough for two. Tacos, burritos, enchiladas — I told them to give me a couple of everything, since I don't know exactly what you like."

"Thanks, but I'm not hungry." Jacquelyn sat at the table and folded her arms. "I don't charge admission — you didn't have to bring my lunch just to check on the dog. There you go again, getting too involved in the personal lives of your patients." She tried to flash him a look of defiance, but a permanent sorrow seemed to weigh her down. Lifting her gaze to meet his, she felt a sharp pang when she saw a pensive shimmer in the shadow of his eyes.

He knew.

With a choking cry she tore her gaze away.

A sense of inadequacy swept over Jonah as he moved toward Jacquelyn. He had never seen such raw pain in a pair of eyes — more than he would have imagined possible for a professional nurse with a loving family and a strong support system.

"How do you know?" Her voice was ragged, as if she had ripped the words from her heart. "Is it written on my face?"

He lowered himself into an empty chair at the table and leaned forward, resting his elbows on his knees. How did he handle *this?* With the detachment he displayed toward his nurses or the compassion his patients desperately needed? He wanted to assure her that she was as lovely as ever, that in her face he could see strength and determination, but she was his nurse, and they were alone in her home. Better to proceed cautiously in what could possibly appear to be a compromising situation.

"No, Jacquelyn. Dr. Shaw called me."

She lifted her head and pressed her lips together, still avoiding his gaze. "Oh. I guess she would. I told her I wanted you to be my oncologist."

He yearned to reach out, to comfort her, but something stopped him. "I appreciate your confidence in me, and I'd be honored to serve as your doctor. Together we will beat this thing."

"We?" The searching eyes she turned toward him were surprisingly hostile. "The cancer is in *me.*"

"But I'll be on your team. Your counsel for the defense. I'll fight for you, Jacquelyn, and together we'll beat this."

Her green eyes clawed at him like talons. "Just shut up, okay? I don't want to hear

157

the usual rhetoric right now." She lowered her head into her hand and Jonah marveled at the power of her anger. She was a fighter and strong anger was good, he could use that strength to help her overcome the cancer. But when she spoke again he heard an edge of desperation in her voice. "I must have been a fool to ask for you. We don't even get along in the office. How are we going to unite to fight my cancer? I don't want to play psychobabble games. There's more than a job at stake here, Doc. It's my life, the only one I have." She sniffed, then wiped her nose on the sleeve of her robe, an unsophisticated, childish gesture that tore at his heart.

"Jacquelyn, I promise you . . ." What? What could he tell her? That he'd been thinking of her since the day she upbraided him in the parking lot? That WVOG and the Holy Spirit were whispering her name in his ear? That she might possibly be the one nurse who could restore his faith in women in general and nurses in particular?

"You've told me that I care too much about my patients," he said simply, noticing that a dim flush raced like a fever across her pale and beautiful face. "Now let me care about *you.*" He heard the warmth in his voice and straightened, afraid he'd said too much. She turned, the heavy lashes that shadowed her cheeks flying up, her extraordinary eyes blazing in surprise. If he wasn't careful he could find himself in real trouble here —

"As your doctor, of course," he added hastily. "During your visits as my patient, I'll be the best advocate you could want. And in the office, our relationship will remain unchanged."

A wall seemed to come up behind her eyes. Her gaze fell to her hands, and her voice, when she spoke, was as cool as ice water. "Yes, doctor," she said, finally meeting his eyes. "I suppose that is the most I can expect. It's what I want, of course. Treat me as a nurse when I'm working, and like a patient when I'm in your office." She hesitated a moment, and seemed to search his face. "Is that why you're really here? To lay down a few ground rules?"

"No." He glanced over at the gingham-accented window, searching for a reasonable explanation. "I don't usually make patient visits on Sunday, but I just felt I needed to drop by. I'd heard the news from Dr. Shaw, of course, and — I thought you might be upset."

"Upset?" Her short laugh was utterly without humor. "I have this strange feeling that my hourglass just got turned upside down. If that's upset, yes, I guess I am."

"Well — don't be. I know I'm new at this hospital, but I've got a good track record with breast cancer cases."

"So this is a *professional* visit." She was staring past him, her voice distant and more reserved than it had been only a moment before.

He lifted his head, about to assure her that his concern was genuine, then realized that she was staring at a large bouquet in the center of her table.

"Lovely flowers," he said, following her gaze.

"From Craig." Her mouth suddenly bent in a dry, one-sided smile. "He sent them after he heard . . . the news."

"Ah." Jonah pulled away. Even though the boyfriend wasn't here, his presence loomed between them. And Jacquelyn had just made certain that Jonah understood his place in the scheme of things — he was Jacquelyn's doctor and employer. He had no place in this cozy gingham kitchen.

She turned and gave him a smile that seemed a little worn around the edges. "Thank you, Doc, for dropping by. Since Bailey and I are both fine, we won't keep you."

He gestured toward the bag of food. "Keep the tacos. You need to eat."

"I'm really not hungry." Her hair shone bronze and gold in the sunlight as she shook her head. "Take them with you. There are several quiet picnic tables across the road by the lake."

"Okay." He stood, picked up the taco bag and walked toward the foyer, understanding. She was glad to have him as a doctor, but she didn't want him as a friend — especially since Craig what's-his-name apparently occupied a primary position in her life. In her own way, Jacquelyn had made herself completely clear.

He paused at the front door. "Will we see you back at work tomorrow?"

She had followed him into the foyer, and her face seemed even paler now than when he had entered. "Yes." She gave him a tight, controlled smile. "I wouldn't want your work to suffer. I'm sorry I missed Friday, but I needed a little time to sort things out."

Not knowing how to answer, Jonah nodded again and slipped out of the house.

Jacquelyn moved to her lace-covered window and watched him stride down the sidewalk toward his car. He'd caught her by surprise, but his presence had briefly brought light to the house, momentarily lifting both her heart and Bailey's. She had been praying for someone to talk to, someone who could understand her fears and worries, someone who would listen to her verbalize the pros and cons of various treatment options — but then Jonah had said his visit was strictly professional.

He hadn't come as a friend. He had come as her doctor.

Jonah Martin was a maverick; she might have known he'd show up on her doorstep. Just like he'd show up at Mrs. Baldovino's door with a steaming lasagna or Mrs. Redfield's with a basket of flowers and a card. He believed in making his patients trust him, he was altogether too personally involved, and for an instant she had almost dropped her guard and believed that he had come because he cared . . . about her.

But he had known she wanted him to be her oncologist.

Okay, so she'd deal with it. She had deliberately chosen him over Dr. Kastner, not because she wanted flowers and tacos and personal attention, but because Jonah Martin's patients *survived.*

Jonah's Mustang pulled away from the curb and sped off around the curve of the lake road until it moved out of sight. She let the sheer lace panel fall back into place, then pressed her fingers to her lips. Cancer treatment meant accepting the good with the bad. In order to kill cancer cells, millions of healthy cells would have to die as well. In order to catch a small cancer, a healthy lump of tissue had to be cut away. In order to stop a larger tumor, sometimes a woman had to part with a breast. Likewise, in order to benefit from Dr. Martin's impressive record for surviving patients, she'd have to endure his questions, his confoundedly personal attention and his probing gaze.

She sighed and closed her eyes. Stacy would have surrendered her firstborn child to have Jonah Martin bring tacos to *her* kitchen, but Jacquelyn didn't think even Stacy would willingly trade places with her now.

"Feeling better?"

Stacy's cheery morning voice broke Jacquelyn's concentration on the stack of patient charts in front of her. She looked up into the sparkling, carefree eyes of her friend and felt a surge of pure, elemental jealousy. Would she ever feel that kind of innocent joy again?

Yes. Right after she'd beaten this disease.

She clung to the familiar stability of the nurses' desk, praying she wouldn't betray her agitation. She would be quietly and totally honest. And she'd show them all that Jacquelyn Wilkes could be just as brave — even braver — than the patients who routinely walked through that door to face cancer with dazzling determination.

"Stacy —" she imposed an iron control on her voice "— I wasn't able to work Friday, but I wasn't exactly sick — at least, not like you think. I guess you could say I was recovering from a shock — my gynecologist told me that a lump in my breast is malignant."

Stacy's mouth dropped open. "What?"

Jacquelyn turned back to the charts stacked on the counter before her. "Apparently my mother's history puts me at high risk. I don't suppose I should be surprised."

"But you —" Stacy sank gracelessly into an empty chair at the nurse's station, and her voice trembled slightly as if she were on the verge of tears. "Jacquelyn, I'm so sorry! Have you made arrangements to see an oncologist?"

Jacquelyn opened the first chart and pretended to skim it. "I've spoken with Dr. Martin and he's agreed to take my case. I have my first consultation with him later today."

"Wow." Stacy pushed her bangs away from her forehead in a distracted gesture. "That will seem strange, won't it? Your boss as your doctor? Maybe you should think about seeing an oncologist at one of the other hospitals. I mean, it's obvious you don't even *like* Jonah —"

"His patients like him," Jacquelyn countered. "And they seem to do well on his protocols, haven't you noticed? Anyway, it's no big deal. It's a small lump. I'll have it cut out and be done with it."

"Cancer. You." Looking away, Stacy whistled softly. "I never would have imagined it. But I'm glad you're handling it so well." A moment of awkward silence passed, then Stacy stood and moved away, tapping her nails over the surface of the plastered wall.

Jacquelyn sighed. How many other explanations would she have to give? She'd have to tell Lauren and Holly the lab tech and probably even Gaynel at the reception desk. She might as well print a newsletter or stand in the middle of the office with a megaphone: I, Jacquelyn Wilkes, have breast cancer. But I'm not going to fall apart, so do me the favor of not treating me like I'm

165

as frail as a lily. Thank you very much.

"Hey." Stacy's head popped back around the corner. "There's a party Friday night over at Bojangles. Want to go? It might lift your spirits."

Jacquelyn closed her eyes and resisted the urge to scream. "No, thanks. I've made other plans."

Staying home alone. Staring at the wallpaper. Wondering if she would ever marry and have children, or if she would die before reaching the ripe old age of thirty.

She fought hard against the tears she refused to let fall.

CHAPTER NINE

"Mrs. Redfield." Out in the clinic hallway, Jacquelyn greeted the tall woman with a calm smile. "Welcome to your first day of chemo. Dr. Martin has asked me to go over some information with you. I know this is a lot to give you in one day, but we want you to understand every aspect of your treatment."

"Oh, I don't mind." Daphne moved into the chemo room with the sure grace of a forest creature. She settled into the deep cushions of the chemo chair and automatically thrust out her arm.

An old pro, Jacquelyn thought, recalling that Daphne had undergone chemotherapy before. "Thanks," she murmured, smiling stiffly. She swabbed the skin and then efficiently inserted the IV. Maybe I'll be an old pro, too, before I'm done.

As the antinausea medication slowly dripped into Mrs. Redfield's vein, Jacquelyn wheeled her rolling stool to the other side of her patient's chair.

"These," she said, placing a stack of pamphlets in Daphne's lap, "will tell you more than you ever wanted to know about cancer and its treatment. I have given you brochures on radiation therapy, tumor markers, blood counts and infections, breast cancer, adjuvant therapy, eating hints for cancer patients, the importance of social support and taking time with your loved ones —"

"Save your breath, sweetie," Daphne said, putting her free hand on Jacquelyn's arm. "I've been through all those booklets with my other doctors. I've had the mastectomy, I've been through a round of chemotherapy. I can tell you all about tumor markers and CA 15-3, the breast cancer antigen." Her eyes gentled. "I've been around the block a few times, Nurse Jackie. The big C and I are old friends."

"Friends?" The horrified whisper slipped out before Jacquelyn could stop herself. In all her days as an oncology nurse she had never heard anyone describe the dread disease as a *friend.*

"Yes." Daphne's eyelids lowered as if the medication were making her drowsy. "God has used my cancer to bring me closer to

168

Him. And though it hasn't been an easy cross to bear, some people carry far heavier loads than I do. And I'm not alone. I have my husband, my sons and a caring church family. The pain is bearable, and the fear — well, I've given that over to God. He holds my life in His hand, so nothing can harm me without His permission."

Denial, Jacquelyn thought. Religion as painkiller. She'd seen it a thousand times, though none of her other religious patients had managed to smile through their denials as easily as Daphne Redfield. From where did the woman find such peace? Jacquelyn considered herself a Christian, though not a live-it, breathe-it fanatic like Mrs. Redfield. Still, if such peace was real, maybe Daphne could help Jacquelyn find it.

The comfortable chemo chairs, coupled with the warmth of the sun from the wide windows, often put patients to sleep. Daphne's eyes were about to close, so Jacquelyn gently prodded her. "Tell me about your sons," she said, leaning forward to adjust the IV line. "How old are they?"

"The twins are almost eighteen." Daphne's eyes widened. "Tall, handsome boys, they are. Young men, really. They'll be graduating from high school this June. I used to think I couldn't wait until they could drive, now I can't wait to see them graduate."

Jacquelyn nodded as she monitored the flow of antinausea medication. "You'll have to bring them up to meet us sometime."

"I will," Daphne answered. "They'd be thrilled to meet a pretty girl like you." She swiveled her head and glanced pointedly at Jacquelyn's hand. "No wedding ring, I see. A steady boyfriend, maybe?"

Jacquelyn leaned back and crossed her arms. "Not anymore," she said, lowering her voice lest Stacy should overhear. She didn't want to give the other nurses a long explanation of what had happened with Craig, the pain was still too fresh. "I guess you could say the going got rough, and Mr. Tough Guy bailed out. I'm afraid I'm going to be single for a while . . . a *long* while."

"I'm sorry." Daphne rested her chin on her free hand, a faint smile on her lips. "But what happened? If my memory serves me correctly — and the older I get, the less often it does — you were supposed to go see your doctor." She gave Jacquelyn a compassionate, troubled look. "Did you go?"

"I did," Jacquelyn said, feeling her throat begin to close up. She didn't like talking about personal things in the office, but she pushed the words out. "And it was a malignant lump, not a cyst. So I'm meeting with Dr. Martin this afternoon. I imagine I'm facing a lumpectomy in the near future."

Daphne's eyes darkened with pain. "Oh, sweetheart, I'm so sorry."

Jacquelyn looked away, unable to bear the sight of such compassion. Why had she said anything to this woman? She didn't want pity or commiseration. She only wanted to get the thing cut out and get on with her life.

"I'll be praying for you." Daphne reached over and squeezed Jacquelyn's hand.

Because the unexpected gesture brought tears to Jacquelyn's eyes, she rose quickly from her stool and hurried toward the small room where the chemo medications were mixed. "I'll be right back," she called over her shoulder, grateful for work to keep her hands and mind occupied. "It's time to mix up my magic medicines."

Jonah fumbled in the file and pulled out two films, then snapped them into the groove at the top of the light box on the wall. He frowned at the X rays. Jacquelyn Wilkes's mammograms showed a definite mass in the left breast, but nothing, thank God, in the right.

171

He stepped back and leaned against the edge of his desk, ice spreading through his stomach as he stared at the films. How — and what — did he tell her? She would demand the truth, plain and unvarnished, and he might have to recommend options far more severe than what she was expecting. Everything depended upon the size of the actual tumor inside the mass. If the nodule was one centimeter or less with no lymph nodes involved, she might be able to have a lumpectomy only. If the lump was one and a half centimeters, he'd probably prescribe tamoxifen or radiation after the lumpectomy. But if the tumor was closer to two centimeters, he'd have to consider so many other things — the lymph nodes, the type of tumor, her age and family history . . .

A headache began to pound at his temple. Should he treat her at all? Maybe Dr. Shaw was right; he should have sent her to Dr. Kastner. The voice of an old medical school professor echoed in his memory: You cross a dangerous line when you treat someone you love. Can you separate your emotions from your regard for good treatment?

He'd never come near that dangerous line before. But no one had ever affected his emotions quite like Jacquelyn Wilkes.

What if "good treatment" required a mastectomy? Would such a disfiguring operation traumatize her? Despite her professionalism and her knowledge about cancer and cancer patients, she was only twenty-eight and unmarried. No single woman wanted to think about facing the future with a vivid scar across her chest, but anything less might prove to be a death sentence.

And that, Jonah knew, he could never accept.

He stared at the shadow on the films a moment longer, then turned off the light box and watched as the films went black.

Something in Jacquelyn rebelled at the thought of climbing onto the exam table in Dr. Martin's treatment room. She took a chair at the desk, knowing the doctor would have to stand when he entered. She didn't care. She'd been on her feet all day. The work, combined with her mental exhaustion, left her so tired her nerves throbbed.

She felt momentary panic when the doctor politely rapped on the door — he's here, it's really happening — but forced her face into calm lines. Jonah — Dr. Martin, she reminded herself — did not remark on her odd maneuvering when he entered, but gave her a brief smile and perched on the end of the exam table himself, her chart in his hand.

She murmured some inconsequential greeting and he responded in kind while he studied her chart as if he had never seen it before. What *was* that expression on his face? He kept his eyes averted as he read a note from Dr. Shaw. She couldn't tell if she'd be facing Dr. Jekyll or Mr. Hyde when he finally lifted his gaze.

"I won't go through the usual drill, Jacquelyn, since you already know it," he said, lowering her chart to his lap. He looked up and clasped his hands, his eyes searching her face. "But it's good we caught this as soon as we did. The radiologist and Dr. Shaw believe the cancer is infiltrating ductal carcinoma. And because these cancer cells stimulate the growth of fibrous, noncancerous tissues in the vicinity of the tumor, it's possible that the actual malignant cancer is smaller than your lump may suggest. The radiologist estimates your mass at just over two centimeters. If the tumor inside is significantly smaller, a T1, lumpectomy and radiation are definitely in order. We can save the breast, and with follow-up radiation treatments we can almost guarantee that there will be no reoccurrence."

"I thought there were no guarantees with

breast cancer," she said, impaled by his steady gaze.

"Well," he said, tilting his head, "you're right. But the risk is minimal. Women with T1 tumors who undergo a lumpectomy and radiation face less than a two percent chance of reoccurrence within the same breast."

She stared stonily at the floor. "What if the invasive component is a T2? That would make me a stage II cancer case, and the treatment is entirely different —"

"Jacquelyn," he interrupted her with a raised hand, "I have every reason to hope it's a T1. We'll go in, do the lumpectomy and check the lymph nodes. After surgery, we'll make arrangements for radiation treatment at the hospital."

"And if I don't have the radiation?"

Surprise blossomed on his face. "Why wouldn't you? It's a simple procedure, far less stressful than chemotherapy —"

"It is not simple." She shook her head. "Radiation therapy requires five daily visits to the hospital for five weeks. For five weeks I'd be exhausted, burning and peeling while I'm trying to work."

"You could take a medical leave —"

"I — I won't," she stammered, wondering if she could make him understand. If she stopped working, she'd be admitting that she was sick. She'd be alone in her house with only Bailey for company, *alone* for more than five weeks, once she included the time she'd need for surgical recovery. "Radiation would drop my white cell counts," she continued. "I'd catch every cold between here and California."

"Would you rather have a cold or increase your risk of recurring cancer?" His tone was light, but his meaning was not.

Her eyes caught and held his. "You said we caught it early."

"But as you pointed out, we won't know exactly what we're dealing with until the pathologist looks at the tumor. We also have to dissect the axilla —"

"I know the drill." She drew a deep breath. The axilla housed the lymph nodes, part of the system that removed wastes from body tissue as well as carrying cells that helped the body fight infection. If the malignancy had spread beyond the lump in her breast, the lymph nodes under her arm would contain cancer cells.

"If my lymph nodes are clean," she said, speaking in as reasonable a voice as she could manage, "what are the chances the cancer will reoccur if I don't have radiation therapy?"

Jonah frowned in exasperation. "Thirty percent. Too high a risk, if you ask me. The figure might be higher in your case, considering your family history."

She looked away and ran her hand through her hair, thinking. He was looking at the negatives; she wanted to focus on the positives. Of one hundred women like her who had lumpectomy only, seventy survived with no return of the cancer. A large majority. They ate well, exercised, loved their families and firmly put cancer behind them. Why couldn't she be one of those seventy?

"I'll make you a deal, Doc," she said, looking up at him. "If you find even one positive lymph node, I'll undergo radiation. But if my lymph nodes are clean," she said, holding up a restraining finger, "you're going to leave me alone. I'll do my monthly breast self-exams, I'll eat right, exercise and have a yearly mammogram, but you're not putting me through radiation. I don't want five weeks of sickness. I don't want to even *think* about cancer for that long."

"You shouldn't be thinking about cancer. You should be thinking about getting better. Fighting back. Doing all you can to stop it."

"That's exactly what I'm going to do." She rose from her chair. "So refer me to a good surgeon, schedule me for the lumpectomy and let me know when to report to the OR. I'll be a model patient, but if my lymph nodes are clean, you'll excuse me from your class, Doc. I know all about cancer — I don't need any more lessons."

"Jacquelyn Wilkes," Jonah answered, his eyes flashing with a maddening hint of arrogance, "you are a stubborn woman."

"I know." She lifted her chin as she moved toward the door. "Deal with it."

Two weeks later it was all arranged. Standing at the nurse's station near the end of a busy day, Jacquelyn reached for the large calendar on the desk and marked Thursday, October ninth, with the words "Jacquelyn out." Of course, she'd be out longer than one day, but hopefully not more than two or three. Lumpectomies usually healed quickly.

At 6:00 a.m. tomorrow she would report to the admissions office at Chambers-Wyatt Hospital where surgeon Thomas Wilder would perform a lumpectomy and axillary dissection.

She had already met with Jonah Martin to discuss the final details, and as a matter of routine she signed consent papers allowing Dr. Wilder to immediately perform a modified radical mastectomy in case the tumor proved to be two centimeters or greater in size. "Everything in me says the tumor won't be that large," Jonah had told her, "but if it has grown to that size in so short a time, we don't want to take a chance. And I don't think you want to undergo two separate surgeries."

"That makes sense," Jacquelyn answered, scrawling her name across the bottom of what was certainly an unnecessary consent form. The hospital covered its bases like a New York Yankees infielder; the nurses weren't allowed to dispense even an aspirin without the proper signed document.

Jacquelyn had slid the stack of consent forms back across the desk toward Dr. Martin, ready to be finished with the entire situation. She had kept herself busy in the past two weeks, purposely trying not to think about anything beyond a lumpectomy. Radiation was an extreme possibility she might have to face, but she'd cross that bridge if — and only if — it proved absolutely necessary.

Now she fidgeted at the nurses' desk, making a series of last-minute reminders for Stacy, Lauren and the temp nurse who'd be covering for her while she recuperated.

"Jacquelyn, if you've got a moment —"

Jacquelyn looked up from her paperwork into Lauren's questioning eyes. "Sure, I was just finishing up a few notes."

Lauren leaned against the counter at the nurses' station and spoke with a depth of concern Jacquelyn had never heard in her voice. "I know your surgery is tomorrow. And I just wanted you to know that I'll hold a good thought for you."

Hold a good thought? As if that would do any good! Jacquelyn swallowed her exasperation and flashed a smile of thanks. "Thanks, I appreciate it. Are you sure I've covered everything? I'll only be out for a week, maybe even less —"

"Take all the time you need," Lauren said, gathering a stack of reports from her basket on the counter. "Relax, enjoy your time off and luxuriate in the deep sleep of drugs." She tilted her head and gave Jacquelyn a jaunty smile. "That's the best thing about surgery. When I had my impacted wisdom teeth removed, I went home, went to bed and let my family fend for themselves for twenty-four hours. I haven't had as good a rest since."

The phone cut into their conversation. Lauren moved to take the call while Jacquelyn tried to ignore the mocking inner voice that wondered how an oncology nurse could compare breast cancer surgery to impacted wisdom teeth.

Stacy came around the corner and brushed a tendril of brown hair out of her eyes. "Five o'clock, thank goodness! Sometimes I think quitting time will never get here."

Jacquelyn glanced at the charts still on the desk. "Is the last patient gone?"

"Yes, thank goodness." Stacy blew at the stubborn lock of hair, then tossed Jacquelyn a grin. "Want to go grab some Chinese food? Sort of a last fling before you're laid up?"

"No Chinese food, no anything." Jacquelyn shook her head. "The liquid surgical diet, remember? Twenty-four hours before surgery, only liquids and gelatin allowed. And nothing after midnight." She lightened her voice. "For lunch I feasted on a cup of chicken consommé. I think for dinner I'll go with lime Jell-O."

"You must think I'm an awful ditz." Stacy's expression clouded for an instant, then she reached out and patted Jacquelyn's arm. "I'm so sorry. I didn't mean to be insensitive. It's just that you look so good, I can't believe you're going under the knife tomorrow. If it were me, I'd be home in bed with my feet propped up, milking sympathy

181

from everyone I know."

Lucky girl, to have people in her life. Jacqueline only had Bailey.

"I guess we're different then." Jacquelyn smiled and set aside her cynicism, trying to find the nerve to ask the question she'd avoided all day. "Stacy, I do need some help. I might be in the hospital for two or three days and I don't have anyone to look after Bailey. If you can't do it, I'll understand, but I hate to take him to a kennel when he could stay home where he feels secure."

"You want me to take care of that monster?" Stacy took a hasty half step backward. "Jacquelyn, he'd bite my head off. Dogs know if you're afraid of them, and that big brute just terrifies me."

"That big brute —" Dr. Martin's voice came around the corner, joined an instant later by his imposing, self-confident presence "— is as gentle as a kitten." He paused by the desk where his eyes met Jacquelyn's. "You don't have anyone to take care of the dog?"

"It's okay, I can take him to the kennel," she said, heat stealing into her face. She'd simply *die* if he thought she was hinting that he ought to step in. He'd done enough by saving Bailey's life; he didn't have to dog-sit, too. "It's not a big deal."

"Jacquelyn —" his voice was crisp "— I'd like to see you in my office, please. Now."

The commanding tone in his voice caused Jacquelyn's pulse to beat erratically.

"Uh-oh," Stacy whispered as Jacquelyn slipped away. "I don't know what you did to set him off, but maybe he'll go easy on you, seeing as how you're having major surgery tomorrow."

When Jacquelyn reached his office, Jonah was leaning against his desk, his arms folded tightly across his chest, one hand pressed to his chin.

"Doctor?" Jacquelyn steeled herself for whatever rebuke might come. Had she been too distracted by her own upcoming surgery that she overlooked something on a patient's chart? Had she unintentionally snapped at someone? She had been a little curt with Daphne Redfield yesterday; she simply hadn't felt like listening to the woman's saccharine assurances that God had everything under control. . . .

Jonah's eyes were as flat and unreadable as slate. "Jacquelyn," he said, lines of concentration deepening along his brows and under his eyes, "if you don't have anyone to take care of the dog, who is going to take care of *you*?"

Her dread and embarrassment shifted

183

quickly to annoyance. What right had he to pry into her personal affairs? She hadn't intended to involve anyone from the office in her illness. She would have to consult with Dr. Martin after the surgery, of course, but he didn't need to know her plans. She would hire a day nurse from a temp agency for the first day or two of her recovery; she'd already placed one call and received an excellent reference. After that, she'd take care of herself, warm her own soup, change her own sheets. She was strong and she knew what had to be done.

She swallowed hard, trying not to reveal her irritation. "I've made arrangements. I'll be fine."

His expression clouded in anger. "I don't know why you insist upon being so independent. Let us know if we can help. You can't take care of yourself right after surgery —"

"I'll be fine," she insisted, her voice sharp. Why was he doing this? She didn't need his personal attention; she didn't want it. Most of all, she didn't want him to know how utterly and completely alone she was.

She whirled and moved toward the doorway, but paused just before leaving his office. "If you think of it tomorrow, say a prayer for me. And if you don't pray —" she shrugged, not looking at him "— then hold a good thought."

On the verge of tears, she turned and fled through the office hallway.

CHAPTER TEN

After a frantic, last-minute phone call, Jacquelyn's veterinarian agreed to board Bailey for five days. After work she drove the dog to the vet's office, hugged the big dog goodbye, then drove back to her empty house. She slept little that night, feeling that a stranger — cancer — slept in the bed with her. She sorely missed Bailey's chain-saw snoring; the house had never seemed so quiet.

She woke at 5:00 a.m., reminded herself not to drink anything and brushed her teeth in the dim glow of the bathroom night-light. She tossed a loose-fitting top, jeans, a hairbrush, toothbrush, toothpaste and clean underwear into an overnight bag, then picked up her wallet and stepped out into the garage. The sharp October air was as astringent as alcohol. The sky was just beginning to glow in the east when the cab driver picked her up and threaded through the city on his way to the hospital.

At the hospital admissions office she signed a half-dozen additional consent forms. She had dropped by at lunch yesterday to give them a blood sample, and she was led to the labs again where more blood was taken. The lab tech there asked her the usual questions about heart, lung and circulatory disease, and Jacquelyn shook her head after each inquiry. Before this lump, she'd been as healthy as a May morning.

"One more thing —" The technician glanced at her chart. "The admissions clerk forgot to ask — who do we notify in case of an emergency?"

Jacquelyn sank back in her chair and closed her eyes. Her father wouldn't want to know about any trouble, he hadn't even called to check on her since she'd told him about the cancer. And Craig had proven himself as intangible as a shadow.

"In case of emergency, call my employer, Dr. Jonah Martin," she said finally, looking the technician in the eye.

He lifted an eyebrow. "I think they really want the name of a family member or close friend —"

"He's also my doctor." She gestured abruptly toward the paper. "Just write his name down. Nothing's going to happen, so don't worry about it."

The technician shrugged and scrawled the name in the blank space. "That's it for the paperwork," he said, standing. "In a few minutes a nurse will come in to make sure your armpit is completely shaved and ready for the lymph node dissection. And I'll need you to remove any contact lenses, dental bridges, or nail polish."

"Already done, done and done," she answered. "I knew what to expect."

"Good." The technician gave her a brief smile and moved toward the door. "Your gown's on the table."

"Thanks." She waited until he exited the room, then slowly began to unbutton her blouse.

Cold.

Voices buzzed above her while someone swabbed an icy liquid over her chest. She wanted to speak, to tell them she was freezing, but her tongue would not move, nor would her hands.

Someone lifted her right arm and slipped a blood pressure cuff around her biceps. Someone else pressed electrocardiograph monitors to her chest wall — *cold* — then professional fingers firmly taped them into position. A slight snip on her fingertip meant the clip to measure her blood oxygen was in place. Somewhere in the darkness an IV poured a blessed anesthetic into her body, numbing her wits and sensations.

So cold. She felt her skin contract and tried to open her eyes, wanting to tell these invisible people that the sheets beneath her were like ice. They should have warned her about the chill. But they were lifting her now, transferring her in one swift movement from the gurney to the operating table.

Cold, the table. Cold, her skin. Cold, the knife — or could she feel it yet?

She lay on a slab of black ice amid a sea of buzzing voices while somewhere, far in the distance, an orchestra played Mozart.

Jonah paused outside the wide windows of the operating room. He hadn't scrubbed in, so he couldn't enter the sterile environment, but he wanted to be nearby, just in case.

Just in case of what? He had perfect confidence in Dr. Wilder, even though the man was as brusque and detached as any surgeon Jonah had ever met. A peculiar breed, surgeons. Slice and dice, splash and dash, cut and send the patient back to the oncologist. He'd spoken to Dr. Wilder last night, following up on Jacquelyn's case, and the older man had seemed almost offended that Jonah had taken the time to call.

Soft strains of Mozart vibrated in the operating room, a rhythmic counterpoint to the steady beeps of the cardiac monitor. A half-dozen people surrounded the table, masked figures in blue, all but obliterating his view of the patient. Jonah shifted his position and caught a glimpse of Jacquelyn's face, pale under the bright lights of the operating room. Her gorgeous red-gold hair had been caught up and covered by a cap; the anesthesiologist's plastic mask covered her nose and mouth.

Someone laughed in the operating room, and Jonah frowned. Though he knew surgical teams did better work when they were relaxed, for *this* patient he wanted to see them taking extreme care.

Get it all, he silently urged the surgeon. Every blasted cell.

"So what do you want to do, Doctor?"

Dr. Wilder looked up at the resident who was eyeing him with a critical squint. The young punk behind that surgical mask probably thought he could do a better job, but Thomas Wilder didn't become the chief of surgery at Chambers-Wyatt on account of his looks.

He turned to the nurse at his left hand,

who ceremonially swabbed perspiration from his forehead. "Give me the findings again," he told the nurse at his right. She consulted the report, which had just come from the pathologist's lab.

"High S phase index, indicating active growth and cell division. Aneuploid tumor cells, high aggression. Mass measures three centimeters, invasive component, two. Invasive ductal carcinoma —"

"TNM stage?"

"Two-B, Doctor. The nodes are N1, involved but still movable."

Wilder weighed his options. The patient had expected this procedure to result in a lumpectomy, but the tumor was significantly larger than it had appeared on the month-old mammogram. Assertive little sucker. The patient had signed consent forms in case a mastectomy was necessary, but he had no idea how mentally prepared she'd be to wake up with half her chest sliced away. She'd done most of her pre-op counseling with her oncologist, the new man at the cancer clinic —

"Who's the new guy in oncology again?"

His resident's brow furrowed. "Martin. Moses Martin, I think."

"Page him." Wilder's eyes flitted to the cardiac monitor. Slow and steady. They could wait this one out and keep the woman on the table. He wasn't about to make a snap judgment and have a lawsuit on his hands.

"You don't have to page him, doctor." The soft voice of his nurse broke into his thoughts. "It's *Jonah* Martin and he's in the observation room."

"He is?"

Wilder turned, and through the reflective windows caught sight of a blond man in a lab coat, a worried look on his face, a cup of coffee in his hand. Their eyes met for the briefest instant, but Jonah Martin's thoughts must have been miles away, for he did not acknowledge Wilder's glance.

"Is that Martin?"

"Yes, Doctor."

He looked at his nurse with sharp curiosity. "What's he doing here? Is this woman a relative?"

"I believe she's his nurse."

Beneath his surgical mask, Wilder felt one corner of his mouth rise in a sly smile. The young dog! Falling in love with a nurse wasn't necessarily taboo, but it definitely wasn't good business . . . or good medicine. He closed his eyes for a moment, wiping all trace of his thoughts from his face, then nodded at his head nurse.

"Show him the pathologist's report and let him make the call. Tell him I'll wait."

"Open your eyes if you can hear me, Jacquelyn."

She could hear, but she couldn't move. Surely someone had taped quarters to the folds of her eyelids.

"Jacquelyn! It's time to wake up. Open your eyes."

The woman's commanding voice jolted Jacquelyn like an electric charge. Her eyes opened, blinked.

"That's better. How are you feeling?"

Jacquelyn let her eyelids relax and forced words over her thick tongue. "Cold."

The nurse laughed — a rich, throaty sound. "That's normal, honey. You're doin' fine. Now try to wake up."

Jacquelyn retreated from the woman's voice, wanting nothing but sleep. Her fingers were still absent, gone with all the other feelings that had fled her body. She could feel nothing but . . . cold.

"Jacquelyn?"

This voice was masculine, and the shock of hearing it brought Jacquelyn as awake as if she'd just had an intravenous dose of caffeine. Her eyes opened into a bright and

193

unfocused room.

"Jacquelyn, I'm Dr. Wilder, your surgeon. Are you awake enough to understand me?"

Dumbly, she nodded.

"Good. We removed the tumor and a one-centimeter margin of healthy tissue for the pathologist. I also took the axillary lymph nodes, and you'll be pleased to know that though they were involved, they were movable, not fixed in place by the spread of cancer. We have every reason to believe we got it all. There was no metastasis."

"Thankgoodness." The words came out in a jumble, and the surgeon's stone face cracked into humanity. "You're a fortunate young woman. The tumor was an aggressive one, infiltrating ductal carcinoma, as we suspected. It was a T2, just over two centimeters, so we took the breast as well."

You took my breast? Jacquelyn couldn't speak; the drugs and shock held her voice hostage.

The surgeon's heavy face melted into a buttery smile. "I was quite pleased with the result, actually. After the drains have been removed, the final scar will be thin and flat on the chest wall. If you wish to consider breast reconstruction, I've left the surgeon with good options."

His hand fell upon her arm. "You're a

fortunate young lady," he repeated, nodding sagely. "You may just beat this thing."

Darkness pressed down on her, and she closed her eyes. She had wanted to hear that the lymph nodes were clear. She had wanted to know that the evil entity was gone from her body. She had wanted to be clean — and whole. And this man had just told her that not only had she been deformed and carved up like a Christmas turkey, but the cancer had galloped out of her breast and into her lymph nodes. And yet she just *might* beat this thing.

She couldn't face it. Frightened beyond thought, she retreated back into the blackness of forgetful, drug-softened sleep.

Someone moved at the side of her bed, and Jacquelyn forced her eyes half-open. She was in a different place. A window at her left side brought the soft gray light of dusk into the room, and a curtain separated her bed from the doorway.

Her hospital room.

Voices murmured from behind the curtain — nurses tending the other patient, she presumed — but a shadowy form stood by her bed. She turned her head slightly, struggling to focus through the haze of painkillers, and caught sight of wide shoulders and a tentative smile.

Craig. He had come when she needed him. Maybe he'd been here all day, and she hadn't known.

Her visitor bent and leaned forward on the bed railing. "Hello." Despite her bewilderment, the masculine whisper brought a drowsy smile to her face.

"Hi yourself," she whispered, struggling to keep her heavy eyelids open. "I'm glad . . . you came."

"Are you in any pain?"

Letting her eyelids fall, she smiled and managed to shake her head. There was no pain in this heavy sleep. This drugged doze was a welcome relief from worry and fear.

"No pain," she murmured, trying to open her eyes again. "I'm just . . . tired."

"Is there anything you need? Anything I can do?" A wonderful degree of concern echoed in the whispered voice. She hadn't heard such warmth since she was a little girl.

"One thing." She felt the corner of her mouth lift in a sleepy smile. "My hair. It feels . . . tangled. Messy. Would you —" She heard a plaintive tone creep into her voice. "Could you help me with it? Sometimes I feel like cutting it all off. . . ."

"Don't you dare." He moved away, then

she heard the sound of a drawer opening and closing. Someone had brought her purse and overnight bag to the room, maybe one of the nurses had even unpacked her things.

A warm, capable hand slipped under her neck and lifted her head, then she felt her hair being pulled from beneath her heavy shoulders. She smiled, caught up in the sensation of pampered care. Then, with a caressing touch, a brush moved from her scalp through the ends of her hair, smoothing out the tangles, erasing the clumps, sending her back through time to a sunlit day in church when she had lain her head in her mother's lap and felt the steady stroke of her mother's fingernails through her tresses. . . .

She wasn't sure how long he brushed her hair; she only knew she was more asleep than awake when he finished. "Thank you," she managed to murmur. "I love you, Craig."

He did not answer, but lifted her hand. She felt the brush of his lips across her fingers and then, secure in the knowledge that she was no longer alone, she allowed herself to fall asleep again.

Jonah waited until her breathing deepened,

then quietly released her hand. She hadn't recognized him. She thought he was Craig, who, according to the nurses, hadn't come by or even called to check on Jacquelyn's recovery. Jonah's breath burned in his throat. Where on earth was the guy?

He stepped out into the hall, returned Jacquelyn's chart to the nurses' station, then took the crowded elevator down to the first floor. He stood patiently, his arms crossed, as an elderly woman in a wheelchair and her daughter exited the elevator. Someone had tied two shiny "World's Greatest Grandma" balloons to the wheelchair, and Jonah felt his anger rise as he stared at the tributes.

Why hadn't the boyfriend sent Jacquelyn flowers? Why hadn't *anybody?* Surely she had parents, friends, relatives, neighbors — so why hadn't anyone stopped to care for her?

He strode off the elevator and went into the small gift shop. An elderly volunteer, her hair a cobweb of silver atop her head, caught his eye. "Can I help you, Doctor?" she asked, snapping to attention at the sight of his white lab coat.

He pointed to a large bouquet of daisies and roses in the refrigerated case behind her. "I'll take those flowers, please. Send them to a patient named Jacquelyn Wilkes, room 513."

The clerk's eyes glittered with curiosity. "It's not often that we get doctors down here. This patient must be *special*." She winked. "What sort of card would you like to go with that?"

"She's my nurse," he replied gruffly. He glanced at the rack of gift cards displayed at the counter. It wouldn't be improper for a doctor to send flowers to a recovering employee, and he could sign the card "From all of us at the office." But she'd recognize his scrawled handwriting, and the boyfriend, when he finally showed up, might think it odd that a doctor and not one of the nurses had arranged for the flowers.

"Just pick a plain card," he told the clerk, giving her a careful smile. "And would you sign it for me? Just write, 'From Bailey, with Love.' She'll understand what it means."

"Bailey?" She gave him a look of faint amusement. "Not Doctor Bailey?"

Jonah shook his head. "Just Bailey." He pulled three twenties from his wallet and laid them on the counter, then pulled out another five and waved it before the woman's wide eyes. "Go have yourself a cup of coffee and a slice of cheesecake," he said, watching her eyes. "Right after you personally see that those flowers are delivered. I'd like them to be in her room when she wakes up, and that's likely to be soon."

The woman plucked the five from his hand like a hungry trout after a worm. "Thank you, Doctor Bailey," she cackled, her powdered face splitting into a wide grin. "I'll take care of this for you right away."

"I'd appreciate it," Jonah said, turning away. His cellular phone shrilled through the silence of the gift shop, and he felt a twinge of guilt as he glanced down at it. Jacquelyn Wilkes was only one of his patients, yet he'd spent nearly the entire day absorbed in her case. If she were in mortal danger he might have been able to understand his concern. But Jacquelyn was well on the way to recovery . . . and clearly in love with another man.

You've fallen about as low as you can go, he told himself, flipping the phone open as he moved into the wide hospital lobby. Are you so afraid of women that you're only attracted to one who hates you? Maybe Jacquelyn is right; your personality *is* seriously skewed.

The call was from Lauren, a routine question he answered immediately, then disconnected. He snapped the phone back onto his belt and paused on the curb as a tank-like sedan pulled up and disgorged a series of sober-faced visitors. Would any of them visit Jacquelyn? Somehow, he doubted it. But it was really none of his concern. She'd made that perfectly clear.

Thrusting his hands into his pockets, Jonah lowered his head and strode across the parking lot.

CHAPTER ELEVEN

"Up now, Jacquelyn. No more sleeping, it's morning."

"No." Clinging to the soft darkness of sleep, Jacquelyn tried to turn onto her side. But a weight fell onto her arm, the pressure of something foreign, heavy and . . . *not her.*

Bandages. Pressure. A dull, aching pain in the tissues over her chest and under her arm.

Jacquelyn's eyes flew open. The white hospital ceiling was above her head, broken only by the stern, broad expanse of a nurse's face. "Nice of you to join us," the nurse said, her shiny eyes as determined as a whirlwind. "Time to wake up. I need you to get out of bed and use the restroom."

Get out of bed? For an instant the suggestion seemed unspeakably cruel, then Jacquelyn remembered that the sooner a patient got up, the sooner she could go home. She put her hand on the railing and struggled to lift her head. "Give me a minute," she said, blinking at the unexpected brightness of the room. White stripes from the rising sun had penetrated the slits of the window blinds and lit the walls. On a small stand in the corner, a brilliant bouquet of white daisies and pink roses bloomed.

The corner of her mouth crooked in a half smile. "Wow, flowers," she whispered, accepting the nurse's freckled arm around her shoulders as the woman pulled her to a sitting position. She had no strength whatsoever on her left side; her left arm might as well have been amputated. But strength and feeling would come in time. She looked again at the gorgeous bouquet. "Who sent those?"

"There's a card," the nurse answered, releasing Jacquelyn's shoulders. In an instant, she had efficiently lowered the bed rail. "Want me to fetch it for you?"

Jacquelyn nodded.

"Tough luck." The nurse stepped back and folded her arms, grinning. "I'm not a retriever. If you want to know who sent the flowers, you'll have to walk over there and find out for yourself. Now, swing those legs around and let's get you out of bed."

Jacquelyn groaned, but inwardly she admired the nurse's pluck. She'd often used similar tactics with her own patients: Let's just get through today's chemo, shall we? Would you like to watch a movie while you're here? We've got all kinds, but you'll have to sit still so the medicine can drip into your veins. . . .

"My dad wouldn't have sent them," she mused aloud, obediently swinging her legs toward the side of the bed. Her head swam for a moment, but she focused her thoughts and kept moving. "Maybe they're from his wife. Or the girls at the office."

The nurse made certain Jacquelyn's bare feet were firmly planted on the floor, then she stood back with an arm extended in case Jacquelyn began to fall. "You'll find out as soon as you make your way over there."

"I'm okay, just a little woozy." Jacquelyn took her first step with more confidence than she felt, and then hung on to the mattress with her right hand as her stomach did an unexpected flip-flop. "Uh-oh. Maybe —" She closed her eyes, waiting for the room to right itself, then gave the nurse a quavery smile. "I'm fine."

"Prove it."

Jacquelyn lifted her chin. Bracing herself against the bed, she took three small steps toward the bathroom — and the flowers. As she neared the bathroom, she paused to drink in the flowers' aroma and peek at the florist's card in the arrangement.

"From Bailey?" She sent the nurse a quizzical glance. "My *dog* sent me flowers?"

The nurse, who hovered a careful two steps away, laughed. "That's some considerate dog."

Jacquelyn moved gingerly into the bathroom. Who would have sent flowers in Bailey's name? Stacy? That wasn't likely, she hated the dog. Maybe Dad had done it out of shame about how he'd ignored her illness, or maybe this was Craig's way of making up.

Momentarily confused, she doublechecked her memory. Craig *had* come to see her, hadn't he? She remembered a man by her bed, a masculine voice, someone brushing her hair . . .

"Nurse," she said, gripping the edge of the sink to steady herself, "do you remember a man stopping by to see me yesterday? It would have been after I was brought up, probably late yesterday afternoon or even early evening —"

"I go home at four," the nurse called. "It wouldn't have been my shift. You'll have to check with the night nurse."

"Ouch." Jacquelyn leaned against the

sturdy sink and again felt the tug of the bandage on her chest. She'd look at it later, when she could bear the thought of —

We took the breast as well.

She sat down heavily upon the toilet seat as her mind burned with the memory.

"Nurse," she called, staring fixedly at the floor. "My chart — exactly what happened in my surgery yesterday?"

She heard the swish of the nurse's polyester slacks as she came closer. "Didn't the doctor explain it to you?"

"I think so." Jacquelyn struggled to focus her thoughts. "But *you* tell me — what does the chart say?"

The nurse paused outside the bathroom door. "Modified radical mastectomy, left breast," she recited. A momentary look of discomfort crossed the woman's sturdy face as she met Jacquelyn's gaze. "Honey, weren't you prepared for this?"

"Of course. I'm a nurse, I'm prepared for anything."

We had to take the breast.

Surgical shorthand for the entire breast *and* the underarm lymph nodes, the lining over the chest muscles, and perhaps even the minor pectoral muscles. The major pectoral muscle would have been left intact, making it easier for Jacquelyn to flex and rotate her arm, easier to do the wearisome exercises that would be part of her life for the next several months.

The nurse moved away, and Jacquelyn sat in lonely silence as reality opened the door on a lot of memories she'd tried to bury. She'd seen her mother's livid scars after the mastectomy, seen her pitiful shrunken chest. Of course surgery had advanced by leaps and bounds since those days and Jacquelyn's surgeon had been one of the hospital's best. But still —

Unbidden, her right hand rose to the protruding lump beneath her light cotton hospital gown. What lay beneath the layers of gauze? What *didn't* lie beneath her bandages?

"Why?" she whispered, lifting her eyes to the ceiling, not knowing where else to turn. Why hadn't she prepared herself for this? Jonah Martin had assured her that mastectomy was only a remote possibility. What had they discovered, an entirely cancerous breast? What in the world could have induced them to disfigure her like this? She had expected only to have the tumor cut out, but now she was left with nothing but — *nothing*.

Her mind withdrew to a safe, remote distance, filling in the clinical images her experience lacked. She knew what lay under the bandage — two drainage tubes, one of which would be removed before she left the hospital; the other would remain in place until all the swelling had gone down. The neat, dark line of surgical sutures would be absorbed into her body. The staples holding her flesh in place would come out during her follow-up visit to the surgeon's office.

Why? An inner voice insisted on answers. Why hadn't Dr. Wilder considered a partial mastectomy or why hadn't he taken a chance and gone ahead with the lumpectomy? Given the unexpected size of the tumor, she'd have willingly gone through radiation therapy. She'd have even undergone chemo to avoid the scarring of a mastectomy.

What could have induced the surgeon to chop off her breast?

She felt herself trembling all over. She would never be healthy or whole, thanks to the arrogant attitudes of certain surgeons and doctors. . . .

"You okay in there?"

The nurse's ruddy face appeared again in the doorway. Her broad face cracked into a grin at the sight of Jacquelyn safely seated. "You're doing good, we'll have you out of here in no time. Within five or six days for sure, if you pass muster with the surgeon. Now come back to bed, and I'll have your breakfast sent in."

Jacquelyn clung to the edge of the toilet seat, grappling with her thoughts and feelings. She had to calm down. Anger would only cripple her recovery and weaken her defenses. She could put aside her misery and bitterness until she was stronger, then she'd confront Dr. Wilder and demand to know why he'd taken such an extreme step. For now, she had to concentrate on getting well.

More shaken than she cared to admit, she leaned forward and eased herself off the toilet, allowing the nurse to guide her back to the bed. She stretched out and lifted her whole, unwounded arm above her head, biting her lip to restrain the tears that bubbled just below the surface.

"Anything you need, hon?"

Jacquelyn felt a sudden chill. "A blanket would be nice."

"*That* I can get you," the nurse said, pulling a blanket from a compartment in the nightstand. With military precision she shook the blanket over the bed, then tucked in the edges and carefully folded it back so that none of the weight fell upon Jacquelyn's chest. "Now you just hurry and get well, 'cause I'm sure there's a world of folks who miss you."

Jacquelyn bit her lip again and looked away. Apparently Bailey was the only one who missed her. The flowers were probably from the office; they knew she adored her puppy and signing the dog's name had been easier than spelling out everyone else's.

"Thank you," Jacquelyn murmured, turning her face toward the window. As the nurse padded away on silent soles, Jacquelyn curled around the wounded place over her heart and tried to stanch the tears that flowed from the corners of her eyes into her hair.

CHAPTER TWELVE

"Here we are. Doesn't it feel good to be home?" Amid the impatient blare of horns from cars behind them on the street, Stacy slowly turned her car into Jacquelyn's driveway.

"Stacy, you don't have to drive like a grandma. I'm not a china doll — I won't break," Jacquelyn fussed as she glanced at her house. She had expected to see newspapers piled on the front porch and mail bulging from the box, but the house seemed as tidy and neat as she'd left it.

"Did you come and pick up my mail?" Jacquelyn asked as Stacy cut the motor. "You didn't have to do that. I just left my key with you in case of emergency — I didn't expect you to come over here and house-sit."

"Maybe the mail fairy moved in." Stacy got out of the car and hurried to the passenger's side, but Jacquelyn had already opened the door and swung her feet to the ground.

"I don't think so, but somebody took care of things," Jacquelyn pointed out, slowly standing as Stacy pulled Bailey's now-faded bouquet from the backseat. "Either that, or my newspaper boy and mail carrier have decided to go on strike."

"I think you worry too much." Stacy held her arm out like a waiter and Jacquelyn playfully pushed her arm away as they made their way to the porch.

"I'm not an invalid, I'm quite able to walk. My nurse was a Nurse Rachet clone, and she wasn't about to let me loll around in bed. So who's been in my house?"

As if in answer, the front door opened and a cheery voice sang out, "Welcome home!" Jacquelyn stared in surprise. A tall, thin woman stood in the doorway, a brightly patterned scarf tied around her head and Bailey's leash looped over her slender wrist. For a moment Jacquelyn couldn't place the woman's face, then the features came together in a rush of memory.

"Daphne Redfield?" At the sound of her voice, Bailey howled and strained at the leash. Jacquelyn looked at Stacy, dumbfounded. "You enlisted one of the *patients* to help me out?"

Stacy lowered her voice to a discreet whisper. "Daphne knew about your surgery and asked if she could do anything to help. And don't say anything about the scarf — she shaved off all her thinning hair a couple of days ago, and I think she might be a little sensitive."

Jacquelyn cut a quick look from her friend to the woman on the porch. "I don't get it. Daphne asked you if she could help me?"

"She asked Dr. Martin," Stacy explained. "And he knew I had a key to your house, so he arranged everything. Daphne has been stopping by every morning to take care of your house and the dog."

"But Bailey was in the kennel!"

"Dr. Martin knew you wouldn't want him to be crated there for five long days. So he signed your dog out of the kennel and brought him home to wait for you."

"Down, Bailey!" Daphne cried, struggling to hold the leash.

Jacquelyn glanced up. The one-hundred-and-seventy-pound puppy was no match for Daphne. The huge dog, eager to greet his long-lost mistress, lunged forward. The leash flew from Daphne's hands, and Bailey broke into a gallop down the walk.

Daphne clapped her cheeks. "Oh, I'm sorry. I — oh, no!"

Jacquelyn closed her eyes, bracing herself for a ferocious embrace that might knock her flat, but the dog only circled her in a wriggling exhibition of love, then sat at her feet, his chocolate-brown eyes snapping with joy.

"Bailey!" Jacquelyn bent to croon into the dog's soft ears, her own heart welling with affection. "I'm so glad to see you! And I'm so glad you're home!"

The gigantic tail thumped in mute appreciation, and Jacquelyn breathed in his warm, doggy scent and smiled. She couldn't be angry with Daphne and Stacy, no matter how much she wanted to be. They had no business going into her house and taking responsibility for her, but they'd done it anyway — and she was grateful. But for Jonah Martin, M.D., she reserved the right to be angry . . . maybe even furious. In her meeting with Dr. Wilder this morning, when he'd removed one of the drains and okayed her release from the hospital, he'd told her that Dr. Martin had cast the deciding vote and approved the mastectomy.

"Come, Bailey," she said, slowly straightening. The dog seemed to sense her physical discomfort, and he slowed his step to match hers as they climbed the front porch stairs and entered the house.

"Daphne, you don't have to stay with me." From the center of her makeshift bed on the living room sofa, Jacquelyn lifted her voice and peered out into the foyer for some sign of the woman. "After all, you're a chemo patient. Someone should be taking care of you."

"Nonsense." Daphne bustled in from the kitchen, a tray laded with cookies, teacups and a teapot in her hands. "I'm in between treatments and I feel fine, even though I look a little — how do my boys put it? — *funky* without my hair." She lowered the tray to the coffee table and paused to scrub the scarf on her head with her knuckles. "It was falling out so fast I had one of the boys give me a buzz cut with an electric razor — but they didn't tell me it would itch!"

Jacquelyn stared at the scarf in horrified fascination. Would she be wearing one of those things some day?

Daphne smiled and inclined her head. "Would you like sugar, cream, or both in your tea? I made us a pot of Earl Grey, which should put a wee bit of zip back into your smile."

"Thanks," Jacquelyn answered, admitting that the idea of tea did appeal to her. "But

215

after we have tea, I'll let you get home. I know your sons and your husband need you."

"Nonsense. I left them a casserole in the refrigerator, and both my boys know how to use a microwave. My family knows how debilitating surgery can be." Daphne perched on the edge of a chair and poured with the grace of an accomplished hostess. "Now was that cream, sugar, or both?"

"Both, I think." Jacquelyn folded her hands. She had to admit that Daphne's help was a luxury she hadn't expected. Without Daphne, poor Bailey would still be in the kennel, because Jacquelyn wasn't able to restrain him on the leash or lift his heavy bags of dog food. She wasn't sure where frail Daphne found the strength. "Thank you," Jacquelyn said as the woman handed her a steaming cup of tea. "I appreciate this more than you will ever know."

Daphne gave her a smile of pure sweetness. "It's no more than sisters in Christ should do for each other. You would have done the same for me."

Would I? Jacquelyn felt the tea burn her tongue. This was exactly the kind of personal involvement she would never allow herself. This was the sort of thing Dr. Martin instigated regularly — the meddling,

216

supervisory caring that a professional simply could not manage for a large number of patients. It was one thing for family members and church people to look after their own, but doctors and nurses had no time for this sort of thing.

An idea slowly germinated within her as Jacquelyn sipped her tea, then she cast the older woman a conspiratorial smile. "Time to confess, Daphne. You sent me flowers and signed Bailey's name, didn't you?"

One of Daphne's carefully penciled brows lifted. "I'm sorry, dear, but I didn't send flowers. I thought about it, but decided I could be more helpful here."

Jacquelyn leaned back on the mound of pillows, perplexed. There had been no messages from Craig on the answering machine and in the mail she found only a small "thinking of you" card from Helen and Dad — probably sent by Helen alone. But hadn't Craig come to see her in the hospital? She *thought* she remembered a man at her bedside and a hand around hers, but in the past few days the memory had faded like a shadow at dusk. Perhaps she had dreamed it all.

She sipped her tea. Whoever had sent the flowers obviously had no intention of stepping forward to receive her gratitude.

"Well," she murmured, dropping her hand to scratch Bailey's ears, "maybe my dog *did* send flowers. I once read in the newspaper about a choking cat who called 911 for help."

Daphne's blue eyes twinkled as she raised her teacup in salute. "Anything is possible."

"Is it?" Jacquelyn lifted her gaze, her heart brimming with a thousand questions and troubling thoughts. Her feelings about the mastectomy, the cancer and Dr. Wilder's comment that she just *might* beat it were still raw, and other disturbing thoughts had crept into her consciousness during her hospital stay.

"I'm not talking about cats and dogs now." She paused as the gold in Daphne's eyes flickered with interest. "I need to know if anything really is . . . possible. If I can be cured. Dr. Wilder said my lymph nodes were just beginning to be involved, and he assured me he got all the cancer. I know that if the margins around the tumor were clear, then the cancer is supposed to be gone, but I don't know if I can ever be at peace again." Frowning, she looked out the window next to the couch. "I mean, how do you live with not knowing? I have another breast that could develop cancer next year. And there may be other malignant cells hiding out somewhere, slipping through my bloodstream."

"You can't know." Daphne spoke with quiet emphasis and her words sent prickles of cold dread along Jacquelyn's back. "They told me they got it all after my mastectomy. And after my first chemo. But even if the cancer comes back, you don't give up, Jacquelyn. You keep living — every day as if it were your last."

"But I-I'm not like you," Jacquelyn stammered, not able to meet Daphne's eyes. "You're such a religious person, you talk to God as easily as I talk to Bailey. I'm a medical professional — I know what this disease can do. I know it will be ten years — I'll be thirty-eight — before I can even begin to consider myself cured." She shivered through fleeting nausea. "I don't see how you can know that you might have more yesterdays than tomorrows and still be so golly-gee happy all the time. Doesn't denial have its limits?"

Jacquelyn propped her good arm on the back of the couch and stared out the window, almost afraid to look at Daphne. Through her outburst she felt as though a heavy weight had been lifted from her heart, but perhaps she'd been wrong to poke pins in Daphne's religious bubble. The woman had been the embodiment of kindness, offering to help a nurse she barely knew outside the confines of the clinic, and Jacquelyn had just selfishly reminded Daphne that she was losing the battle. The compassionate-to-everyone-but-his-nurses Dr. Martin certainly wouldn't have laid this burden on one of his patients.

"You think I'm in denial?" A tinge of wonder laced Daphne's voice.

Jacquelyn looked over to see the woman grimace in good humor. "Denial," she said, looking at Jacquelyn with a secretive smile, "would be nice."

Jacquelyn's blood ran thick with guilt. "I'm sorry. I didn't mean —"

"Do you ever go outside to look at the clouds?" Daphne interrupted, stirring her tea.

"Sure." Baffled by the shift in the conversation, Jacquelyn shrugged with her good shoulder. "When I was a kid, I'd imagine all sorts of things in the sky."

"You should keep looking up." Daphne set her teacup and saucer on the table next to her chair. "And I don't mean that as only a figurative expression. The Bible has a lot to say about clouds. A cloud covered the holy mountain where Moses spoke with God, and the Lord often appeared to the

Israelites in a pillar of cloud. God told Moses that He would come in a cloud so the people would hear and see and put their trust in the Almighty. Clouds are a sign that God is near."

Jacquelyn frowned. "Those were Old Testament times. Now we know that the noise we hear booming from clouds isn't God, it's thunder."

"That's only one perspective." Daphne smiled and locked her hands around her knee as she leaned forward. "I like to think of clouds as the suffering in my life. We naturally think of clouds as dark, gloomy and oppressive, and yet when they darken the sky, I know God is near. If there were no clouds in my life, I would have little need for God. As it is, I depend upon Him utterly."

Jacquelyn let her gaze drift to the lace-covered window. Outside, beyond the ligustrum hedge and the colorful crotons, white, fluffy shapes blew across an azure sky.

"I guess I tend to think of clouds more as shade," she said, turning back to Daphne. "You know, a convenience. Something to keep the hot sun off my face for a few hours."

"That's a good analogy. God can bring shade, too. But I'm not talking about those

221

scribbles of cotton clouds that fly by. I'm talking about those days when your life is covered by dark, boiling masses, when gray clouds swirl over your head like angry, vengeful dragons." She tilted her head. "Have you known days like that, Jackie?"

"Sure," Jacquelyn answered dully. "More than I care to remember."

Daphne nodded. "So have I. And when the clouds come, I am glad to know that God has drawn near, too. In every cloud, He is there."

"Waiting to teach me a lesson, right?" Jacquelyn gulped the last of her tea and slammed the cup down to the saucer. "He's out to punish us when we stray. Well, I know I haven't been the perfect Christian. I stopped going to church after my mother died, and then my Dad remarried and — well, I just haven't felt it necessary. Sometimes I watch church services on television, and I pray . . . when something comes up."

Daphne said nothing, so Jacquelyn leaned her head on her hand and sighed. "I suppose this little brush with cancer is God's way of whipping me back into spiritual shape. I've already decided to go back to church. Maybe this was a wake-up call, something to teach me a lesson."

"I don't think so."

Jacquelyn looked up, caught off guard by the sudden vibrancy of the woman's tone.

"I have found — always," Daphne said, her voice warming as she spoke, "that through every cloud God wants me to *unlearn* something. He wants me to simplify things, to put other things and other people aside until it is just me and Him. He doesn't want me to *do* anything more, He wants me to sit at His feet and listen to His voice. When once again He is the Father and I am the child, our relationship is restored."

Jacquelyn stared, intrigued by Daphne's suggestion. "So you're saying I should — what?"

"Rest, Jackie. You need to rest." Daphne stood and took Jacquelyn's cup and saucer from her hand. "You should turn your thoughts toward your loving Father. After all, He's the one who sustains your life — not the hospital, the lab, or your doctors."

Jacquelyn sank back to her pillows and watched the graceful woman retreat into the kitchen. With stage IV cancer inexorably eating away at her one hundred and two pounds, how could Daphne Redfield rest? The enemy still raged in her body, her battle had not yet been won.

And neither had Jacquelyn's. She still had to confront Jonah Martin about his decision

223

to leave her permanently scarred. He'd approved her mastectomy, a treatment far too radical for her situation, and last night she'd even dreamed of gleefully filing a lawsuit against him.

If Craig had run at only the thought of cancer, what would any other man do at the sight of her misshapen torso? Jonah Martin was a male; he would never understand a woman's feelings about her breasts or her body. And Jacquelyn had never even known the pleasures of intimacy in marriage, of giving herself fully to the man she loved . . .

Now she never would. Jonah Martin, in one passing moment, had practically guaranteed that no man would ever look upon Jacquelyn with desire in his eyes. Oh, sure, she'd heard women at the clinic talk about how their husbands loved them no less than before their mastectomies, but they were married when the cancer attacked, their husbands had already fallen in love with them.

Everyone from Stacy to Ivana Trump knew that today's single men looked on the outside first. What man would stick around long enough to get to know Jacquelyn? Oh, she might be able to fool new acquaintances for a short period of time, but she wasn't the type to hide significant details. She'd be up-front and honest with anyone she dated, and what man would want damaged goods when he could have a healthy, unmarred woman?

She closed her eyes, and a series of images from the "Know Your Prostheses Options" pamphlet danced across the back of her eyelids. In the months ahead, while Stacy and her friends went out to parties and trolled for young doctors, Jacquelyn would be dating a fake breast: getting to know it, trying it on for size, finding the right one for her lifestyle. What filling should she choose — water? Air? Gel? Foam rubber? Maybe, she thought, she should make her own beanbag breast, which would probably be more realistic looking than some of the sorry things she'd seen her patients wearing. The shape that looked good standing up wouldn't look natural if she lay down, and she could never, ever wear anything that showed even the tiniest bit of cleavage.

"Where do they sell those long-sleeved swimsuits from the roaring Twenties?" she whispered, scratching Bailey's head again. The dog rolled his dark eyes toward her and thumped his tail in answer.

Jacquelyn heard footsteps and knew Daphne would soon be coming back either to talk or to remind her to do her arm and shoulder exercises. Not in the mood for either, Jacquelyn gingerly folded her hands over her chest and pretended to sleep.

Two weeks after her surgery, Jacquelyn stiffly lowered herself into a chair in Dr. Martin's office. Her chart, she noticed, was spread on the desk even though Jonah was nowhere in sight. She was glad she could steal a moment to orient herself and harness her emotions in a tight rein. She had worn her uniform to the office, hoping to assume as many of her duties as possible, but before she could return to work, she needed to win Dr. Martin's approval . . . and vent her repressed feelings.

She had not seen Dr. Martin since before her surgery. He had called the house two or three times and checked on her progress through Daphne. The few times Stacy dropped over she had brought greetings from all the people at the office, including, Jacquelyn supposed, Jonah Martin. This morning, Lauren, Stacy and Gaynel had welcomed her in the hallway with bright smiles and cautious, light embraces, then Jacquelyn's eyes darted toward Jonah's office. The light was on, the door open.

"He stepped out to get his coffee," Lauren said, noticing the direction of Jacquelyn's glance. Her lips curved in a slow, secret smile. "Why don't you do us all a favor and go straight in?"

"What do you mean, do you a favor?" Jacquelyn asked, her heart skipping a beat.

"Never mind." Lauren gave her a playful nudge on the shoulder. "Just go in and keep the good doctor happy. He's been as grim as a hangman since you've been gone, even with his patients. He keeps running more behind than usual, and of course he blames Stacy and me. Apparently you're the only nurse who can keep him on schedule."

Jacquelyn squared her shoulders as she walked toward his office. He may have been unhappy with her absence from the clinic, but his feelings certainly couldn't compare with hers. And she wasn't helping by letting her resentment build and grow. She needed to confront Jonah Martin right away. She'd let him do his routine exam and discuss her prognosis, and then she'd let him have it with both barrels. For days she'd been thinking about his actions — good and bad — on her behalf, and with every hour his decision to order her mastectomy seemed more reprehensible and illogical. Was he an absolute schizophrenic? How could the man who had arranged for someone to take care of her house and her dog also have maimed her for life?

Now she sat before his desk, clenching her hand until her nails entered her palm. Only the sound of Jonah's athletic step in the hall kept her from breaking the skin.

"Jacquelyn!"

Startled at the sound of his voice, she glanced up and heard his quick intake of breath. A strange and unexpected warmth surged through her when surprise and delight blossomed on his face. "Nurse Wilkes! You're looking —" He paused and bit his lip, then moved behind the safety of his desk. "What I meant to say," he said, carefully setting his coffee mug on the desk, "is that you're looking well. Dr. Wilder said you'd made remarkable progress."

"Not as remarkable as I'd hoped," she said, finding his nearness both disturbing and somehow exciting. "I would have been back at work last week if I'd had only a lumpectomy."

"Well, I'm sorry about that," he said, sinking into his chair. "But let's review your case." He looked up, and she saw a gleam of some deep emotion in his blue eyes. "How are you feeling?"

"As well as can be expected, I suppose."

"Good." Jonah shifted the pages of the

pathology report. "The margins around the tumor were clear. And the lymph nodes hadn't yet attached to one another or to adjacent blood vessels. Of course we had hoped they'd be clear, too, but —"

Jacquelyn sighed. "I know the details, Doc, just pronounce me fit, please. I'm going bonkers from boredom at home."

Jonah lifted his gaze to hers. "Any pain at the site of the surgery?"

"None, only a little tightness. But that's normal."

"Any numbness?"

"No."

"Any edema? Any swelling of the left arm whatsoever?"

"None. I'm fine, I promise. No phlebitis, no edema, no pain. I've been doing my exercises faithfully and I'm ready to go back to work."

"Not yet." Jonah dropped her chart and folded his hands, studying her thoughtfully. "I want to know what you're feeling about the mastectomy. Given the size and rapid growth of your tumor, Dr. Wilder and I thought it best to go ahead and remove the entire breast."

Her irritation veered sharply to anger. "How can you blame Dr. Wilder? I *know* what happened in that operating room. *You* decided to remove my breast, Doctor, after you'd told me that I wouldn't need a mastectomy!"

He lifted his hands, his eyes glittering with repudiation. "That's not fair. You and I discussed the possibility of a mastectomy. You signed the consent forms. You're an oncology nurse, you know how dangerous these infiltrating cancers can be —"

"But I wasn't prepared!" Her accusing voice stabbed the air. For an instant she considered lowering her voice, then rejected the idea. Let Lauren and Stacy and Dr. Kastner hear. She didn't care if even the patients knew what their sainted Dr. Martin had done to her. "You didn't tell me I'd lose my breast."

"I said you might." His voice simmered with some barely checked passion, but Jacquelyn didn't care to stop and analyze it.

"You should have warned me!"

"I did." His voice, without rising at all, had taken on a subtle urgency. "I showed you the statistics, I warned you about the risk, I demonstrated the long-term prognosis. What more could I have done?"

The question caught her unprepared. What else, indeed, could he have done? He had warned her thoroughly, and technically he didn't even need to. She was a nurse, she knew all about cancer. Why, then, was she so angry? Was she as deeply in denial as her father?

All too quickly, she ran out of diversions. The truth was, she hadn't *wanted* a mastectomy, hadn't wanted to lose any part of her life or her body to cancer. Her anger had turned toward Jonah because he had been the one to authorize her loss, but more than that, he was the only one . . . around.

She balled her hands into hard fists, fighting back the tears that swelled hot and heavy in her chest. There was no escaping the undeniable and dreadful truth. She was alone, and she had no one to blame for her situation but herself. She should have gone to the doctor sooner, she shouldn't have trusted in her own silly self-diagnosis.

"Jacquelyn." The sound of mingled pity and compassion in his voice compelled her to look away. Behind her she heard a definite click and knew that Stacy or Lauren had mercifully closed the door.

"Just tell me why you did it, I want to understand," she said, her tears choking her. "Why did you elect such a radical approach? It was only a stage II tumor. You could just have easily elected lumpectomy and radiation. And then I wouldn't be scarred. I'd be whole."

He did not answer for a long moment, and when she lifted her tear-blurred eyes, she saw an almost imperceptible note of pleading in his face.

"You don't know how I agonized over that decision, how I still agonize over it," he said, one hand clutching the edge of his desk, the other mindlessly tapping a pencil on her chart. "Dr. Wilder could have gone either way, even though he was surprised by the tumor's rapid growth and he knew about your family history. But he left the decision up to me. And though I knew you really didn't believe a mastectomy would be necessary, I told him to go ahead and take the breast." A glaze seemed to come down over his swimming eyes. "Because I'd rather have you alive than not have you at all."

The tenderness in his words amazed her, and for a moment she could not speak or move. Her breath caught in her lungs, and she stared, speechless, at the pencil he tapped as steadily as a metronome.

What in the world had he meant? Did he realize he had just admitted that he cared for her . . . or had he?

There was a flash, like light caught in water, when she looked up and her gaze crossed his. "Jonah, I —"

He held up a quieting hand. "Let's not

talk right now. I think we're both a little agitated. Cancer is serious business, and as you've often told me, I tend to become too involved in the lives of my patients."

Jacquelyn listened with rising dismay. His *patients?* Was that the only reason he cared — because she was one of his blessed *patients?*

Suddenly she was humiliatingly conscious of his scrutiny. He was weighing the effect of his words and she couldn't let him see that for a moment. A thrill had shivered through her senses at the thought that he might feel more for her than for any other cancer patient.

"I understand, Dr. Martin," she said, feeling her face flush. She clenched her jaw to kill the sob in her throat. "I know you'd hate to lose an excellent nurse."

There. Meet arrogance with arrogance.

"Quite right." His concerned expression relaxed into a tight smile. "And if you don't mind, let's continue this discussion later this afternoon. I have a nine o'clock appointment with a new prostate patient, and I need a few moments to look over his chart."

"No problem." In one swift movement, Jacquelyn rose and moved toward the door.

CHAPTER THIRTEEN

Jonah felt a wave of relief as Jacquelyn left his office. He'd nearly blown five years of determination in the brief moment he nearly admitted to her — and to himself — that his reasoning had been befuddled by longing.

But his feelings for Jacquelyn were, had to be, the last thing on his mind for more than a few important reasons. First, she had a boyfriend. Jonah's brief encounter with her in the hospital had proved that she loved Craig what's-his-name whether the guy deserved her or not. Second, the flail of bitter experience had taught Jonah that romance didn't belong in the office. And third, a doctor should not allow his emotional feelings for a patient to cloud his judgment about what would be the most prudent medical treatment.

And the most prudent treatment for Jacquelyn Wilkes was mastectomy followed by chemotherapy. Though his throat had ached with regret when he advised Dr. Wilder to proceed with the more radical surgery, he had been certain he was acting in Jacquelyn's best interest. Women with a family history of cancer typically developed more aggressive tumors at a younger age, and the cancer had already spread to the lymph nodes. Despite her denial, Jacquelyn should have known and understood his concern.

Then why did he feel such torment?

"Dr. Martin?" Jacquelyn leaned into the doorway of his office, feeling as hollow as her voice sounded. Her back ached between her shoulder blades, and the skin across her chest felt like the head of a drum against which her heart thumped in a tired, repetitive motion.

But she was grateful for her weariness. Right now she was too tired to care about Jonah Martin, and felt reasonably sure nothing he would say could upset her.

Jonah was seated at his desk, tape-recording notes the medical assistant would later transcribe onto patient charts. He looked up briefly, saw Jacquelyn, and motioned her in, apparently without breaking his train of thought.

Good, she thought, eyeing the empty chair

in front of his desk as if it were an island in the midst of a troubled sea. Dr. Porcupine was back.

He finished his notes, snapped off the recorder, then noticed that she was still standing.

"Please, sit down," he said, color rising into his face. While she collapsed gratefully into the chair, he shuffled a few papers scattered over the surface of his desk.

"Whew," he finally said, running his hand through his hair as he glanced over at her. "Quite a day, huh? I'm worn out, and I'm not recovering from surgery. I can guess how you must feel."

"Can you?" She lifted a brow. She didn't like him in this warm fuzzy mode, right now she would rather deal with Dr. Porcupine.

He seemed to take the hint. "All right then." His mouth took on an unpleasant twist as he pulled her chart from a stack on his desk. His voice was controlled now, almost tight. "You know the drill, Jacquelyn, but let me give you the refresher course. You know we can't say you are cured until ten years passes without a recurrence of the cancer — well, let's just say that from this day forward, I expect you to faithfully perform monthly breast self-examinations as well as having an annual mammogram."

He glanced at her for a sign of objection. "Understood?"

She nodded, too drained to speak.

He paused and drummed his fingers on the desk. "Next week," he said, a look of intense, clear light pouring through his eyes, "I want you to begin chemotherapy here. Just in case one or two of those rebellious cells slipped by Dr. Wilder's scalpel."

"Chemo?" She tensed at the horrified sound of her own voice. "You cut off my breast and you want me to take *chemo* right away?"

"Jacquelyn." He spoke with quiet firmness. "It's standard procedure. Stage II tumors with lymph node involvement, especially from patients with a strong family history of breast cancer, have a high risk of relapse that can be significantly reduced by taking chemo, followed by hormonal therapy."

"But — here?" She spread her hands wide. "I can't take chemo here, not in front of my own patients! I'm the one who's always telling them to be brave, that nausea won't kill them, and that those silly wigs look natural. For heaven's sake —"

"Afraid you can't take your own medicine?" The words were cold, but when she looked up he wore a pained expression, as though he regretted his bluntness.

How could she explain? It wasn't fear, pride, or self-consciousness that kept her from agreeing, but a combination of all those emotions. How could she, the stalwart, no-nonsense Nurse Jacquelyn, let her patients see her vulnerability? They needed her strength . . . and she *didn't* need their pity.

She gazed speculatively at her doctor. "You wouldn't do it if you were me," she said abruptly. "You wouldn't take chemo in front of your own patients."

By his slight squint and the sideways movement of his jaw, she knew her words had hit home. Oh, it was fine for him to challenge her, but woe to any nurse who dared suggest that a revered *doctor* take his own advice.

When he drew a breath, she mentally braced herself for a rebuke.

"Okay, Jacquelyn." His voice was surprisingly tender. "You're right. I'll administer your treatments myself. We can set up the treatment after hours. I'll respect your privacy."

The offer caught her unprepared. Disconcerted, she crossed her arms and pointedly looked away. "I could go to another hospital. I could even find another doctor."

"You don't have to do that." She could feel his warm eyes boring into her. "Jacquelyn, I'm your doctor, and I'd like to be your friend. We've come this far together, so let's keep moving forward, shall we? Your chemo will be completed in sixteen weeks. You can receive your treatment on Thursday or Friday, rest over the weekend and return to work on Monday. If your blood work is clear at the end of six months, you can forget you ever had cancer. I feel certain we'll be safely rid of it all by then."

Forget the cancer? Impossible.

She shrugged to hide her confusion, then dropped her head so he couldn't study her face. What should she do? The practical, logical side of her brain knew he was right about everything. He'd been right to take the breast. He was right to order chemotherapy. She was upset because she was tired and weak, and for the first time in her life cancer had turned on *her.*

Mixed feelings surged through her as she lifted her head. Why was she always so reluctant to concede to him? Something in her wanted to deny him and please him at the same time.

"All right, Doc." Somehow she forced a smile through her mask of uncertainty. "I'll put myself in your hands. I'll be your nurse from eight to five, and your patient from five for as long as it takes on chemo days."

"Good." Before his appealing smile, her defenses melted away. "Jacquelyn, I promise, I'll take every consideration of your feelings."

"You already have," she whispered, thinking about all the things he had done for her in the past two weeks. Was it possible that his concern was rooted in a feeling deeper than his unusual compassion for his patients? She rapidly dismissed such thoughts. Jonah Martin was an anomaly, a one-in-a-million doctor, and though he might be a trial to work for, she felt fortunate to have him as her physician.

"Have no fear, Dr. Martin." She smiled with all the enthusiasm she could muster. "I intend to eat right, to take my vitamins, to exercise and be happy. And —" the thought of Daphne Redfield suddenly flitted through her brain "— I'm going to start going to church again. This — *situation* — has reminded me that I'm not as close to God as I should be."

A strange, faintly eager look flashed in his eyes. "The church I'm attending is wonderful, if you're looking for someplace new. I'd be happy to meet you there for the Sunday service." Like an afterthought, he added,

"Of course Craig is welcome, too."

"Craig?" Even his name tasted like gall. She shook her head and laughed. "I wouldn't look for him in church." She wanted to add, I wouldn't look for him anywhere, but she bit her lip. Dr. Jonah Martin certainly didn't want to hear about her sad, nonexistent love life.

"All right, then." His tone deepened to a husky whisper. "Well, I want you to know that I don't exactly approve of you coming back to work so soon —"

She sputtered indignantly, but he held up a quieting hand. "But since you have, I insist that you eat a hot lunch every day in our cafeteria so I can check up on you." A faint light twinkled in the depths of his blue eyes. "If you don't have the energy to pack something microwavable, let me know, and I'll send one of the girls out for something. And every night you're not having chemo, you are to leave here promptly at four and go home to rest. If you need help with that canine pony, you must call me, Stacy, or Daphne."

She swallowed hard, lifted her chin and boldly met his bright gaze. "You're not my —" *Boss,* she almost said before realizing that he was. Struck by the silliness of her rebellious attitude, she shook her head and smiled. "Well, *that* was certainly juvenile," she finished, barely able to keep the laughter from her voice.

He regarded her with open amusement. "No arguments, Jacquelyn. If you want to be well, you will do *what* I tell you, *when* I tell you."

She tilted her head and pursed her lips. It was obvious he'd been listening to her little speeches in the office; he sounded exactly like her when she addressed new patients.

"Yes, sir," she said, standing. She let out an exaggerated sigh. "I hear and obey. All but the lunchroom thing. I'm your patient, not your slave, and you can't shackle me to this office. If the weather's nice, I'd like to eat outside on the lawn."

"That could be a problem." His voice had roughened, but his lips trembled with the need to smile. "I'm your supervising physician, but how can I supervise you if you're out of my sight?"

A foolish, bold reply rose to her lips, and before she could bite it back the words spilled from her tongue: "You could join me."

In heaven's name, what was she *doing?* He would think she was shamelessly flirting, as bold and brash as Stacy.

An inexplicable look of withdrawal came

over his face, then vanished as an easy smile played at the corners of his mouth. "You could let me take you out to dinner." The words came out at double speed, as if they'd been glued together. "You name the night, this week or next."

She froze, shocked. Was he teasing? Surely he was. He'd just told her to invite Craig to church. And he openly flirted like this with half his women patients, though most of them were old enough to be his mother. This invitation was about as genuine as his long-standing threat to show up at the Baldovino's house for lasagna.

A cynical inner voice cut through her confusion. This was his office. Though at this moment she was his patient, she was also his nurse. Hospitals were not appropriate for romantic rendezvous, so he couldn't have meant the invitation seriously.

She drew a deep breath and forbade herself to look in his eyes. "I'll go out to dinner with you, Dr. Martin," she said, tossing him the sauciest smile she could manage, "when you can scratch your ear with your elbow."

Jonah felt his smile freeze as Jacquelyn turned and left his office. What a fool he was! At least she'd kept her head and put him in his place, or he'd have spilled his feelings, which at this point were far more dangerous than his careless words.

It's a good thing you're renting that apartment, he thought, swiveling in his chair until he faced the window. If you don't get a hold of yourself, you're going to be moving sooner than you intended.

And yet he didn't want to leave Chambers-Wyatt Hospital until he knew Jacquelyn Wilkes was on her way to a complete remission. So he couldn't afford to be distracted by romantic notions, hormones, or whatever it was that made him want to yield to the dynamic vitality she exuded like a scent. He'd certainly met women as beautiful, and one or two as intelligent, but he had never before met a woman who made him want to surrender his iron-forged resolutions and dismantle the barriers around his heart. With her dogged determination and steely courage Jacquelyn Wilkes had stolen his affections . . . along with most of his good sense.

Why in the world had he blurted out such an open, obvious come-on? No woman in the world would want to think romantically of a man who had just finished discussing her medical records and ordering her life, but he had been emboldened by the sorrowful look that filled her eyes at the mention of Craig's name. The boyfriend had never once showed up at the hospital to visit Jacquelyn; Jonah had checked. And in casual conversations with Daphne Redfield, he had learned that Craig did not stop by the house to visit, either.

"It's really pitiful, Doctor," Daphne told him when he called to check on Jacquelyn's progress. "She reads on the couch all day with that giant dog by her side. The animal's a blessing, though, because she seems to have no one else. Her father did call on Saturday, so I introduced myself. Of course I assumed he knew everything about Jacquelyn's condition, but when I said she was recovering nicely from her surgery, the man mumbled something about someone at the door and hung up without another word."

Daphne's horrified wonder had rolled over the telephone line. "I can't imagine a father leaving a daughter alone like that. If one of my boys were sick, I'd be at his side in an instant, no matter how grown up they were."

"I'm sure you would," Jonah answered. He finished by asking a few questions about Daphne's health, then he had hung up and stared at the wall in his austere apartment.

So Jacquelyn Wilkes was alone. That

explained a lot — her devotion to duty, her fanatic obsession with her dog, the steel beneath her smile.

Jonah and loneliness were well-acquainted. His weapons against loneliness were his busy schedule and the emotional demands of his patients. If not for patients like Daphne Redfield, Concetta Baldovino and young Michael Richards, he'd be as nutty as a mouse in a milk can. Jacquelyn Wilkes would be, too, if he didn't allow her to stay busy and fill her life with something meaningful.

He'd do anything in his power to keep Jacquelyn from feeling the pain that walked with him daily.

The phone at his belt chimed, snapping him out of his reverie. One of his patients needed him, probably Michael Richards, the kid with bone cancer. He had received a strong dose of Adriamycin and Cytoxan that morning, and his mother had been as anxious as a hen with one chick.

Jonah picked up the phone and tried to settle into his professional demeanor. If the chemo didn't work, Michael would lose his right leg. Jonah didn't want to disappoint the world by sidelining an enthusiastic future quarterback.

He cleared his throat and flipped the

phone open. "Dr. Martin here."

On Friday afternoon, October 31, Jacquelyn waited until the office emptied, then sank into one of the cushioned chemo chairs. Someone had hung a string of construction paper jack-o'-lanterns across the wide window of the treatment room and outside, on a distant street, she could see that the parent-and-child patrols for Halloween candy had already begun.

How ironic. She'd begin her chemo treatments on a night primarily noted for goblins, ghouls and cheap horror movies on television.

"Should I give the speech you drill into every new patient?" Jonah asked, his eyes bright with mischief as he entered the room. He straddled Jacquelyn's little rolling stool, his lab coat trailing behind him like a medieval king's robe.

"You can skip the speech." Jacquelyn thrust her arm toward him. "Fill 'er up, Doc, and pop a good movie into the VCR."

Jacquelyn had to admire the skill with which Jonah slid the needle into her vein. Her own technique wasn't nearly as smooth.

"There," he said, attaching the IV drip to the tube that now ran into her arm. "These antinausea medications should keep your night and weekend from becoming too unpleasant. When they're in, I'll give you the injectable cocktail and send you home. We're going to follow the 'dose dense' protocol, Cytoxan and Adriamycin once every two weeks for four doses, followed by Taxol every other week for four doses. It's a fairly intense treatment but usually well tolerated."

Jacquelyn's gaze lifted to the pouch on the IV pole. "You don't have to stay," she whispered, feeling suddenly guilty. He was here, willingly working after hours, on account of her foolish pride. "This is going to take some time, and I know you're busy —"

"I have some things to do in my office." Jonah slapped his hands on his knees, then pushed back, propelling the stool across the gleaming floor. "And nothing to do at home." He stood, but paused to lower his hand to her arm as if to check the IV site. "Call if you need anything," he said, the touch of his fingers warm on her skin. "I'm here and I'll be listening."

She nodded, too overcome with sudden emotion to speak.

CHAPTER FOURTEEN

"Mrs. Redfield?"

Two weeks later, Jacquelyn hesitated at the edge of the reception area and looked around for Daphne. She bit her lip, torn by conflicting emotions, when she recognized the slender woman rising from the couch. Daphne wore her usual bright head covering, but the eyes beneath the scarf today seemed tired and dim. She moved stiffly across the lobby area, leaning hard on the handle of an umbrella. The smile she cast toward Jacquelyn held only a ghost of its former energy and warmth. How could she have weakened so quickly?

Assaulted by a terrible sense of guilt, Jacquelyn pressed her lips together. She had been looking forward to telling Daphne about how well she was doing after two weeks of chemo — she hadn't lost much of her hair, and she still had an abundance of energy — but her eagerness faded as the older woman carefully made her way toward the nurses' station.

"How are you feeling today?" Jacquelyn asked, then she blushed at the stupidity of the inane question. She glanced down at Daphne's chart to disguise the emotion she knew her eyes revealed. "You know, Dr. Martin will love that red scarf. I think red is his favorite color."

"So why are you wearing white?" Daphne teased, but her voice seemed to come from far away. "Sometimes, Jacquelyn, I think you have too much brain and too little romance in your life."

Jacquelyn lifted a finger in rebuke. "That's not true. I love my dog."

"You are deliberately being obtuse." Daphne wagged her head, but her mouth curved with tenderness. "Look at you! You look great."

"I'm bouncing back to my bossy self." Jacquelyn took Daphne's arm and helped her to the chair where she would take a blood sample and a blood-pressure reading.

"You look beautiful." Daphne nearly collapsed into the chair as her knees buckled, then she propped the umbrella between her legs and sighed in relief. "You're as pretty today as you were before your surgery," she went on, ignoring her own obvious discomfort. "You look too good for a cancer patient — the rest of us will have trouble keeping up."

She paused, breathless, while Jacquelyn fumbled with the blood-pressure cuff. Why were her eyes stinging? She couldn't cry in front of a patient! She never had, but Daphne's rapid decline had caught her by surprise. This woman had been on her hands and knees scrubbing Jacquelyn's kitchen only a few weeks ago.

"I think you're just being kind," she said, wrapping the cuff around Daphne's arm. She had to be careful with double mastectomy patients, any undue pressure on the arm could lead to edema or swelling. She would always have to remind the other nurses to take her own blood-pressure readings on her right arm, not her left.

"No, I'm being truthful."

Jacquelyn let the comment slide as she studied the sphygmomanometer gauge. "Umm, your pressure's pretty low. Let me stick your finger and see what the lab tech says. You may not get your treatment today after all."

"Treat me or not, it's all the same to me." Daphne held out her hand. "I enjoyed coming out into the sunshine. The house has been too quiet, with the boys in school and

Dan at work."

The blood ran bright red from Daphne's bruised fingertip, and Jacquelyn placed the micropipette under Daphne's finger to catch a crimson drop. She then placed the micropipette into the CBC machine, then hummed while it printed out the results.

She pulled out the paper report and frowned. "Your neutrophil count is two. No chemo for you today."

The absolute neutrophil count, or ANC, referred to the actual number of white blood cells a patient had to fight infection. An ANC of less than one would put a patient at risk for serious infection while a patient with an ANC of less than .5 would be placed in protective isolation. A healthy person's ANC fluctuated slightly from day to day, but a cancer patient with an ANC of less than 2.5 would never be able to withstand the chemical onslaught of a chemo cocktail.

Daphne wouldn't get her treatment. And she needed it desperately.

"Good news." Jacquelyn pasted a bright smile on her face. "You get a vacation. I'm going to give you Neupogen to raise your white blood cell count, then you can go home and get some sleep. Eat good foods, all you want. If you follow my orders and rest, you can come back in a couple of days and take your treatment then."

"Whatever you say, dear."

In the light of Daphne's gentle, understanding eyes Jacquelyn managed a tremulous smile. "I'm sorry you had to get out of bed to come down here."

"Nonsense." Daphne shook her head. "When you believe God controls all things, you begin to see everything in your day as a divine appointment. So since I'm here, I'd like to hear how you're doing."

Jacquelyn slid into her chair, eager and yet not eager to share her news. An hour ago she had been glad to see Daphne's name on the appointment list, wanting to share how her discomfort with the chemo had been minimal. But how could she speak of health and life when the woman next to her was literally wasting away?

"I'm doing well," she said finally, edging her words with caution. "I feel pretty good. I've been working full days with an hour nap in the afternoon, and I'm eating — a lot. Some of the other patients have told me about things I thought might help, so I've been taking blue-green algae supplements and sticking to a diet high in beta-carotene. One of our afternoon patients is bringing me some pills made from shark cartilage."

Daphne crinkled her nose. "Sounds like old wives' tales in new wrappers, if you ask me. I'm glad you're doing well on the chemo, but what I really wanted to know is —" she leaned forward and placed her cool hand on Jacquelyn's arm "— how are you and Dr. Martin doing?"

Jacquelyn sat back, stunned. What in the world could Daphne mean? She shivered as a shudder of humiliation ran through her center. Had she said or done something to imply — to *reveal* — that she thought a great deal about Jonah Martin?

"Dr. Martin is fine," she stammered, coloring fiercely while she searched for a way to ignore Daphne's obvious meaning. "Though we get along better as doctor and nurse than doctor and patient." She turned and gestured down the hall. "If you want to see him today, I know he'll tell you to go home just like I did. He's with someone now, but if you want to wait —"

Daphne's mouth twitched with amusement. "Heavens, Jackie, don't play games with me. I don't want to see him. I want to know if *you've* seen him — outside the office, I mean."

Jacquelyn managed a choking laugh. "Why would I want to do that? The man is hard enough to escape *in* the office. He's always spying on me and ordering me around. He even tries to dictate what I eat for lunch."

"He likes you." Daphne folded her arms on top of the umbrella. "And I'm pretty sure God wanted me to tell you that Dr. Martin may feel something for you that goes deeper than friendship. Though I don't know why *he* doesn't say something."

Surprise caught the words that would have slipped from Jacquelyn's tongue. She could scarcely imagine God gossiping with this woman, but the idea that Jonah Martin might honestly care for her . . .

She stared, tongue-tied, at her patient.

"He was very concerned about you during your surgery," Daphne continued as if she hadn't noticed Jacquelyn's astonished reaction. "More than any other doctor would be concerned, if you get my meaning. What other doctor would call and find the help you needed? Not many, I can assure you! But Jonah Martin did."

"He's — he's my boss," Jacquelyn stammered. "He went the extra mile because he's my employer."

"Would Dr. Kastner have done the same thing? He's your boss, too."

"But he's not Dr. Teddy Bear!" Jacquelyn flung up her hands in helpless frustration, then squinted at Daphne in embarrassment. "Listen. You adore Dr. Martin and I can understand why. He *is* special, I'll admit that. He takes a lot of extra care for his patients and I suppose that's why I wanted him to be my oncologist. But Daphne, he doesn't think of me as . . . well, you know. As anything special."

Daphne didn't answer. She merely sat there, smiling at Jacquelyn with an "I'm right and there's no sense in arguing" expression on her face.

Indignation surged through Jacquelyn's veins. "This is how rumors get started." She lifted a scolding finger and lowered her voice to an intense whisper. "Someone out in the hall overhears a story like this, and the next thing you know, the rumor mill is reporting that the good doctor and I are engaged. Well, it's not true and it's not fair. So please, Daphne, don't mention your little idea to anyone. I have to work with Dr. Martin and I wouldn't want a story like this to complicate things."

Daphne held up her hand. "Excuse me. I thought you might have seen what I saw." Her smile flashed briefly, dazzling against her jaundiced skin. "I guess I'll have to keep on hoping."

Jacquelyn groaned.

"And if you didn't see what I saw," Daphne whispered, leaning closer with a teasing smile, "then you, Nurse Jackie, are simply blind."

"I saw Mrs. Redfield today," Stacy said, dipping a potato chip into a tub of cottage cheese. She and Jacquelyn were eating lunch at one of the two small tables in the lounge, a makeshift cafeteria for the employees of the cancer clinic. None of the others had come in yet.

"I sent her home," Jacquelyn said, hoping Stacy hadn't overheard any of her conversation with Daphne.

Stacy daintily wiped a smudge of cheese from the edge of the chip. "She looked awful. What was her white cell count?"

"Two." Jacquelyn popped open the plastic container of veggies she'd brought from home. Inside, like decapitated warriors from a vegetable army, neat broccoli florets and cauliflower crowns lay bunched together, intertwined with carrot ribbons. She picked up a carrot curl and tossed it into her mouth, determined to eat no matter how much her spirit rebelled at yet another serving of rabbit food. "I couldn't believe it," she said, munching. "Daphne said she was actually grateful for the chance to come out of the house. Most people would be frustrated to make the trip for nothing — especially since I know she isn't feeling well."

She looked away, wondering if Stacy would mention the astonishing question Daphne had asked Jacqueline before leaving. Stacy was a veritable outpost on the front of the rumor wars, and Jacquelyn had been sincere when she told Daphne she didn't want stories about her love life bandied about the clinic and the hospital. It was hard enough to maintain a decent reputation when you were young and single. Jacquelyn certainly didn't need to deal with rumors about her involvement with a doctor.

"Hi, girls." Sighing heavily, Lauren sank into an empty chair at the second table. She rubbed her temples for a moment, then began to unroll the top of a plain brown lunch bag.

Jacquelyn paused with a broccoli floret between her fingers. "Headache?"

"A little one." Lauren pulled out a sandwich and a container of juice. "My kid. My daughter and I are constantly at war over the most mundane things." She shrugged and picked up her sandwich. "Typical mother–teenage daughter stuff, I guess. But

I'm not far from putting her in a locked box and throwing away the key until she's eighteen."

"Better make that twenty-two," Stacy said, grinning. "I gave my parents the most trouble during my college years. My mother's hair went white in two weeks the year I dated one of my professors."

Lauren's elegant brow lifted. "I hope you at least got a decent grade for the effort."

Stacy shrugged, then winked at Jacquelyn. "Anatomy was my hardest subject. I had to do something to get through it."

"Get through what?" When Jonah's baritone voice cut into the feminine chatter, Jacquelyn lowered her eyes. If she looked at him, she'd remember what Daphne Redfield had said — rats, wasn't she thinking about it anyway? How could she *help* thinking about him when he insisted upon poking his head into the lunchroom every day?

"Ladies," he said, moving toward the small refrigerator, "not one of you is eating a substantial lunch. If you're going to keep pace with the workload around here, you're going to have to eat more."

"My kids cleaned out the fridge before I got to it." Lauren held up her sandwich, made of the brown ends of a bread loaf.

"Peanut butter and jelly is the best I could do."

"At least you're doing better than the others." His blue eyes flitted disapprovingly over Stacy's chips and cottage cheese, then came to rest on Jacquelyn's dismembered vegetables. A muscle flicked at his square jaw. "Nurse Wilkes," he said, his eyes sharp and assessing, "I certainly hope that tonight you're dining on proteins and carbohydrates. Your body needs food to heal."

"I'm healing very well, thank you," she answered, her tone sharper than she'd intended. Stacy looked up, surprised, and even Lauren lifted a brow.

Jacquelyn glanced down, embarrassed by the heat in her face. Good grief, even if the entire office hadn't heard Daphne's question, from Jacquelyn's own rash actions they'd soon guess that something was in the air.

"I'm delighted to hear of your progress." Jonah pulled a paper bag out of the refrigerator, then turned. The empty seat at Lauren's table beckoned like a lighthouse, but with stiff dignity he moved toward the table where Stacy and Jacquelyn were sitting.

"Do you mind?" He paused behind an empty chair and looked directly at Jacquelyn.

Was Stacy snickering? Whatever that muffled noise was, Jonah seemed not to notice it. As Jacquelyn stared, he sat at the table and opened his lunch bag, pulling out a sandwich, potato chips, a container of fruit juice and a package of chocolate cookies. Stacy, her eyes bright and amused, dipped one last chip into her cottage cheese, ate it and dramatically proclaimed that she needed a breath of fresh air. As she stood and moved away, she nudged Lauren, who hurriedly picked up her sandwich and mumbled something about the pleasure of lunching on the lawn.

Their crepe-soled nurses' shoes made no sound as they moved away, and Jacquelyn stared numbly at her vegetables, wondering if she should follow. She couldn't help feeling as though a giant web of conspiracy had been woven around her and even the patients knew something she didn't. Well, this foolishness would have to stop. Jonah Martin cared for her only as a patient and fellow professional. It would be wrong for her — or anyone else — to assume anything more than that.

She took a deep breath and faced him. "I hope you realize you have effectively chased the entire nursing staff from the lunchroom." She snapped the lid on her container of vegetables. "Didn't anyone ever tell you about the unspoken law against fraternization between doctors and nurses?"

"No one needed to tell me," he said, staring down at his food. His tone was heavy with sarcasm. "I wrote it." He picked up his sandwich, then looked at her with something stirring in his eyes. "And you're wrong. I didn't chase *all* the nurses away. You're still here."

"I'm on my way out." She couldn't bear the touch of his eyes upon her, and the uneasy look of longing behind his gaze. She pushed back her chair and stood, ready to leave — until he spoke again.

"I thought this was the twenty-first century," he said, then he paused to take a bite. He chewed slowly, knowing simple politeness would force her to wait for the end of his declaration.

She tried to hurry him along. "So?"

He swallowed, then gave her an innocent smile. "You nurses are liberated. You own your bodies, your hearts and your lunch tables. So in the spirit of fair play, you shouldn't mind if Dr. Kastner or I choose to eat lunch in here."

"Dr. Kastner doesn't eat, he dines." She pushed her chair to its proper position under the table. "He saves his eating for evening, when he goes out with his wife and various other important people. You, on the other hand, never even leave the office until late and then —" She paused, aware that she was about to cross an invisible line. The conversation was becoming too personal. What Jonah Martin did away from the office was his business, certainly not hers. And she shouldn't criticize. He'd been uncommonly cooperative in his willingness to give her chemo treatments after hours and in relative privacy.

"Well, I don't know much about you," she finished lamely, pressing her hands to the table. "So I'll let you eat in peace while I join the other nurses."

"Wait —" His hand fell upon hers and she had to fight the impulse to pull away. "Jacquelyn, I am serious about your lunch. While you're on chemotherapy you need to eat more than vegetables and salad."

"Thank you, Dr. Martin." She shot him a cold look. "But you don't have to worry about me. I'm doing well. I feel strong, I haven't had much nausea and even my hair is hanging on."

"You've only had two treatments. Some of the drugs' side effects aren't visible for ten to fifteen days."

His words lit a hot, clenched ball at her

center and she whirled away, her heart hammering under her scarred chest. Why was he always looking for what might go wrong? Alarm and anger rippled along her spine as she turned back to face him. "I thought you were Dr. Compassion. I can't believe you would be so pessimistic —"

A swift shadow of anger swept across his face. "Just because I believe in giving my patients hope doesn't mean I will lie to them," Jonah answered. "I tell them the truth. I'm glad you're doing well, but you can't place your faith in vegetables. Last week I attended the funeral of a patient who did all the right things for five years, but she still lost the battle."

Jacquelyn wanted to throw her hands over her ears, but instead she turned toward the window, her breath coming raggedly. Oh, what she'd give to force him to spend a week recuperating from some dire surgery in one of his own hospital's beds!

"I am fine." She reined in her temper. "I prayed there would be no cancer outside the lymph nodes or in the tumor margins, and there wasn't. God answered my prayers, and I know I will be okay. And God will see me through this chemotherapy."

"Good." His voice sounded flat, tentative. "But you can't stay healthy eating grass."

"I'll show you how healthy I am." She turned toward him, confused and crazily furious. "I challenge you to a run. A race. Meet me Saturday morning, nine o'clock, along the lakefront by my house. If I beat you, you'll have to admit my diet is working and you'll agree to leave me alone. My life is my own business — I can take care of myself."

For a moment he rolled his eyes, then the beginning of a smile twisted the corners of his mouth. "I'm a pretty fair runner. So what happens if I beat you?"

"Then —" She faltered, having no idea how to answer.

"If I beat you," he leaned toward her, "you will go to dinner with me Saturday night. I'll order you a steak, a baked potato dripping with butter and French silk pie for dessert. And you'll eat it, as much as you can, without complaint."

She hesitated, blinking with bafflement. What had she done now? She had wanted to show him that she was strong enough to stand up to him and suddenly she'd found herself on the losing end of a bet that would inevitably end in a date.

She couldn't beat him. She couldn't have beat him when she was healthy. But neither could she back down. She'd thrown down the gauntlet and he had astonished her by picking it up.

She thought she detected laughter in his eyes when he extended his hand. "Do we have a deal?"

If she refused, he'd tell everyone in the office. She'd never hear the end of it.

So she took his hand and shook it, then ceremonially tossed her container of vegetables into the trash can. Before he could taunt her with anything else, she hurried down the hall, her mind reeling with the realization that though she'd never wanted to date a doctor, without a doubt she'd be out with one Saturday night.

And she had instigated the entire fiasco.

Jonah smothered a smile as he watched Jacquelyn flee the room. The red-haired nurse was neutral in nothing, and though he'd seen the flash of regret in her eyes after issuing her "challenge," he knew her pride wouldn't allow her to quit. After the loneliness and depression she'd experienced following her surgery, he was glad to see the flare of her fighting spirit.

He turned back to his sandwich and wondered if he'd been wise to challenge her. She took her chemo on Friday nights, and a Saturday morning run would not be a good idea. Even if the chemo did not make her sick, fatigue was one of the most prevalent side effects. He *could* hang back and let her win, but she'd resent that . . . and he'd lose her company at dinner. And this was the age of equality, wasn't it? She had challenged *him,* probably in a burst of temper.

"Wow." Stacy's voice broke the silence as she entered the lunchroom. "Who put a bee in Jacquelyn's bonnet?"

Jonah turned back to his lunch, afraid the other nurse would see the look of delight on his face. "Jacquelyn waved a red flag in front of my nose. I think she was surprised when I accepted her little challenge to a race."

"A race?" Stacy's voice rose in surprise. "Dr. Martin, I'll never understand you." She came over to his table and lowered her voice to a subtle purr. "And I'll never understand why you are wasting your time with the least willing woman in the office. There are dozens of girls at the hospital who'd love to go out with you, but you and Jacquelyn —" Her mouth quirked with humor. "Well, it just wouldn't work."

Jonah gave her a narrow glinting glance. He knew he was treading the knife edge of his own personal boundaries, but he had to know. "If I were interested in her — which

I'm not — why wouldn't it work?" He dropped his eyes before Stacy's steady gaze. "And, for the record, I'm definitely not interested. So you can pass that word on to her boyfriend."

"Craig Bishop?" Stacy frowned. "He hasn't been around for weeks. No, you and Jacquelyn wouldn't work because . . . well, because you're different, that's all. You're —" Her smile deepened. "Well, Jacquelyn calls you all kinds of names when you're not around. She doesn't like you, but don't take it personally. Jackie's just not very outgoing. Sometimes I think the only thing she cares about is that dog."

"That's not really true." Jonah looked away and considered a bland, nondescript seascape someone had hung on the wall. "She's logical and independent, but she can be warm and caring."

"Yeah, Jackie's the first person at our Christmas party to put a lampshade on her head." Stacy shook her head as she moved toward the sink. "And if you believe that one, I've got property in the Everglades I want to sell you."

Jonah picked up a newspaper someone had left on a chair and pretended to read, effectively ending the conversation. But his eyes merely stared at the words while his thoughts raced. There was no boyfriend. Craig Bishop, no matter what he'd meant to Jacquelyn, was out of the picture for good.

Smiling to himself, he shook out the paper and exhaled a long sigh of contentment.

Saturday dawned in a beautiful burst of reds and golds. Jacquelyn looked out the window and groaned, half-convinced that God held something against her. Slanted sunlight shimmered off the glowing evergreen foliage around her house, and across the street the lake shone like silver below an endless cobalt sky. The November air was pleasant, not too hot, not cold, a perfect day for running. And though she searched from horizon to horizon, not a single cloud marred the perfect bowl of blue overhead.

"Come on, Bailey," she said, urging the dog from his bed. The mastiff snorted and unfolded, then slowly stood, yawned and lumbered toward the door. Jacquelyn let him out, set his breakfast on the porch and then hurried toward the bureau where she kept her running clothes.

She could call Jonah and cancel. But what excuse could she give? She couldn't say she was sick after insisting that she was doing well, especially since something had come up yesterday and he had insisted on moving her treatments from Fridays to Mondays. Even the excuse of a common cold would be an indictment against her "healthy eating" regime and she would never stoop to some feminine excuse like menstrual cramps. Men never understood women's problems, anyway. Her father was a classic example. During the worst part of her mother's illness, when she had to be diapered and changed regularly, Jacquelyn's father had left the task to his daughter or the part-time nurse.

Did he even look at Mom? Jacquelyn wondered, taking clothes from a dresser drawer. Did he see the scars from the mastectomy? Did he hold her and assure her that he loved her, or did he turn away while she dressed?

She pulled her nightgown over her head and tossed it into the laundry hamper, then turned to stare at her own scar in the mirror. The incision was still red and bumpy over the flatness of her chest, a visible seam, but the skin had knit together very well. In time, perhaps, the ridge would become less evident, but on Jacquelyn's wedding night it would still be there, an ever-present reminder of the darkest days of her life. Maybe someday she would come to see it as a survivor's badge of honor, but now it was an ugly scar, pure and simple.

She shrugged off the thought and reached for the prosthesis she had recently received. A volunteer from the American Cancer Society's Reach to Recovery program had visited her in the hospital — the mastectomy Welcome Committee, Jacquelyn had bitterly joked — bringing her a bra that contained a temporary cloth model. Her permanent prosthesis, which she'd just picked out from the lingerie department of her favorite department store, was a soft plastic form containing silicone gel. It slid easily into her sports bra, and Jacquelyn stared at her new shape with a mixture of revulsion and pleasure. The prosthesis felt alien next to her body, and in a fit of temper she gave it a name: Myra, the same name she'd bestowed upon the invisible playmate of her childhood.

"Myra, you look okay — now," she told her reflection after slipping into her shorts, "but what are you going to look like when we're jogging around the lake?" She turned to study her profile. "Do you promise not to move around? I can't cross the finish line and find that my breast has migrated to some place around my ear."

Giggling at her own foolishness, she

slipped a T-shirt over head, fluffed out her hair, then reached for her socks and running shoes. Her pride and temper had landed her in the middle of this mess. Maybe, if she was lucky, Jonah Martin would pull a hamstring or be paged for an emergency call. Those were the only two ways she could imagine coming out of this event a winner.

CHAPTER FIFTEEN

Though Bailey wanted to go along, Jacquelyn put the dog in her fenced backyard, then crossed the street and stretched out in a patch of grass. Even from here she could hear Bailey's frustrated whine, and the sound grated on her nerves. At nine o'clock, if Jonah Martin hadn't shown up, she'd go home.

When at five minutes after nine Jonah still hadn't appeared, she smiled in satisfaction and lifted her arms in a victory salute. "I win, by default," she called to a car passing by. With an odd twinge of disappointment, in a quieter voice she added, "So from this day forward Jonah Martin has to stay out of my life."

She was about to cross the street and return home when the roar of a car's engine startled her. Jonah's Mustang swung around the corner and veered toward her, coming to rest under the shade of an oak tree. She lifted her good arm and pointed to her watch.

"I'm sorry," Jonah said, slamming the car door. His blond hair was a tousled mess, his eyes still clouded with sleep. He wore a faded T-shirt over cotton sweats that had been chopped off above the knee. High-top tennis shoes covered his feet, their tongues hanging out like a panting dog's, while long black shoelaces dragged along the ground.

Well, he'd certainly placed a high priority on *this* meeting. If she had any illusions that he harbored special feelings for her, his appearance this morning had certainly swept them all away. A truly *interested* man would have set an alarm clock, dressed neatly and at least combed his hair. No man who wanted to impress a woman would show up eight minutes late and dressed like a walking garage sale.

"I overslept." He flashed a killer smile while he knelt to tie his shoes. "Had a late night."

"I don't care to hear what you were doing last night," she remarked, pleased at how nonchalant she sounded. She didn't want to hear about his date, and she didn't want to know whom he had taken out. She knew half the nurses in the hospital would give their eyeteeth just to have him look in their direction.

"But I was with a friend of yours."

Stacy?

As if he'd read her mind, he turned and eased into a smile. "Daphne Redfield. She wasn't feeling well, so I went over to see her and the family. I gave her an injection of morphine, then her boys and I played basketball until midnight." He tugged on his shoestrings, then stood. "I think the kids needed to burn off some energy."

The biting words Jacquelyn had prepared fell, useless, back into the blackness of her jealousy.

"Have you stretched?"

All business, wasn't he? No small talk, no admiring of the weather, no inquiries into Bailey's health or her own, for that matter. He probably had a lunch date. He'd have to get this over with so he could go home, shower and clean up for whatever lucky lady would meet him for lunch.

"I'm ready." She bent to touch her toes. "You should get a penalty or something for being late, shouldn't you?"

His smile turned to a chuckle. "You're right. Tell you what — I'll give you a head start. Since I was five minutes late —"

"Eight."

"Okay, eight. I'll give you those eight minutes to run ahead of me. How long is the trail around this lake, about a mile?"

"Two miles. I usually run it in twenty minutes, when I'm not pushing. Eight minutes — that's quite a lead you're giving me." Her mind raced. He didn't want to win, he'd had second thoughts about taking me to dinner. He couldn't win, not with her halfway out in front. . . .

"I was late, I'll pay the penalty." His smile shimmered like sunbeams on the water. "So are you ready, Nurse Wilkes?" He lifted his arm and studied his watch. "Anytime you're ready, take off. I'll leave eight minutes behind you."

Sure he would. He was so eager to lose, he'd probably give me a ten-minute lead.

Jacquelyn took a deep breath, shook out her arms and legs one final time and then took off, willing herself not to think about Jonah Martin. Whatever he decided to do was fine. If he wanted to lose, she'd have something to brag about in the office. And if he won . . . but he didn't want to. She'd spoken on impulse and so had he; now they both regretted it. So he'd arrived late and offered her this unbeatable advantage. He'd had second thoughts about the propriety of a doctor and nurse going out for what would certainly look like a date, and he didn't want to complicate things.

Her feet pounded the asphalt running path as her mind ran in relentless circles. The lake was quiet this morning; the usual picnickers and dog-walkers were still lingering over Saturday morning papers and cups of steaming coffee.

Why was she doing this? Her arms hung like lead weights and she felt pressure near the incision under her arm. Myra bumped up and down like a beanbag in a pocket, jostling against already irritated skin. Since she was going to win, she should turn around right now and call the whole thing off. But if she stopped running, Jonah would say she forfeited. He'd win and be forced to take her to dinner, which he didn't want to do. So she *had* to finish at this foolish breakneck pace instead of her usual leisurely run, because if she slowed down he'd think she was pursuing him, that she *wanted* him to take her out, which she definitely did *not* want to do. . . .

How long had she been running? Five minutes? The time felt like an eternity. She heard no footsteps behind her, and she could see nothing through the dense cattails at this edge of the lake. He should still be at their starting point, unless he'd started early in order to beat her, but *that* he did *not* want to do.

Pound, breathe, pound, breathe, swing arms, keep steady, run, win, run run run.

How long now? She risked breaking stride long enough to lift her watch. Straining to see the blurred numbers, she saw that nine minutes had passed. He should be on the track now, quite a distance behind her. She found it difficult to calculate while her body labored to keep up the pace, but if he ran a six-minute mile while she ran an eight, he'd take twelve minutes to run the lake, minus the eight he'd allowed her . . . she should beat him by at least four minutes. Even if he was a bona fide sprinter and ran a five-minute mile, she should still beat him by at least two minutes, even at her slower pace.

The asphalt ahead broke into pieces where an oak's roots had pushed upward from the soil, and Jacquelyn adjusted her stride to jog around the uneven surface. They really should fix that, she thought, pushing her arms and feet again into an even rhythm. It's dangerous, really, to allow something unexpected to just jump up at you like that. There you are, just running along, and suddenly something pokes up at you and messes up your pace, your life, everything you had going for yourself. . . .

Her arms weren't cooperating; they hung from her shoulders like weights. Wounded muscles around her lungs screamed from the unexpected strain and she felt suddenly achy and exhausted, as if she'd abruptly come to the end of her energy reserves.

Good grief, what if she couldn't finish? What if Jonah Martin came chugging along and found her breathless on the ground? He'd never cease to preach at her. He'd hover over her even more closely and would probably order her one of Mrs. Baldovino's lasagnas, the Seventh Carbohydrate Wonder of the World. . . .

There. Just ahead, beyond the curve of the road, she saw the blackened top of her chimney. Almost home. And yet she heard nothing of Jonah Martin. Even though she was definitely not running as well as usual, she'd still managed to beat him.

Because he let her win.

Because he didn't get involved outside the office.

Gasping in the uneven rhythm of her pounding feet, she pushed herself forward. An elderly woman in a pink sun visor and yellow housedress walked ahead on the trail, leading a fluffy white wisp of a dog. The animal turned to gape at Jacquelyn with wide eyes and a laughing pink tongue.

Ignoring the ankle-biter, Jacquelyn pushed her sour thoughts aside and breezed past, giving the woman a wide berth.

"Excuse me, please."

The masculine voice rose from someplace behind her without a note of breathlessness. Jacquelyn bit her lip and resisted the urge to scowl. Jonah! Where he had come from she couldn't say, but he approached and passed her effortlessly, each stride fluid and strong.

As he ran effortlessly ahead, Jacquelyn felt her feet grow heavy. The pressure on her lungs increased as her steps slowed. Pride reared its head and snarled at the thought of defeat, then wonder silenced it.

Why did he pass her? He had chosen to run at a sprinter's pace. For some unimaginable reason, probably male pride, he wanted to win. Which meant dinner . . . and a date.

If she survived. Her breath came in shallow, quick gasps as she rounded the corner and saw her house, prim and pretty, on the opposite side of the street. But like a balking dog that recognizes the vet's office, her legs faltered and then stopped, refusing to go farther. Jacquelyn leaned forward, her hands on her bony knees, her head hanging low.

She was dead empty; for the last mile she'd been running on fumes. In that, at least, Jonah had been right. Vegetables and water weren't enough to fuel a frantic run around the lake.

"Jacquelyn! Are you all right?"

Jonah's voice, rough with anxiety, came to her through a whirling fog. Her eyes watered as her vision faded to black and her ears began to ring.

Good grief, I'm about to faint!

"Lie down. I'll get some water."

Strong hands helped her to soft ground. His voice, infinite in its compassion, seemed to come from some unearthly realm. She pressed her hand over her wet eyes and obediently lay back, not caring whether she lay on dirt or asphalt. She was depleted, overheated and probably close to losing consciousness, but conscious enough to feel intense humiliation. If there was any blood left in her head, she knew it was concentrated in her cheeks.

"Drink this."

She parted her fingers enough to see Jonah kneeling over her, his jaw tensed, his eyes dark and serious. He was holding out a plastic bottle of some sports drink and scanning her with concerned eyes.

She felt his hand at the back of her head,

lifting her until she could sip without difficulty.

"That's enough, thank you," she whispered, frowning at the slightly salty taste of the drink. She lowered her head back to the ground and heard an annoying yapping sound. The old woman and the dog had reached them, drawn by the universal human tendency to gawk at tragedies and overt humiliation.

Had Myra stayed in place? She threw a hand over her chest to be sure.

"I'm fine," she gasped, squinting into the sunlight. "I just need to get my breath."

"Is she okay?" The woman's quavering voice cut through the silence.

"She'll be fine." Jonah spoke in his Confident Doctor voice. "She has overexerted herself."

Even through the pain of exhaustion, Jacquelyn managed to scowl.

"See?" Liquid laughter filled his voice. "She's better already."

Furious at her vulnerability, Jacquelyn forced herself to sit up, then waited until the lake and horizon stopped spinning and resumed their proper places. "I'm okay," she said, noting with clinical curiosity that tiny water droplets covered the skin of her arms like glistening pearls. Perspiration: the body's foremost cooling mechanism. At least some systems in her body were still working at full capacity.

The pink-visored woman hesitated, then nodded at Jonah and led the little yapper away.

Jonah lowered himself to the path, resting his arms atop his bent knees. "I think you gave her a scare. I know you gave me one."

"I'm okay," Jacquelyn repeated, feeling like a parrot. "I just need a minute. I haven't run in a long time and I started out at too fast a pace. I should have taken it slower."

"Slow and steady wins the race." He looked at her, his gaze as soft as a caress. "There's a lesson here. You shouldn't take anything, including your recovery, too fast. You've done very well — in fact, I was beginning to think I was too generous with my eight-minute handicap."

"You've run before," she managed to say. Her heart was still hammering in her ears.

"Yeah. My dad went to college on a track scholarship and I followed in his footsteps." The faint glint of humor in his eyes faded. "I guess I should have warned you, but this race was your idea."

She leaned forward and used her aching left arm to wipe a stream of water from her forehead. "Until today, I thought I was a good runner."

"You are. But I'm afraid I pushed you too hard."

Worrying about her physical condition again, was he? Always the compassionate doctor, never anything more.

"You don't have to worry about me, Doc." She ignored the hand he offered and stood without his help. "You won the bet, fair and square. So tonight I'll choke down whatever you feed me."

He flushed at her words, but kept his features composed. "You don't have to go if you don't want to. I wouldn't force you —"

"You won." She forced her lips to part in a curved, still smile. "You don't have to spare my feelings — unless you don't want to be seen with me."

His breath quickened. "Any man would be proud to be seen with you, but I don't want you to think this has anything to do with your employment. This is strictly voluntary — come only if you want to."

"Ask," she said, feeling an unwelcome blush creep onto her cheeks, "only if you want me to come. You don't have to do this."

"All right, then, I'm asking." He stood in one athletic motion. "Why don't I pick you up at six? We'll eat at one of those casual tourist places, so you can wear whatever you want."

"Fine."

She waited at the curb until an approaching car passed, then lifted her chin and crossed the street, keenly aware of his scrutiny until she entered the house and closed the door.

"Ohmigoodness, this is wonderful." The Caesar salad dripped with dressing and grated cheese. Jacquelyn had forgotten how delicious forbidden foods could taste.

"Good?" The glow of Jonah's smile warmed her across the table. "Wait until you taste the steak. Then you'll understand why we had to stand in line forty-five minutes."

Jacquelyn hadn't minded the wait. She wasn't surprised when Jonah chose one of those cookie-cutter steak houses that cater to tourists because she knew they weren't likely to see anyone from the hospital there. Away from the formalities of the office, the man had proven to be very good company. He was neither aloof nor unduly attentive, not quite the stern employer or the overly compassionate doctor. Nibbling at her salad, Jacquelyn tilted her head and gazed at him, irreverently wondering if he did have a split personality. The Jonah Martin who sat across from her seemed to be a blend of two opposite natures.

Now relaxed and rested, she and Jonah talked about their pets — he once had a tabby cat named Smoke — their favorite books and movies, and the funny things they had believed as children.

"I still can't believe that you thought rabbits laid eggs," she said, spearing a bit of slippery lettuce on the bottom of her salad bowl.

"What else could I think?" Jonah shrugged, his eyes shining in the pale light of the candle on the table. "The Easter Bunny brought colored eggs, chocolate eggs and marshmallow eggs. And rabbits live in those little burrows like ducks and ducks lay eggs, so . . ."

She laughed. "When did you find out the truth?"

"Fifth grade. The science unit on mammals. I learned that except for the dodo bird, mammals don't lay eggs. So I ran to my mother for an explanation of where mammal babies came from." Teasing laughter filled his eyes. "In those days, life seemed to be a series of contradictions."

"What did your mother tell you?"

"To go ask my father." His golden eyebrows arched mischievously. "And he tried to explain the biggest contradiction of all — that men and women, who were designed to be complete opposites, must join to create life. I suppose that's when I first became interested in medicine." His face shone like gold in the flickering candlelight. "I got a very complete explanation, when all I wanted to know was why rabbits didn't lay eggs."

Jacquelyn smothered a smile. "Your father wasn't a doctor?" Most of the doctors Jacquelyn knew were pedigreed third-and fourth-generation physicians, destined from birth to practice medicine and drive luxury cars.

"Dad is a pastor. The shepherd of a little flock in Oak Woods, Virginia."

"I see." So that accounted for Jonah's unusual compassion, his unfailing optimism in the face of death, the almost-visible halo around his golden hair. He'd been born and bred to care — for his patients, at least.

The waiter cleared their empty salad bowls away, and for an instant the expanse of wooden table between them seemed as wide as a church door. Jacquelyn laughed awkwardly. "I've never been out with a minister's son."

"Is the experience so different?"

She shrugged. "I don't know. I've never been out with a doctor from my office, either." She reached for the straw in her iced tea and stirred it slowly. "I don't know if I should even be here. I know you're only doing this because you try to encourage your patients. In fact, I fully expected you to let me win the race this morning."

One corner of his mouth twisted upward. "Afraid not. My masculine pride couldn't have withstood defeat," he said, a note of mockery in his expression. "Besides, I didn't think you'd appreciate it if I let you win."

"You're right." Jacquelyn stirred her tea again, suddenly at a loss for words. Thankfully, the waiter chose that moment to appear with two sizzling platters.

"Two filet mignon, medium-well," he announced, deftly placing the dishes on the table. "Is there anything else I can bring you?"

"This will be fine for now," Jonah answered. The waiter gave Jacquelyn a final smile before departing, and for a moment she wished she could jump up and join him in the kitchen. She shouldn't have been so honest with Jonah about her feelings; the atmosphere between them now felt stiff and uncomfortable. The easy camaraderie had vanished the moment she mentioned that she knew he was only taking her out as a gesture of goodwill. He was silent now, probably embarrassed by her forthrightness. Well, after dinner she could plead a headache and beg him to take her home.

"Thank you, Father, for this meal and this company."

Jacquelyn looked up, startled. Jonah had uttered the prayer with the casual ease of one who had grown up with public displays of piety, and he didn't seem at all embarrassed to bow his head in a restaurant. She and her family had always said grace before meals, but they would never have done so where others could see. It was so . . . obtrusive.

"Dig in," Jonah challenged, picking up his steak knife and fork. "This steak is delicious. God made red meat, Jackie, and he meant for you to enjoy it. Along with sugar and the butter dripping all over that baked potato."

"How can you say that?" She picked up her knife and fork, too, but frowned at him. "Research has proven that broiled meat can be carcinogenic. And everyone knows butter is loaded with cholesterol."

"Eating too much of anything is bad for the body," Jonah answered, popping a slice of steak into his mouth. He chewed slowly, grinning at her, then swallowed. "But just enough is great. Do you know how much red meat you'd have to eat to expose yourself to enough carcinogens to do damage? A lot. And cholesterol is the buildup of too many fats, which people wouldn't have if they didn't eat all the time. Three hundred thousand people in this country die every year from complications arising from obesity, while this year only 43,300 women will die from breast cancer. Think about it."

Jacquelyn stared at him blankly, her knife and fork frozen in her hands.

"My theory is simple," Jonah went on, cutting another slice of steak. "God made the human body — He designed it with exquisite care. We don't worry about breathing — our lungs tell us when to inhale and exhale. It's an involuntary function. You don't worry about telling your heart to beat. Why should you worry about eating?"

"Because eating is a *voluntary* function," Jacquelyn pointed out. "You don't do it automatically."

"We should," Jonah answered. "Our body gives us a hunger signal and a fullness signal. We only get into trouble when we ignore what our body tells us. People should learn to eat when they're truly hungry and stop when they're full. That's God's way, and it's logical. Look at me." He lifted his hands, and Jacquelyn had to admit that he was a perfect weight, neither too heavy nor too thin. And he had already demonstrated that he was physically fit.

"I eat *what* I want, when I'm hungry," he went on. "God programmed our bodies to crave variety, so one day I'll eat veggies, another day I'll go for a greasy hamburger. But I can't believe that the God who designed fat to be delicious and sugar to be sweet would want me to avoid his gifts. Everything in moderation, though, that's the key."

Jacquelyn found his unconventional ideas more than a little disturbing. Had she entrusted her health and future to a crackpot? "You really trust this haphazard diet of yours?" She squinted up at him. "You think it's healthy?"

Jonah smiled. "I know it is. I've never eaten any other way. Oh, I studied nutrition in medical school, and I read all the studies. But 99 percent of Americans with nutritional problems have forgotten to listen to their bodies." A warning cloud settled on his clear features. "I guess what I'm saying, Jackie, is that you shouldn't put your trust in broccoli and cauliflower. It won't hurt you to eat them, but don't think they're going to keep you safe from cancer. They don't have that kind of power. My father would tell you that only God does."

She glared at him. "You think I should ignore the fact that I've just gone through a mastectomy? That I should forget about cancer?" Her voice grew hoarse with frustration. "If that's true, then why are you making me go through chemotherapy? If God will protect me, why am I doing anything about my cancer at all?"

"God uses all sorts of things, including medicine and doctors and beta-carotene." The corner of his mouth twisted with exasperation. "But nothing, including chemotherapy, is foolproof. I think God expects us to use all the means we have at our disposal, and then pray like everything depends on Him — because it does."

"You believe that?" She ripped out the words. "When is the last time *you* prayed with a patient? For a patient? For me?"

A guilty shadow crossed his face as he looked away. "I'm just telling you what my father would say. I'm no expert on religion. I guess you could say that a few years ago God and I had a falling out." He transferred his gaze back to her. "But you said you had grown closer to God since your surgery. I thought you might be interested in what a man like my dad would tell you."

He was obviously angry — and hurt — at something or someone in his past, and she felt suddenly vulnerable in the face of his hostility. Unable to look into his flashing eyes, she glanced down and stabbed her baked potato with her fork. "*Now* I feel like I'm out with a minister's son."

"Is that so bad?"

"Yes." Her anger swiftly abated. "You don't understand where I am, Jonah. I had cancer, the same cancer that killed my mother. My tumor — an extremely nasty and aggressive variety — could return if a single cell broke lose and is still gallivanting around in my body. And yet you're telling me not to worry, not to do everything I can to save my own life."

"I'm not saying that at all." His voice was calm, his gaze steady. "I'm saying you should admit that you can't control everything. You could do all the right things and still find another lump next year." His face went a shade paler as his fist clenched on the table. "I don't want that to happen, so I think you should consider depending on God. There have been many studies lately proving that surgical patients with strong religious faith do better than irreligious patients —"

"Daphne Redfield trusts God." She boldly met his gaze. "What has He done for her?"

CHAPTER SIXTEEN

Jonah felt his mouth go dry at the mention of Mrs. Redfield's name. He'd given Daphne a double dose of pain medication last night, hoping it would help her rest. Her husband, his expression pinched and worn, had been grateful, holding Daphne's hand as she gradually stopped moaning and fell asleep.

"Thank you, Doctor," Joseph Redfield had murmured, his eyes fastened to his wife's pale countenance. Pain had carved merciless lines across Daphne's elegant face, muting what had once been vibrant beauty. "The boys and I were praying you'd be able to give her something. She's so tired — she needs to rest so she can regain her strength. For the boys."

"I know." Feeling helpless and frustrated, Jonah had gone outside where Justin and Jed, the Redfield twins, sat like forlorn statues on the darkened front step, a basketball between them. Within a few moments the three of them were slamming the ball toward the basket over the garage, playing a silent, furious game which drained their anger, frustration and fear.

Yet Jonah was a doctor. He wasn't supposed to fear death. He had studied it in all its clinical forms; he knew from his Christian upbringing that to be absent from the body was to be present with the Lord. And yet when he thought of Jacquelyn, so vibrant and alive, wasting slowly away like Daphne, his heart turned to stone within his chest.

"Jonah?" Jacquelyn's voice broke into his thoughts. "Don't you have an answer?"

He stifled the urge to laugh. Sometimes he wasn't even sure of the *question*. His patients thought him God's gift to medicine and most of the time he either provided solutions or bluffed his way by trial and error until he was able to find some protocol that provided a workable resolution to the problem at hand. But Jacquelyn knew too much, a bluff would never work with her.

"I don't know what God is going to do with Daphne Redfield," he admitted. He forced himself to look into Jackie's wide green eyes. "And I've never had cancer, so I can't empathize with you. But I know enough about God to know that if I were dying, I could trust in His loving kindness and tender mercies. I know His touch is gentle."

She shuddered and lowered her gaze. "His touch isn't always gentle," she answered, her voice a thin whisper across the table. "Sometimes it's harsh and it hurts. It took major surgery for God to get my attention, but He got it. I prayed. I'm trying to read a little bit in my Bible every day, and I've started going back to church." With the sense of conviction that was part of her character, she explained, "But God helps those who help themselves, right? So I'm doing all I can to help Him. He gave me a brain, He expects me to use it. I've learned all I can, I'm doing all I can, I'm exercising and eating right, and putting myself through chemo because *you* convinced me I need it."

Almost without meaning to, his hand found its way across the table and clasped hers. "Jackie, listen to me." His voice echoed with the same sincerity, the same words his father would have used. "God doesn't help those who help themselves, He helps those who call on Him. I think that's what He wants you to do. Stop doing so much on your own. You can't do it all."

Her eyes, dark and questioning, came to

rest on his and for a long time she said nothing. When she spoke again, she had changed the subject: "So where did you ever get the idea that rabbits laid eggs?"

Two nights later, Jacquelyn awoke in a cold sweat. She stiffened, momentarily paralyzed by fear, then heard the familiar sounds of Bailey's deep breaths and the pounding of her own heart. Across the room, the red numerals on her alarm clock glowed like steady, unblinking eyes. Despite the reassuring sights and sounds of her own room, she shivered.

She'd had a black dream. She'd heard her cancer patients talk of them; they usually began after the second or third course of chemotherapy. They were nightmares that terrorized without faces or forms — mysterious, ugly terrors that jerked patients from sleep in the dead of night. Until now Jacquelyn had never realized how honestly frightening, how truly *real* they could be.

Rest in the Lord, she told herself, remembering what Jonah had said at dinner. Rest in the Lord, but resting wasn't as easy as it sounded. For the past two days she had tried to take his advice. She had awakened with the light heart of the well rested and told herself that she would trust God and not worry. After all, it would be a relief not to fret about what she ate and how many hours of exercise she fit into her busy schedule. And she was absolutely *sick* of carrots, broccoli and a breakfast plate of vitamins and algae capsules.

And so she had gotten up, taken Bailey outside and headed into the shower. And as she'd lathered, her hand had run over the ridge of scar tissue on her chest, and a biting, dark fear had sniped at the peace in which she'd enveloped herself. Was that a bump or another malignant lump? Though she knew the voice of fear was her enemy, she shivered under the hot shower, knowing she couldn't outrun her fear, she couldn't rest. Jonah could dispense advice all day long, but he had never known cancer. He had never lain awake at night, knowing that only through pain and suffering could the Death Angel be avoided.

She pressed her hand over her mouth, trying to steady her breathing. A hard fist of illogical, undeniable panic grew in her stomach until her gorge rose and blood roared in her ears. She sprang from the bed and ran for the bathroom. It was what — 1:00 a.m.? — at least five hours since she had finished her weekly chemo treatment. She had endured two treatments with scarcely any effects whatsoever, but this time she was not going to get off so easily. . . .

Ten minutes later she lay flat on the chilly tiles of her bathroom floor, perspiration staining her nightgown, her hair streaked with tears and sweat. She gulped back a sob and ran her hands over her damp scalp, then gasped in disbelief when her fingers came away covered in shimmering, silken strands.

She would lose her hair. Not just the hair on her head, but her eyebrows, her eyelashes, even the fine hair that covered her arms. . . . Don't worry, it will grow back, she could hear herself cheerily reminding her patients. You might want to cut all your hair short to lessen the shock, or perhaps you'd prefer to invest in a natural-looking wig.

In no time at all, she'd be wearing scarves like Daphne. Or one of those polyester-looking wigs some of the older women wore. She swallowed the sob that rose in her throat and looked up at the ceiling. *God, everything I dreaded is happening.* . . . She bit her lip until it throbbed like her pulse, and then her stomach heaved again.

The night seemed eternal. Lying on the cold floor, Jacquelyn faded in and out of consciousness, realizing that she had never felt more alone in her life. She knew she ought to get up and drink some water, but the room swirled around her every time she lifted her head and she didn't want to fall and crack her skull on the porcelain toilet. If she did fall, who would come to help her? No one. No one would hear her cry or the thump of her body hitting the floor.

Don't call the doctor; call one of us nurses if you have a problem.

How many times had she made that statement? And yet she, one of those confident nurses, couldn't rise from the floor of her bathroom, couldn't even make it to the phone.

Mustering her strength, Jacquelyn pulled herself across the tile, finally reaching the cordless phone she kept on the counter. She dialed the clinic number from memory, then grimaced when the answering service operator curtly asked what the emergency was. "I need Dr. Martin," Jacquelyn said, lowering her head to the cold tile of the floor. "Tell him it's Jacquelyn Wilkes. I'm having a bad reaction to the chemo, and I'm . . . alone."

Shivering with chill and fatigue, she relaxed her fingers and could do nothing to stop the phone from clattering over the bathroom tiles.

Jonah's eyes were sandy and his bones

ached as his car roared up Jacquelyn's narrow drive, but his heart pounded in an erratic rhythm. The operator from the service said Jacquelyn sounded bad, and Jonah winced at the thought. He should have kept her at the office for another hour or two, perhaps treating her after hours was a bad idea altogether. But she had insisted on privacy, and he would have done anything to make things easier for her.

Her front door was locked, and as Jonah pounded on it he heard a low, menacing growl from the other side. Bailey, of course. Jonah shook his head and hoped the dog had a good memory.

Hesitating only for a moment, he found a fist-sized rock in the border of Jacquelyn's flower bed, then used it to smash one of the side lights edging the door. Bailey was now barking in earnest and Jonah wondered if he'd have to call 911 for Jacquelyn *and* a dog-bite victim. He slipped out of his jacket and wrapped it around his forearm, then eased his padded limb through the broken pane, all the while calling, "Bailey! Good boy, remember me? Sit, Bailey!"

By some wonder, Bailey didn't bite. Jonah's fumbling fingers felt the dead bolt and flipped it. In another moment he had opened the door, and in the steady glow from a hall light he could see the huge dog, teeth bared, the hairs along its neck lined up at attention.

"Bailey!" He deliberately injected a note of happiness into his voice and knelt, a suicidal position if the dog had malicious intentions. There was no way he could wrestle the dog to the ground and he'd never rise quickly enough if the big brute decided to charge. . . .

But Bailey came over slowly, his nose erect, his tail steadily lowering. The dark muzzle slowly relaxed, the lips relaxed from a snarl to what could best be described as a grin. Bailey gave Jonah a cursory sniff, then barked and ran back toward Jacquelyn's room.

Jonah followed, his heart thumping against his rib cage. From the hallway he could see Jacquelyn facedown on the bathroom tiles, the phone halfway on the floor as if it had been shot from her hands —

"Jacquelyn!" Fear of the unknown knotted and writhed in his stomach as he hurried forward and knelt by her side. Had she been experiencing side effects she'd been too proud to report? He turned her carefully and smoothed her wet hair from her face. With an almost clinical detachment, he noticed that the reddish-gold strands stuck to his skin as if he'd coated his fingers with honey.

He ran his hand down her arm to her wrist, feeling for her pulse. It was there, steady and slow. She was most likely dehydrated, sorely in need of fluids and rest. Their race this past weekend had probably exacerbated the effects of today's chemo. He drew a deep breath, struck by sudden guilt. He should never have taken her up on that bet. No one in the midst of chemotherapy had any business racing around a lake —

"I'm sorry." Her eyelids fluttered open, and the words were so soft for an instant he wondered if he'd imagined them.

"No, I'm the one who should apologize," he said, sitting on the floor next to her. "I should have known better than to accept your challenge. And then I probably made things worse, taking you out and making you eat all that rich food."

Though she shivered, a smile played briefly on her lips. A wave of warmth pulsed along his veins, and he pulled her into his lap, cradling her head in his arms. "Does it hurt a lot?"

The blush on her pale cheek was like the flush of sunset on snow. "It doesn't really hurt," she said, her voice like two sheets of sandpaper being rubbed together. "But I've never felt so bad in my life. I'm sick as a dog."

Something in the old metaphor made Jonah smile. This wasn't a medical emergency, he could see that now. But, looking around, he could see that she'd passed a couple of miserable hours in this bathroom. The toilet and sink needed cleaning, and she needed a bath. . . .

But right now she needed someone to hold her, and Jonah was grateful he'd come.

Jacquelyn slept for half an hour in Jonah's arms, then he put her back in her bed so she could rest while he rummaged for clean sheets and linens in a hall closet. When he'd found what he was looking for, he carried them out to the living room sofa, where he knew she'd spent most of her convalescence from surgery. Daphne had mentioned that Jacquelyn liked being able to look out the window, and he had a feeling she wouldn't want to look at her messy bed for a while.

After spreading sheets and arranging pillows on the sofa, he carried her to it, tucking in the blanket under the soft cushions. When he was certain she slept soundly, he also found a plastic waste can from her guest bedroom and placed it by the side of the sofa, just in case her stomach heaved again. No sense in finding her on the bathroom floor a second time.

Dawn had begun to brighten the horizon when he tiptoed through the living room, a bucket and bottle of disinfectant in one hand, a scrub brush in the other. He wasn't prepared for the soft sound of laughter from the sofa.

"Doctor, where did you find that apron? And why in the world are you wearing it?"

Her voice was ethereal, almost without strength, but in it he heard a trace of humor . . . and gratitude.

"My mother always wore an apron to clean." He dropped the bucket and brush in the hall. "I found it wadded up in one of your kitchen drawers. I can tell it's not something you use very often." He pulled the wet rubber gloves from his hands and stepped into the tidy living room. "I see you made it through the night without using your waste basket as an emesis basin. That's good, Jacquelyn."

"I feel like something left by the side of the road." She lifted her hand as if to push back her hair, then apparently thought the better of it and let her hand fall across her chest. Her eyes shimmered with light from the window. "I don't know how to thank you. I'm glad you came, but you didn't have to clean my bathroom."

"You were in no shape to do it," he said lightly, moving back toward the hallway. "And I couldn't call Daphne to help again."

He immediately bit his lip, wishing he could take the words back. He didn't want to remind one sick patient that another wasn't doing well at all. But if Jacquelyn was discouraged by his words, she gave no sign of it. She simply turned her head toward the window and closed her eyes, leaving him alone to finish the cleaning.

Half an hour later, after changing the bed linens upstairs, tossing a mismatched load of laundry into the washer, and making certain no trace of last night's episode remained in either the bedroom or bathroom, he moved into the living room and perched on the edge of the antique trunk Jacquelyn used as a coffee table. Dehydration had tightened her skin over the ridge of her cheekbones, but a few glasses of water and a sports drink would restore her fluids in no time. Red-gold hair littered the pillowcase like cast-off threads, and he knew it'd only be a matter of days before she bought a wig or came to work in a hat. Most of his female patients were more troubled by the temporary hair loss than any of chemo's other side effects, but though Jacquelyn's hair was lovely, he couldn't see that its loss would diminish her beauty. Her fair skin magnified the deep depths of her emerald eyes, and even now there was soft color in her sweet curled lips.

What was she dreaming about?

His pulse quickened when her lashes lifted and she caught him studying her. But she didn't seem surprised.

"You're not going to be fit for your patients today," she said, her voice a soft whisper in the room. "And we're both going to be late for work."

"Everyone else can wait." He took her hand, so small and slender, and balanced her palm upon his, marveling that the skin could feel so warm and supple after the difficult night she'd passed. She didn't pull away from his touch.

"Is there anything else you need?" he asked, pushing the words past a sudden lump that rose in his throat. "Anything I can do before I go home to shower? I'm going to bring you a glass of water, and I'll see if I can't find some juice or something in your kitchen."

"I'm fine, Jonah." The gratitude in her voice tugged at his heart. "I just need to get my strength back and the juice will help.

I'm planning to come in to work today."

"Don't push yourself. Lauren and Stacy can handle things."

"I'll be fine." Determination lay in the firm set of her chin. "I may not make it in until lunchtime, but I'll be there."

"All right." Still holding her hand, he enclosed it in both of his. "Jacquelyn, if you ever need anything, all you have to do is call. I'll give you my home phone number. I want you to know —"

Her fine, silky brows rose a trifle, waiting to hear his next words, and Jonah suddenly realized he could say no more. What was he doing? He couldn't deny his attraction for this woman, but this was not the time to lose his heart. She was sick, he was a doctor, and his compassionate instincts had scored a knockout blow against his common sense. . . .

He leaned forward and let his lips graze the spot where her hairline met her forehead. "Take your time this morning, get some rest. Before I go I'll leave water and juice for you here on the coffee table. And I'll tell Lauren you had a rough night. She'll understand."

Jacquelyn nodded sleepily. He placed her hand on the blanket over her chest and patted it as tenderly as a brother might, and then turned into the kitchen. He had to tape a piece of cardboard over the window pane he'd broken and call a glass company to repair it. And then he would place Jacquelyn's fluids on the table and slip out as quietly as he could. Later, when he was alone and out of this cozy house, he'd be able to think clearly about what he had to do next.

Jacquelyn opened one eye as she heard the front door close. He was gone. A pitcher of ice water and a huge tumbler of orange juice sat on the table at her left hand. She sat up, pausing as her riotous stomach rebelled and then began to settle. When the churning and aching subsided, she lifted the juice glass, held it aloft for a moment as if in salute to Jonah, then slowly brought it to her lips.

The sweet, ripe taste brought tears to her eyes, and she drank greedily. After the ravages of the night before, her body cried out for nourishment, and the juice was exactly what she needed.

Just as Jonah Martin, she now saw clearly, was exactly what she needed. She didn't need some undependable, ambitious lunk who would have left the room with a pillow over his face at the first sign of her queasy stomach. Would Craig Bishop have donned her apron and rubber gloves to scrub a toilet and sink?

"When pigs fly," she whispered to Bailey as she leaned down to scratch the mastiff's ears. As always, the dog was by her side on the floor, and at her acknowledgment his tail thumped rhythmically on the wooden floor.

She now saw with crystal clarity that Daphne was right — Jonah Martin cared for her. He was unusually compassionate with his patients and he did involve himself too much in their lives. But though he might have held Mrs. Baldovino's hand or kissed Daphne Redfield on the forehead, he never would have offered them his home phone number. That number was the measure of his commitment, proof that his feelings for Jacquelyn went beyond the confines of the office, deeper than his concern for her as a patient. His feeling went deeper than professional concern, Jacquelyn knew, because she had seen the masculine hunger in his eyes and felt the brief shiver that rippled through him when he took her hand. He had come running when she called, he had held her head when she was sticky with stale sweat, and no man did those things for a woman unless he loved her beyond all doubt. Unless he loved her as much as . . .

I love him.

She sat back, stunned by the sudden thought. Why did a knot rise in her throat every time she glanced toward his office? In the beginning she had assumed that he affected her because she thoroughly disliked him, but she had to admit that she admired his professionalism, his intelligence, even his meddlesome compassion. And now that she had been on the receiving end of that mercy, she would never again take it lightly. Jacquelyn Wilkes, Chamber-Wyatt Hospital's Nurse of the Year, would never be as orderly, as quick, or as proficient with her patients, because Jonah Martin's love had changed her.

She had seen love in his eyes and recognized it as the same gleam she'd been denying in her own. How long had she loved him? Probably for weeks. She should have realized it when she asked Dr. Shaw to refer her to Jonah instead of Dr. Kastner. She'd known then that Jonah was what she needed . . . but too many other things had blocked her vision, kept her from seeing what really mattered.

"What do I do now?" she asked the air, then looked down at Bailey. Despite her physical weariness, her heart skyrocketed with happiness and she felt a foolishly wide grin creep over her face. "I suppose there will be a wedding, Bailey. Jonah's certainly old enough to know what he wants, and I think he wants a home and marriage. I know I do."

She leaned forward until she sat nose-to-nose with her pet. "It would be nice to have Jonah here with us all the time, wouldn't it?"

Sensing her excitement, Bailey's tail began to thump the floor in earnest.

CHAPTER SEVENTEEN

Jonah gave Lauren a quick nod, then grimaced at the sight of half a dozen patient charts stacked at the nurses' station. He had never been one for sticking to a rigid schedule, but he'd really have to hustle today. Kastner wouldn't like this backlog.

"Is the waiting room full?" he asked the nursing supervisor as he slipped into his lab coat.

"Yes," Lauren answered sharply, glancing up at the clock. "Dr. Kastner was late this morning, too. And there's no sign of Jacquelyn."

"She'll be late." Jonah spoke without thinking, then immediately regretted his words. Stacy, who was helping an older patient down the hall, jerked her head toward him, curiosity gleaming in her eyes. "I spoke with Jacquelyn this morning," he went on, hurrying to his office. "She had a rough night after her chemo treatment, but said she'd be in later this afternoon. Maybe after lunch."

Once in his office, Jonah checked his messages, fumbled in a drawer for his stethoscope, then took a moment to swipe his hands through his still-damp hair. Stacy possessed a shrewd intuition, and soon she'd be asking Lauren how Jonah Martin knew so much about Jacquelyn's condition. He'd already seen more than a few lifted eyebrows between the two women because he sent them home on Jacquelyn's chemo nights, preferring to administer the drugs himself. He knew they were murmuring about preferential treatment and special attention, and probably wondering what else might be going on. . . .

What *was* going on? He wasn't exactly sure, but he knew it had gone too far. This morning he had hated to leave Jacquelyn's side, even her warm little house. His feelings for her had ripened from admiration to affection to something more, and he had sworn he'd never again become involved with one of his coworkers. He was setting himself up for a tumble and he was putting Jacquelyn in a difficult situation. While it wasn't exactly improper for doctors and nurses to date, everyone knew such a relationship made an already intense working atmosphere almost unbearable. Other doctors at the hospital would say he'd taken advantage of a pretty young woman at the point of her greatest vulnerability. And if they heard that he'd spent part of the night at her house, no matter how innocent or humane his reasons for going over there, Jacquelyn's reputation would be tarnished.

No matter how he considered it, he couldn't deny that trouble was circling again. Once the rumor mills started cranking, Jacquelyn would be portrayed as a gold-digging nurse or he'd be painted as a lecherous doctor who preyed on powerless patients. Lauren and Stacy could — and would — attest that he and Jacquelyn remained in the office alone, after hours. . . .

Whatever this thing between them was, he had to stop it. He hadn't been in Winter Haven long enough to put down real roots, and whatever feelings had begun to blossom in Jacquelyn's heart would shrivel up and disappear in time. If that had been love shining in her eyes, it was misguided, founded on her need and his position as her caregiver. Once she was well, she'd become her old feisty self again. She'd probably be glad to see him go.

He paused, torn between his waiting

patients and what he had to do. Well, the patients had been waiting for an hour; a few more minutes wouldn't hurt. Kastner had been late, too, so he could share the blame for the backlog.

Jonah picked up the phone and dialed Eric Elrod, a friend from medical school who had transferred to a hospital in California. Eric had called a couple of weeks ago, asking if Jonah was interested in a transfer. At the time Jonah had thanked him and declined, but things had changed.

"Hello, Eric?" He'd managed to catch his friend at home, and for once Jonah was glad of the three hour difference in time zones. "Listen, if your hospital still has that opening in oncology, I'd like to hear more about it. Can you fill me in on the details?"

Stacy and Lauren stepped out of Dr. Kastner's office and moved silently to the nurses' station. Stacy found her voice first. "I don't get it. How could they hire him with these kinds of accusations hanging over his head?"

Lauren sank into a chair. "Because nobody puts *accusations* in an official record. Looks like he left before anyone proved anything."

Stacy leaned against the desk. "So how did Kastner find out? Who called him?"

"Someone from the old boys' network, I

guess. And you know what they say — bad news flies around the world while good news is still putting on its boots."

"Do you think — could he have done anything to Jackie?" Stacy asked, anxiety spurting through her. "And would Jackie tell us if he had?"

Lauren's expression darkened with unreadable emotions. "I don't know. The entire story is hard to believe." Her brows slanted in a frown. "He's never approached me in an improper way — but then again, I'm a married woman." She gave Stacy a pointed look. "What about you? Has Dr. Martin ever said or done anything —"

Stacy frowned and shifted her weight, trying to remember every occasion she had been alone with Jonah Martin. "There might have been a time or two when I thought he *wanted* to say something. I mean, he is single, and I'm not what you'd call exactly standoffish." She started to smile, but thought the better of it when she saw the seriousness of Lauren's expression. "He might have tried something if I'd let him. But when Jacquelyn got sick, I think he lost interest in me."

"Such a *nasty* rumor." Lauren shuddered dramatically. "And such a shame. Dr. Martin shouldn't have to pressure any woman for attention. If I wasn't married, I'd have considered going out with him myself."

"So what happens now?" Stacy lowered her voice as she heard someone approaching through the hallway. "What do we do?"

"We steer clear of him as much as possible," Lauren answered, distrust chilling her eyes. "And we wait for Dr. Kastner to confront him about those rumors. Until he does, we carry on and do our best. Our patients don't have to know anything, but be sure you don't leave Dr. Martin alone with a female patient for any length of time. This clinic doesn't need the stigma of a lawsuit. We have problems enough already."

Stacy nodded, then moved away, trying to shake off the dark feeling of foreboding.

As she walked into the clinic's reception area, Jacquelyn felt her heart fill with the wonderful sense of going home. In a way she supposed this place *was* her home; she certainly spent more of her waking hours here than in her house. But the feeling of happiness in her heart could only have come from the knowledge that Jonah was here doing the work he had been called to do . . . which happened to be the same work she now passionately loved.

Jacquelyn saw Mrs. Baldovino waiting on

a sofa, and gave the woman a broad smile as she pointed to the scarf she'd tied around her head before leaving the house. She was shedding like a sheepdog.

"Good morning, Mrs. Baldovino. What do you think of my headgear? You'll have to show me all those intricate knots you use to tie up your scarves. I have a feeling I'll be craving some variety by this time next week."

The older woman gasped and clapped her hand upon her cheek. "Nurse Jacquelyn! You are being treated?"

"Yes, I am a patient here," Jacquelyn answered, smiling at another man who looked up in surprise. "And losing my hair. It's almost gone, but it'll grow back."

"You've been keeping secrets from us." Mrs. Baldovino wagged her finger like a scolding teacher. "I didn't know you were taking the chemo, too."

"Just trying to identify with my patients," Jacquelyn quipped, sinking onto the sofa next to the older woman. The words had barely escaped her mouth before her conscience smote her. Why was she still making light of the most crucial thing in all their lives?

She exchanged a polite smile with her patient, then shook her head. "Mrs. B., I shouldn't have kept this a secret. A couple of months ago my doctor found breast cancer. I've had a mastectomy, and now I'm taking chemotherapy, too. And now I understand, I *really* understand, all the things you've been telling me." She reached out and placed her hand on the woman's arm. "For all the times I must have seemed hard of hearing, I am so sorry. I should have been a better listener."

"Ah, Nurse Jackie," Mrs. Baldovino answered indulgently, "you will be all right." Her eyes brimmed with gentle compassion. "Ernesto and I will say a prayer for you every morning."

"Thank you," Jacquelyn answered, surprised to find her voice thick and unsteady. How could she have ever seen her patients as a collection of arms and vials and charts? Every ear in the crowded waiting room had heard her "confession," and every eye now shone toward her in quiet understanding.

"Well, I suppose I had better get to work," she said, rising from the couch. She caught a little boy's eye and winked. "I'm moving a little slowly this morning — I was up all night tossing my cookies."

The boy grinned while a handful of other patients laughed. Jacquelyn nodded at the assembled room. "I'll be back to get some lucky audience member in a moment. Just let me tell Lauren and Stacy that I'm here."

She hadn't gone far down the winding hallway when intuition told her something was wrong. She heard Stacy's taut whisper before she rounded the corner, but was unprepared for the look of complete and total shock on the younger nurse's face.

"Jacquelyn!" Stacy gasped as Jacquelyn approached the nurses' station. Lauren didn't speak, but her eyes widened in a slight, watchful hesitation.

"I know I look bad," Jacquelyn said, moving behind the counter. She dropped her purse into the deep drawer where the office staff kept their personal possessions. "And this scarf isn't a fashion statement. My hair is falling out. But I can deal with it."

"You do it," Stacy said, turning to Lauren. "You're the supervisor, so you tell her."

Jacquelyn turned. "Tell me what?" The anxiety in their eyes had nothing to do with her appearance, after all. A creeping uneasiness rose from the bottom of her heart when the two women exchanged troubled glances. "Did one of our patients pass away?"

"No one died." Lauren stepped forward and straightened her posture. "Dr. Kastner called us into his office this morning. As you know, last weekend he attended that medical convention in Atlanta —"

"So?" Irritation spiced Jacquelyn's uneasiness. What did a medical convention possibly have to do with their troubled faces?

"While he was there, he met a doctor from the University of Virginia Hospital. A man who knew Jonah Martin. Who knew why Jonah Martin —" she lowered her voice "— had to leave."

Nervous flutterings pricked Jacquelyn's chest. He left to take another job. And another, and then another —

"You wondered why he has worked in so many hospitals," Stacy said, breaking in. "As it turns out, there's a good reason."

Suddenly conscious of an unnamed dread, Jacquelyn hid a thick swallow in her throat and turned away. "He left because he wanted to move on. He's always advancing —"

"He left because one of his nurses threatened to sue him," Lauren answered, an edge on her voice. "Apparently he dated her a couple of times, then something happened and she accused him of sexual harassment. Nothing was ever proved, of course, because the poor girl was too traumatized to press charges. Everything was settled quietly when Martin left the hospital."

Jacquelyn felt a wave of grayness pass over

her. "It can't be true."

Lauren's eyes narrowed. "If it's not true, then how do you explain his record? Six hospitals in seven years? And you're always complaining that he's too close, too *personal* with his patients —"

Jacquelyn closed her eyes and held up her hand, cutting Lauren off as the paraphrase of her own words echoed in her ears. It couldn't be true, and yet there were things about Jonah that had disturbed her from the first day she met him. His two-sided personality, his odd aloofness, the gleam of hunger in his eyes when she caught him watching her in an unguarded moment . . .

"He doesn't seem like the type to harass women," Stacy said, chewing on her thumbnail. "But if it's not true, why would he run? He has to be running from *something*."

A scream clawed in Jacquelyn's throat, begging for release, but her clamped lips imprisoned it. What a fool she was! Jonah Martin didn't love her. What she had seen in his eyes was lust, not love. And she had allowed him into her house, given him free rein to come and go while she was alone and vulnerable.

She staggered toward a chair as her knees turned to gelatin beneath her. He had admitted that he and God had had a falling out! By the looks of things, God was right to turn his back on Jonah Martin! How could she have been so blind, so foolish? Was she so emotionally needy and desperate that she turned to a lust-driven doctor for attention and support? Even Stacy would show more sense!

Stacy's concerned face moved into Jacquelyn's blurry field of vision. "Do you need some water? You really don't look too good."

Jacquelyn felt as if her feelings and brain were paralyzed. "I think," she said, bracing her arms on the sides of the chair, "that I shouldn't have come in today."

Jonah stepped out of his office and shot a look of pure annoyance toward the nurses' station. Lauren and Stacy had been off their game today. Of course he hadn't helped things by being late to work, but though he'd been rushing through his exams to catch up, the nurses hadn't been helping. Now the two of them were huddled behind the nurses' counter with their backs to him, probably indulging in gossip of a uniquely feminine variety.

"Lauren," he called, sighing with exasperation. "Can we bring in another patient, please?"

Lauren turned and gave him a hostile

glare. "Of course, Doctor." She swiped at the stack of patient charts on the desk and moved off toward the reception room.

Stacy turned and eyed him with a similar withering stare, and then he saw Jacquelyn. She sat in the corner chair, her face as pale as snow, a flash of cold in her gaze. She had tied a bright scarf around her head, but hollows lay beneath her eyes, dark, bruised-looking circles.

His first instinct was to gently scold her for bothering to come in. She ought to be home in bed. He'd have taken her home himself, but —

The bitter gall of resolve burned the back of his throat. He had allowed himself to become too involved with an entirely inappropriate person, and Eric Elrod would soon be faxing information about that oncology position in California. Though Jonah's emotions bobbed and spun like flotsam on a Winter Haven lake, he could learn to ignore them. For Jacquelyn's sake.

His thoughts were distracted by Mrs. Baldovino's boisterous greeting. "Ah, Dr. Martin!" she called, breaking away from Lauren in order to hurry over and take Jonah's hands. "Tonight we shall have that dinner date. We will eat lasagna, and my Ernesto has agreed to cook! The tests have come back, and my cancer is in remission!"

"I know, and that's wonderful, Mrs. Baldovino," he said, summoning a smile. "I will be happy to eat with you and Ernesto. Has he thought any more about that tummy tuck?"

"Ah, Dr. Martin, you are naughty!" Mrs. Baldovino shook a finger at him, then reached up, clasped his head, and firmly kissed him on both cheeks. "But you are the *best* doctor. And I shall never forget all you have done for me."

She turned and caught a glimpse of Jacquelyn behind the nurses' desk. "And of course, my dear Nurse Jacquelyn! You are invited to dinner as well. And I will show you how to tie your scarves in pretty knots, and Ernesto will tell jokes to make you feel better —"

"I'm afraid she won't be able to join us," Jonah interrupted, steeling himself not to look in Jacquelyn's direction. "She's not well. In fact, I was just about to send her home."

"I am so sorry." Mrs. Baldovino clasped her hands and gave Jacquelyn a look of pure sympathy. "Should we postpone our dinner, then? Would tomorrow night be better? The weekend?"

"No." Jonah winced inwardly when his

voice sounded more curt than he had intended. "You'll have to make do with me, I'm afraid. You see, I was wrong to include Nurse Jacquelyn in this little venture, and I wouldn't want to put her in an awkward position." He smiled at his patient as if she were a small child and playfully waved her away. "Now go with Lauren and let her stick your finger. And I'll see you tonight for that lasagna."

As Mrs. Baldovino moved away, still chatting a mile a minute, Jonah turned again to the nurses still behind the desk. At the touch of his gaze Stacy threw back her head and defiantly moved toward the patient charts, but Jacquelyn simply stared at him, raw hurt glittering in her green eyes.

What had he done this time?

Jacquelyn went home to bed. She drowned herself in sleep, trying to forget the unimaginable hurt of the last few hours.

Jonah Martin was a liar, a hypocrite and one of the cruelest men she had ever known. His own record indicated something was amiss, and she'd been quick to spot it on her first day back in the office. Why, then, had she put the inconsistencies in his bio out of her mind? How had her innate dislike of him turned into affection? She was no fool, but she was a woman. And Jonah Martin was too good-looking and charming for his own good.

He had not only toyed with her heart, he had taken her life into his hands. He'd ordered a mastectomy, which could have reasonably been avoided, and he'd kept her on an immediate and strict chemo regimen which probably could have been postponed for several weeks. Was he intent on killing her or did he only want to break her heart?

Without ever saying so, he had led her to believe he loved her, and then in front of Lauren, Stacy and even Mrs. Baldovino, he'd proved that he had no interest in her whatsoever. She wouldn't have believed the rumor about his alleged sexual harassment until she saw how boldly and completely he dismissed her today. If his intentions toward her were honorable, he could have announced them right then and there. But he hadn't. He hadn't even remembered to give her his home phone number — so much for the meaning behind that useless promise!

And yet he had the gall to talk about God and tell her to rest in the Lord! Ha! "Even the devil can quote scripture," she murmured, beating the pillow as she tossed on her bed. "And that's what Jonah Martin is — a devil with blue eyes."

Even Daphne Redfield had been deluded. That saintly woman had been fooled by that handsome disguise; she had even believed Dr. Martin's usual overwhelming and unwanted attention toward Jacquelyn signaled something more than mere medical concern. "I guess you got your signals crossed, Daphne," Jacquelyn mumbled into her pillow. "God sent you a message for me, but the devil monkeyed around with the words. God is good — He would have warned me about Jonah Martin."

Jacquelyn hadn't seen Daphne in over a week. Her blood counts had not risen to a level high enough to continue her chemo, and Jacquelyn knew from whispers around the office that the cancer hadn't responded as Jonah had hoped. Her blood work continued to show an elevated CEA level, so apparently the latest round of chemo hadn't been enough to stop its growth . . . or even to slow it.

Jacquelyn knew that even Jonah's perfectly patient temperament had been sorely tried by the protocol's failure to put Daphne's cancer in remission. On the afternoon Daphne left the clinic without receiving her chemo, Jacquelyn had entered Jonah's darkened office to drop off a chart and had been surprised by the sight of him on his knees beside the desk. Apparently he hadn't heard her, so she backed out as quickly as she had entered, the chart still in her hand, an exclamation of surprise muted on her tongue. At that moment she had believed he was praying. Now, of course, she thought it more likely that he was looking for something he had dropped on the floor, a paper clip or something. . . .

Almost, she thought, pulling the covers closer to her ears, *I almost listened to him.*

She huddled under the covers as a cold knot formed in her stomach. She had finally begun to hope for the future, and then Lauren and Stacy had dropped that bombshell. She'd been dreaming of a home and a love completely different from what she'd known with guys like Craig Bishop, but all that remained of her dreams were the raw sores of an aching heart.

She bit her lip and choked back tears. She might be drowning in grief and humiliation, but at least she'd been spared public embarrassment. Jonah had seen to that. There would be no big breakup, no ugly confrontation. Lauren and Stacy would never know the full extent of Jacquelyn's feelings for the handsome doctor, and only God would know how little Jonah had cared.

She would not let this defeat her. This

deep, unaccustomed pain in her heart felt worse than her disappointment with Craig because she was sick, tired and weak. She'd feel sourness in the pit of her stomach for a while, maybe even a long while, and then she'd get on with her life. Jonah Martin may be a wretch, but Jacquelyn Wilkes was no quitter. As soon as she was stronger, she'd request a transfer, maybe to the pediatric oncology ward at the main hospital.

The shrill ring of her telephone broke through her jagged and painful thoughts. Instantly awake, she sat up and grabbed the phone. "Hello?"

"Miss Wilkes?"

The question hit her like a stab in her heart. Only highway patrolmen, doctors and emergency room personnel called in the middle of the night, and no one who knew her called her "Miss Wilkes."

"Yes?" Her stomach was still clenched tight, and despite her control, her teeth began to chatter.

"This is Joe Redfield, Daphne's husband. Daphne asked me to call you. I thought you might like to know."

"Know what?" She knew the question was tactless and rude, but her mind wouldn't function.

"We had to take her to the hospital this

morning and — well, they couldn't do anything else, so they've sent her home. She asked me to call you a while ago, but I waited." Mr. Redfield let out a long, audible breath. "Anyway, she's in a coma now, and I thought you might like to know that her time is coming. She thought a great deal of you, Nurse Wilkes, and I know she'd want to say goodbye."

Goodbye? But she didn't do goodbyes. She didn't go to funerals, she didn't make bedside visitations, she didn't get involved. . . .

Old habits were hard to break, but for Daphne, she'd try. "I'll be right there."

She hung up the phone and pressed her hands to her face, trying to still her quaking emotions and already regretting her promise. Sheer black fright swept through her, terror she had not felt since her own mother's death. Why hadn't she said no? Why hadn't she come up with an excuse? Mr. Redfield would understand, and he'd just said Daphne was in a coma. She wouldn't know if Jacquelyn was present or not, and Joseph Redfield was a stranger, so he wouldn't care. . . .

But Daphne had been there for her. When Jacquelyn had come home from the hospital, Daphne's warm eyes had greeted her;

her comforting voice had talked her through the panic that often welled in Jacquelyn's throat. Daphne had brought her tea, baked her cookies, fed and cleaned up after Bailey. . . .

The big dog lifted his head in surprise when Jacquelyn suddenly threw back the quilt. "I gotta go out," she whispered, hurrying toward her closet. "I'll be back later. In time for breakfast, I promise."

The dog lowered his head to his massive paws as if he understood perfectly.

Chapter Eighteen

Shivering in jeans, a sweater and tennis shoes, Jacquelyn consulted the scribbled note in her hand and compared it to the number on the house before her. She hadn't thought to ask Joe for an address when he called, and she'd had to search for it in the phone book before setting out. Fortunately, the Redfields' house lay on a well-traveled street near Lake Silver, and Jacquelyn had no trouble finding it in the night.

Joe had left a porch light burning and yellow rectangles of light shone from practically every window of the house.

Jacquelyn quickened her steps up the front walk, then knocked lightly on the door. A tall, gangly youth opened it, and Jacquelyn's mind went blank as she stared up at pain in the young man's face.

"I, uh, am Nurse Wilkes," she stammered. The boy nodded and opened the door wider so Jacquelyn could enter the house. Either he was expecting her or he didn't care who she was.

The house was a typical suburban model, probably a three-bedroom, two-bath like hundreds of others in this area. An older man with silver hair sat on the sofa in the living room, a Bible in his hands. Their minister, of course. In the kitchen at the back of the house, Jacquelyn could hear the sound of someone rummaging in a cabinet. She remembered all the players and the parts from another deathbed scene, but her foggy brain couldn't figure out why someone would be cooking at this hour — or why she was here.

The teenager jerked his thumb toward a single hallway that led off the living room. "Mom's in there," he said, his voice thick and heavy. "Dad's in there, too. My brother's making coffee, if you want some."

Jacquelyn shook her head, then walked toward the bedroom, her feet heavy as she trudged through a haze of feelings and doubts. What was she doing here? She had never been to a patient's home, never seen a patient die. She wasn't the type to get this involved. Though she had been blessed by Daphne's life, she wasn't sure she wanted to be part of the dear woman's death.

The bedroom curtains were drawn against

the night, a single lamp burned on a bedside table. A CD player filled the room with soft strains of something that sounded like choir music, and next to the bed, a brown-haired man slept upright in a slip-covered wing chair, an open book on his lap.

Daphne lay silent in the center of the bed, her head elevated on a stack of pillows. Her eternal smile had vanished, but Jacquelyn could still see both delicacy and strength in her face. An oxygen tube ran under her nose, but other than that, she lay unmolested by monitors or other equipment. At peace.

Jacquelyn tiptoed toward the end of the bed, not wanting to disturb either Daphne or her husband. Though she had never hesitated to enter a patient's hospital room, she felt strangely intrusive in the intimate setting. She would murmur a prayer and then slip out, her duty done. She'd send a card to the funeral, and try to put the past behind her. This — the bed, the woman in it, the minister in the living room — reminded Jacquelyn too much of her mother.

She wasn't aware of making noise, but at her approach the man's eyelids fluttered and opened. Though his face was slack with fatigue, his mouth tipped in a faint smile.

"I'm sorry," Jacquelyn said, turning away from the bed. "I didn't mean to wake you. Go back to sleep if you want, and I'll —" What? She couldn't leave after spending a grand total of sixty seconds with the Redfields. "I'll sit with you," she finished.

"No, I shouldn't have been sleeping." The man leaned forward and thrust a broad hand toward her. "You must be the nurse Daphne was so fond of. I'm Joe Redfield, Daphne's husband."

"So I gathered." Jacquelyn gave him a brief smile, then looked around the room. "Is there anything I can get you? One of your sons is making coffee, and I could see if he needs help. I'd be happy to take care of things out in the kitchen —"

"The kitchen's not important." Joe's gaze flitted toward the form on the bed. "I was reading to her and I guess I dozed off. She likes for me to read the Bible — she says it takes the pain away better than drugs. And the doctor won't give her any more morphine. He says it would slow her breathing to the point of — well, it would be dangerous. So she likes me to read. I was reading when she slipped into the coma." His smile brought an immediate softening to his rugged features. "Guess my voice is about to give out."

Jacquelyn stepped toward him. "Let me read."

"Oh, I couldn't ask you to —"

"Mr. Redfield —" she waved aside his objection "— your wife got down on her hands and knees to scrub my bathroom when I was recovering from surgery. Reading is the very least I can do for her."

Joe didn't protest, but lifted the Bible from his lap and offered it to Jacquelyn. She sank to the edge of the bed, careful not to disturb Daphne, and hoped Mr. Redfield would relax and sleep again. He was a handsome, masculine man, but fatigue had settled in pockets under his eyes and his hands quivered with exhaustion.

"I had just finished the top of that page," Joe offered, settling back into his chair.

"All right." Jacquelyn looked down at the Scriptures. He'd been reading from Psalms. If Daphne could hear him, surely she found comfort in the words.

"I look up to the mountains — does my help come from there?" Jacquelyn began.

"My help comes from the Lord, who made the heavens and the earth!
He will not let you stumble and fall; the one who watches over you will not sleep.

Indeed, he who watches over Israel never
  tires and never sleeps.
The Lord himself watches over you! The
  Lord stands beside you as your protective shade.
The sun will not hurt you by day, nor the
  moon at night.
The Lord keeps you from all evil and
  preserves your life.
The Lord keeps watch over you as you
  come and go, both now and forever."

Joe's breathing had slowed and deepened, and Jacquelyn thought he might be asleep again. She lowered the Bible and leaned forward, studying Daphne's face. Her lips were curled as if on the edge of laughter, and a musk-rose flush covered her high cheekbones. Had the flush been there when Jacquelyn arrived? She couldn't remember.

"Does she hear us, do you think?"

Joe's question startled Jacquelyn. "Um, it's possible." She looked down, a little embarrassed to be caught studying her patient so closely. "Some patients have reported being aware of what was going on around them while they were comatose. It's hard to know what the subconscious experiences."

"I think she hears us." Joe spoke in a

certain, clipped voice that forbade any argument. "I know she does. She looks . . . more peaceful when she hears the Scriptures. Will you read some more, or shall I?"

"I'll read." Jacquelyn opened the Bible again. Her eyes skimmed across the page to another psalm. "Those who trust in the Lord are as secure as Mount Zion; they will not be defeated but will endure forever . . ."

Jonah paused in the doorway, surprised by Jacquelyn's presence. What in the world had possessed her to come to the Redfields' house in the middle of the night? Even the minister who had been keeping this vigil had gone home; he and Jonah had passed each other on the front porch.

He leaned against the door frame, momentarily mesmerized by the sweet sound of the psalm on Jacquelyn's lips. "O Lord, do good to those who are good, whose hearts are in tune with you."

Whose hearts are in tune with you . . . When had his heart last been in tune with God? Probably seven or eight years ago, back before the UVA incident. In those days he was honestly trying to please God with his profession, still trying to make a difference in the physical *and* spiritual lives of his patients. His parents had been proud of

341

him, as had the entire congregation of the Oak Woods Community Church. He was the church's missionary to the world, the brilliant small-town boy who would make good and do good at the same time. . . .

But then his name — and theirs — had been disgraced. And human nature, which he had always imagined capable of the highest kind of altruism and selflessness, had proved itself to be tawdry, coarse and selfish. And throughout his ordeal, God had not answered a single prayer for either mercy or justice.

He'd been running ever since.

Just as he was preparing to run again.

But he couldn't leave Daphne. She would be one of the few individuals who thought of him as the kind of doctor he'd dreamed of becoming back in Oak Woods. She'd be in Heaven before she learned that he was a coward, a deserter and a hypocrite.

Daphne hadn't stirred since ten o'clock, the last time he'd stopped by the house. She had been growing steadily weaker over the past few days, despite his frantic efforts, even despite the few prayers he'd forced himself to offer on her behalf.

Her husband, distraught and exhausted, had finally urged Jonah to let her go. "She's ready to leave us — can't you see that, Doctor?" Joe had said that afternoon when they debated whether or not to check her out of the hospital and send her home. "She's worn out. She's ready to meet the Lord."

But there were so many things she still wanted to do! Her boys, still seven months shy of their high school graduation, would walk across the stage and receive their diplomas with only their father in attendance. And if Daphne were well, she'd never allow Jonah to give up his work here and run. She'd never allow him to give up Jacquelyn. Daphne had once confided to Jonah that she'd been praying for Jacquelyn ever since her first day in the clinic. "She's a sweet girl and a gentle soul," Daphne told him, an uncanny awareness in her gaze. "And I can understand why your eyes light up every time she enters the room. But she's an independent sort, Dr. Martin, like I was. God had to teach me how to trust Him alone. And I think He wants Jacquelyn to discover that truth, too."

Maybe your prayers were answered, Daphne. Jonah looked again at the sight of the lovely girl bent over the Scriptures. Only a miracle could have gotten Jacquelyn Wilkes to the bedside of any patient.

"Wait, nurse — do you think she's waking?" Joe called out.

Straightening, Jonah looked over Jacquelyn's head toward Daphne's face. Her flesh had colored and he thought he could see her eyelids trembling. He began to move into the room, then stopped himself. These might be Daphne Redfield's last conscious moments. She wouldn't want to spend them talking to her doctor.

"She's saying something," Jacquelyn said, standing. She motioned to Daphne's husband.

Good call, Nurse Wilkes.

"Come closer." Jacquelyn moved out of the way. "I think she wants to talk to you, Joe."

The burly auto mechanic perched on the edge of the bed and tenderly took his wife's hand. "What is it, honey?" he asked, bending low.

As one, Jacquelyn and Jonah leaned forward to catch her words.

Jonah couldn't hear, but Joe picked up a refrain. ". . . I shall not want. He makes me to lie down in green pastures, he leads me beside the still waters. He restores my soul, he leads me in the paths of righteousness for his name's sake. Yea, though I walk through the valley of the shadow of death, I will fear no evil, for Thou art with me."

Joe's voice clotted; his hand tightened

around his wife's. Jacquelyn cast him a quick glance, then tried to continue the psalm. "Thy rod and thy staff, they . . . comfort me."

She needed help; she didn't know all the words. Jonah stepped into the room, blending his baritone with Jacquelyn's uncertain voice. "You prepare a table before me in the presence of mine enemies," he said, standing behind Jacquelyn. She threw him a quick, expressionless glance, then turned back to Daphne and continued, following his lead. "You anoint my head with oil, my cup runs over."

The lines of pain upon Daphne's face lightened as if an invisible hand had wiped them away. Her countenance relaxed as the faint beginnings of a smile curled upon her lips.

Joe joined them again, resignation and peace in his booming voice. "Surely goodness and mercy shall follow me all the days of my life."

Jonah heard movement behind him, and turned to see Justin and Jed in the doorway. He motioned them in, then moved to make room for the twins.

"And I will dwell in the house of the Lord forever. Amen."

Through the roaring silence that followed,

Daphne Redfield breathed one word: *Jesus.*

Jonah could hear his heart battering against his ears. He had witnessed many deaths, but never one as peaceful, as *right,* as this one.

"She's gone," Joe finally said, speaking in an odd, yet gentle tone. "My bride has gone home."

Jonah moved toward his patient and automatically pressed his fingers to her neck to make sure there was no pulse. Daphne had made it clear there were to be no dramatic efforts to resuscitate a body that had worn itself out in a long, arduous battle. "Two twenty-five a.m.," he remarked, noting the time of death. "Now she's in the presence of the Lord."

One of the boys hiccupped a sob, and Jonah kept his eyes averted as Joe moved to embrace his sons.

"I'll miss you," Joe said, hugging his boys as he stared at his wife's face. Her eyes had not opened since the coma, only the movement of her lips had given them any clue that she'd returned to consciousness just in time to bid them farewell.

Jonah turned toward the doorway to give the family a few moments alone. Jacquelyn, he noticed, had already retreated to the hall outside the bedroom. She stood there, backlit by the bright lights of the living room, her face awash in tears.

He caught her gaze, expecting to see the same peaceful assurance he'd seen in Joe's eyes, but was surprised by the storm stirring there.

Silently, he closed the bedroom door and pulled her out into the living room.

"Jackie, I know you're upset."

"Upset?" Jacquelyn's throat closed around the word. After the single most excruciating, discouraging, horrifying and depressing day of her life, how could he stand there and glibly pronounce her *upset?* Daphne Redfield, the last woman on earth who deserved death, had just lost her battle with cancer. If justice existed anywhere, God should have seen fit to heal *her.* Daphne was a walking saint, a selfless fountain of truth and light, while Jacquelyn, who couldn't even get through the twenty-third psalm without prompting, was on the road to recovery. Why was she standing here, *alive,* while Daphne lay lifeless in the next room with her weeping husband and sons at her side?

Jacquelyn's sense of loss went beyond tears. She flung her hands out in simple despair, unable to speak. She had seen too much today, witnessed too much pain. Daphne, who had bravely battled cancer to the end, had probably not complained in her years of suffering as Jacquelyn had in her single month of chemotherapy. . . .

And they had told Daphne the cancer was gone. After her surgery, and after her chemotherapy. And yet she had just died, a forty-six-year-old woman who should have lived to celebrate at least thirty more Thanksgivings and Christmases.

Jacquelyn covered her face with her hands as grief and despair tore at her heart. She needed comfort and reassurance and she did not protest or pull away when she felt Jonah gather her into his embrace. Forgetting her resolutions of a few hours ago, she reached for the solid comfort of his arms and he held her gently, the touch of his hand on her head almost unbearable in its tenderness.

Move away from him. The man was nothing but trouble. Lauren and Stacy would have a fit if they saw her now, they knew he was a liar and a fraud . . . he would hold her now and break her heart tomorrow.

But now she needed his strength. A war of emotions raged within her, a cyclone of feelings and fears Lauren and Stacy would never understand. Jonah was here. A friend

— for now. She rested in his arms, distantly aware of the comforting scent of his cologne, the languid, slimly muscled grace with which he held her.

She turned her head, resting her cheek upon his shirt, damp with tears she couldn't remember crying. "All Daphne wanted," she whispered, dismayed to hear bitterness spill over into her voice, "was to see her sons graduate from high school. She didn't make it. Why couldn't God have arranged that, Jonah? Was she asking too much?"

"I don't know." His voice trembled, but his hand continued to gently stroke the scarf tied around her head. "Don't you think I've asked myself the same questions? Dad would say God works in ways we can't understand."

"Daphne should have listened to me." Jacquelyn abruptly pulled away and met his wet eyes. "She wasn't eating right. I offered her some of my algae capsules, but she was content to go on, trusting God and you, her doctor —"

"Jacquelyn, don't." Jonah flinched at the accusation in her tone, and she knew her words had lacerated him. She hadn't meant to be cruel, but he had hurt her more than she would ever let him know. And truth was truth. Daphne had stood back and *allowed* cancer to invade her body —

"Do you think she wanted this? Do you think *I* wanted this?" Jonah's voice was harsh and raw. "We did everything medically possible. And I even prayed —"

"With your daddy's faith." She stepped back, throwing the words at him like stones. "Secondhand faith is no good, Jonah. And life isn't that simple. You can't just pray cancer away. You have to fight it."

He closed his eyes and pressed his lips together in an obvious attempt to stifle some emotion. When he spoke again, his voice was more controlled. "Jacquelyn, I understand that you're angry — about Daphne and maybe even about the way I treated you in the office today. And I know you're worried about your own cancer. But you've got to believe that together we've made the right decisions. We can't save every patient — sometimes we just can't fix things."

"But God's supposed to!" A wave of unfathomable, unrealized fury erupted from within her, almost choking her voice. "God was supposed to heal my mother! And I asked Him to heal Daphne. How can I know He'll heal me? Either my prayers aren't working, or God is as ticked off at me as I am at Him!"

"Maybe He's mad at all of us." Jonah's features hardened. "But I won't have you saying things like this in this house. Daphne's husband and sons deserve better. They knew their mother was ready to die. You're angry and afraid, but Daphne wasn't. She always said God's perfect love casts out fear —"

"Shut up, Jonah! I'm tired of hearing you quote other Christians." She pressed her hand over her face, shielding her burning, tired eyes. Like a receding tide, her anger ebbed away, leaving her engulfed in weariness and despair. With a long sigh, she backed away toward the front door.

"I'm tired of everything." She shook her head, stumbling over words and her own confused feelings. "I want to go home and sleep . . . or something. I want my dog."

"Jacquelyn, wait." Jonah stepped toward her with an expression on his face that looked like love, but couldn't be. Her mind reeled in confusion as she pulled the door open, urging her feet to hurry out into the night.

"Jacquelyn!" She scarcely recognized the aching, husky voice that called her name as she sprinted down the sidewalk toward her car. She could ignore him; Jonah wouldn't follow. He would call the funeral home, fill out the paperwork, sign the death certificate and call the minister to comfort Daphne's grieving family. In a few hours, when the sun had risen and he had caught a few hours of sleep, the memory of their brief embrace would vanish like a ghost at dawn. He wouldn't remember; she was no more important to him than any other patient.

Fighting back tears, Jacquelyn fumbled in her purse for her keys and hoped she would forget about him as easily.

Go after her. Stop running.

"I can't." He stood in the dark doorway and listened to the sound of Jacquelyn slamming her car door. In the sound of her curt goodbye he had heard a final dismissal. She needed comfort, but she wanted to find it at her home with that goofy dog. She did not want him.

It was for the best. Dr. Kastner had been decidedly cool to him ever since returning from his weekend convention, and before leaving work tonight he'd stopped in Jonah's office and mentioned that tomorrow they'd have to meet to discuss "a matter of some importance."

Jonah had heard that line before. The rumors caught up to him faster here than in his other positions, but that was okay. He had already decided to leave.

But the people inside this house had no share in his personal misery. In their eyes he was the doctor who had failed Daphne, and it was time to go in and carry his portion of the burden.

He left the quiet of the night shadows and went back into the house.

What was she doing?

Jacquelyn's hands trembled as she fumbled with the keys. The ignition seemed to have changed shape and form since she'd last been in the car. Her gaze clouded with tears of frustration.

"Why can't I get this blasted thing in?" she cried, slamming the jammed key with the brunt of her palm. The blow made her wince in pain, but the key finally slid into the slot.

"Jacquelyn Elisa Wilkes," she moaned, rubbing her injured palm as she lowered her head to the steering wheel. "Can't you do anything right?"

As if in answer, the blackened sky above opened. A flash of lightning lit the eastern horizon behind the Redfields' house, hanging to the earth for a dramatic second before it disappeared, leaving only a pelting rain that drummed overhead on the roof of her car.

A storm — how fitting. Daphne had died, and the hope inside Jacquelyn had died with her. And so the earth wept with Joe Redfield and the two boys who no longer had a mother.

But Jacquelyn couldn't cry, not now. She turned the key in the ignition, threw the car in gear and backed out of the driveway, pausing only long enough to fumble with the switches for her headlights and windshield wipers. The merciful rain blurred the house outside her window, and she pressed her foot to the accelerator, eager to leave the nightmare of this night behind.

What was she to do? Jonah Martin had never said he loved her, had never given her any verbal assurance. Except from the light peck on her forehead this morning — was it only this morning? — he had never even kissed her. Unless you counted that dinner he'd won through that silly bet, they had never even been out on a date.

So why did a rock fall through her heart at the thought of his defeated face? A light had disappeared from his eyes tonight, and for the first time she realized that he might be as distressed by Daphne's death as she was.

Fatigue oozed from every pore; she was tired, that's all. She'd feel better and think more clearly in the light of morning. And tomorrow Jonah would have buried thoughts of Daphne in that dark place where he kept all the secrets of his past.

She coasted to a stop at an intersection and gave the rain-washed road a perfunctory glance. No one was coming, no one but criminals and ministering angels went out at this hour of the night. Looking left, she jerked the steering wheel hard to the right, then felt the car rise and fall in a barely perceptible lurch.

She'd hit something.

Blood slid through her veins like cold needles as she slammed on the brakes. Merciful heavens, what could have been on the road at this hour? She hadn't seen anything, but she hadn't really been looking, either. Had a vagrant lain down by the side of the road? This was a quiet stretch, with a vacant lot on one side and an orange grove on the other. There were no houses, no all-night diners, no reason for anyone to be near.

She shoved the gear into Park, then clawed at the door handle and let herself out. Rain slashed against her skin and scarf as she ran in front of her streaming headlights, then rounded to the passenger's side of the car.

No one there. She slumped in relief. Only a dark lump behind the front tire, probably a hunk of wood or rubber, maybe a wad of clothing that had blown off the back of someone's pickup truck.

It moved. Cold air brushed across the backs of Jacquelyn's legs, and her scalp tingled beneath her damp scarf. *What is it?*

Kneeling on the asphalt, she strained to see through the darkness and the blowing rain. And then, above the sound of the raindrops pounding on the car, a strangled meowing wail broke her heart.

"Oh, you poor kitty." Jacquelyn crept forward and cautiously lowered her hands to the animal's fur. The black cat opened wide green eyes, looked directly at her and rasped another pitiful wail.

Caught up in a sickening sensation of guilt, Jacquelyn gathered the injured animal into her wet and trembling hands. Holding it close to the warmth of her body, she ran to the front of the car and knelt in the wavering beams of the headlights. With the care she'd have shown a wounded child, she lowered the animal to the asphalt and ran her hands over the cat's torn fur. The animal was literally spilling into her hands, there was no help she could give it, she had no tools, no bandages. . . .

"God, why?"

The cat wore no collar, no tag. She felt wetness between her fingers and lifted her hands to the light, only to see that they were undeniably stained with the crimson dye of blood.

"No," she told the cat in her most authoritative voice. "Nothing else will die tonight. You're going to hang on until I can get you to the vet, and then someone will take care of you."

In one swift movement she unwound the scarf from her head, then unfolded it and slid it under the animal. Using it as a bandage of sorts, she wrapped it around the animal's belly and tied it with a swift, sure knot.

"Ready, kitty? I'm going to lift you now."

There was no answering meow, no sound or movement from the animal. As the rough asphalt bit into her knees and elbows, Jacquelyn knelt on the road and lifted the cat's head, stroking its nose, begging. "Come on, breathe! Open those eyes again, let me know you're with me!"

Somewhere behind her lightning cracked the skies apart, and the rain pooled into darkly reflecting mirrors on the glistening asphalt of the road. The animal made no

357

sound. Tears blinded Jacquelyn's eyes and choked her voice. She was helpless. Always helpless, unable to save even one of the simplest of God's creatures . . .

"Jacquelyn!"

Two strong hands gripped her shoulders and lifted her, spinning her around and pulling her away from the injured cat. With every ounce of her strength she resisted the man who repeatedly called her name, pounding his chest with her blood-streaked hands until she could cry no more.

Her head bowed, her body slumped in despair, and she finally surrendered and held tight to the doctor in the raincoat.

Jonah moved silently through Jackie's house, stopping finally in the small powder room near the foyer. He paused before the mirror and ran his fingers through his wet hair, realizing that he looked almost as worn as Jacquelyn. He'd put on a fresh shirt and jeans that he always carried in his car for emergencies like this one, but he wasn't about to take the liberty of rummaging through Jacquelyn's closet to find dry clothes for her. He wasn't certain what her mood would be when she awakened, but he was willing to bet she wouldn't be thrilled to find him in her house.

As much as he wanted to stay, he was going home.

Knowing how upset she was, he had followed her from the Redfields' house as soon as he could get away. Fear like the quick, hot touch of the devil shot through him when he saw her car turned at that odd angle on the wet road. He experienced a gamut of emotions when he saw her kneeling on the pavement, and his stomach tightened when he heard the faint thread of hysteria in her voice as she tried to coax life back into a dead cat. It didn't take a psychologist to understand why the accident had upset her so. Even if Daphne hadn't just died, Jackie had an extremely tender heart for animals.

Jacquelyn had, in fact, a tender heart for almost everything, and Jonah marveled that he hadn't seen the depth of her compassion before. Despite the cloak of self-protective habits she wore in the office, tonight he had seen her deep concern for a patient, and her grief when that patient lost the battle. He had also noticed — though he hadn't wanted to — the way her body flowed toward his when she came into his arms for comfort. He had behaved like a fool and muttered inanities, but it was hard to remain coherent when he stood close to her.

Just the feel of her in his arms had sent his pulses spinning.

He snapped off the light and went back to the living room where Jackie lay asleep on the couch. Out on the road, she had calmed down after he had promised to take care of the cat, and she actually let him put her in his car while he went and bundled the animal in his raincoat. He placed the animal in the backseat, pulled Jackie's car off the road and out of the way, locked it, and then drove her home.

Not once did she speak during the drive. She sat as still as a statue, her eyes closed, her arms crossed over her chest, fending off some invisible enemy he couldn't see. She had even seemed to understand why he'd brought her inside the house instead of dropping her off and leaving her to fend for herself. "I don't want you to think that I'm weak or crazy," she said, pausing at the top of the steps to look him straight in the eye. "I'm not."

"I know you're not," he answered, holding out his hand for her key. "This night has been rough on all of us."

"The cat?" she asked, staring at the door.

"I'll bury it tomorrow."

She nodded slowly, then fumbled in her purse and handed him a key ring. After opening the door, he led her to the couch, still covered in sheets and a blanket from the long night before. She lay down almost automatically and closed her eyes. He thought he might have to give her a sedative to help her sleep, but she immediately withdrew from him into a shallow doze.

Now Jonah found that he didn't want to leave her, but for the sake of her honor, he needed to go. But he'd be back in the morning. He'd come back anytime she called, if he could.

The rising sun had swallowed up the wind and rain, leaving the morning quiet and still. Jonah opened the door to Jackie's house, then let Bailey out into the yard to romp while he searched for a shovel in Jacquelyn's garage. Within half an hour he had buried the cat and placed garden stones over it to keep Bailey's digging paws at bay.

When he returned to the house, the romping dog on his heels, Jacquelyn had awakened. She sat on the couch, the remaining coppery strands of her hair tangled and wild about her face, unspoken pain alive and glowing in her eyes.

"Good morning."

She lifted her chin in answer. "Thanks for taking Bailey out. And . . . thanks for bring-

361

ing me home. I wasn't myself last night. I didn't know I would be affected like that." Her eyes misted. "Daphne was special."

Her eyes narrowed. "Did you — did you spend the night here?"

"Don't worry, I slept in my own bed." He took a seat in the wing chair across from her and rested his arms on his knees. Bailey, his tail swaying like a lion's, sauntered over and rested his majestic head in his mistress's lap.

Her hand fell possessively on the dog's muzzle, but her eyes didn't leave Jonah's face. "I'm sorry. I must have sounded like a heretic or something, but last night was rough. I just don't understand why God allows some things to happen the way they do."

"Wiser men than I have been trying to figure that one out for generations." Jonah heard the dryness in his voice. Two days with little sleep were bearing down on him; he hadn't been this tired since his residency days. He'd have to go home and sleep for a couple of hours, but first he'd have to call the office and stall Kastner. And there was something else —

"I almost forgot, I have something for you." He reached into his shirt pocket and pulled out an envelope Joe Redfield had given him after Daphne's death. "I would have given it to you last night, but you left too quickly. It's a letter from Daphne."

Surprise siphoned the morning blush from her face. "For me?"

He nodded and slid it over the coffee table toward her. "I'll go feed Bailey while you read it. Just tell me where you keep the Monster Mash, and I'll mix up something for him."

"In a big plastic bowl under the kitchen sink," she answered, her sleepy eyes fastened to the envelope. "He gets three cups for breakfast with a big dollop of plain yogurt. The yogurt's in the fridge."

Jonah nodded and rose from the chair, whistling for the dog. Lured by the promise of breakfast, the mastiff took one more look at his somber mistress, then bounded away and followed Jonah into the kitchen.

CHAPTER NINETEEN

Fighting through the lingering cobwebs of nightmare-filled sleep, Jacquelyn opened the letter. In last night's dark dreams, Daphne Redfield, Alicia Hubbard and other deceased patients had risen up from their coffins, lifting bony fingers while their baleful, fiery eyes accused Jacquelyn of not caring. She had tried to defend herself with words from her old philosophy, we've all got to die sometime, but her tongue cleaved to the roof of her mouth, and the words would not come.

She didn't want to die. And she had cancer, too.

With trembling fingers, she unfolded a single sheet of feminine stationery and began to read:

My Dearest Jacquelyn:
I may not have many more chances to see you, and the Lord brought your

name to my mind this morning as I sat outside enjoying the sun. I wish you could see my garden — Joe and the boys have pounded the front yard to smithereens with their basketball games and football throwing, but they've let me keep this little side yard all to myself. I've planted perennials here — Mexican violets and crepe myrtle and butterfly weed, and it's a joy to know the flowers will keep coming back long after I've gone home.

For I am going home, and very soon, I think. And of all the people I know, I think you may now be the most vulnerable. Don't be upset, dear Jacquelyn. I do not fear death. My husband and my sons know I will miss them terribly, but we will be reunited before the threads of eternity have even begun to weave into the Lord's finished pattern. To be absent from this frail, broken body is to be present with my Lord, and I am not reluctant to depart . . . but for you. That is why I have asked Joe to call you when I am ready to go.

I know you, Jacquelyn, and I know you will question whether it was right for God to take me. It is. I am His, and if He chooses to draw me home sooner than later, who am I to complain? I used to desire long life, for I thought I would fill it with wonderful, useful service to my Lord, but through this cancer He has taught me that I should not seek to serve Him at all. It is far more important that I simply *be* — be His child, be obedient, be willing. Life is not about what I *do*, it's about what I *am.*

And faith, after all, is the opposite of common sense. You may think that God is not good because He has taken me home, but He is, and I trust His goodness completely. I have found that the life of faith is one of continual testing, and death will be my final, greatest test. But since Jesus has stood by my side throughout life, I know He will support me through death. And if you were at my side, you now know it, too.

And so, Jacquelyn — my arm is growing tired — I suppose I want to tell you this — I have not been cheated, God has been more than good. It is not what I do for Him that matters, it is only what God can do through my weak vessel, through yours, through Dr. Martin's. God bless Dr. Jonah — he has been more than a doctor. He is a comfort and a friend, though I fear he has lost the joy of his faith somewhere along life's way. Help him find it again, if you can. He loves you, and our Lord loves him.

God bless you, my sister. Do not strive to be so self-sufficient — as long as you are, you do not need God — or your fellow man — for anything. Always remember that *deciding* for God is a far cry from *yielding* to Him.

I am yielded, and I will be watching you from heaven. Rejoice, dear one! I pray that you will truly *live* all the days of your life.

With deepest love and affection,
Daphne

Jacquelyn let the letter fall to her lap and fought to control her swirling emotions. How could such a sick woman know so much? How did Daphne, the most quiet and self-effacing of women, manage to see into the darkest parts of the human heart?

She'd written that Jonah had lost his joy — and Jacquelyn could see that Daphne was right, though Jacquelyn had no clue as to why he behaved so erratically. And she'd written that Jonah loved Jacquelyn — how in heaven's name could Daphne know *that?* Earlier Jacquelyn had thought he might, but those illusions had vanished like the morning mist.

But Daphne had written with confidence and peace. How?

Her words, like a musical refrain, kept slipping through Jacquelyn's thoughts: *Faith, after all, is the opposite of common sense.*

How could Daphne die with a smile upon her face? Because she believed and faith, after all, is the opposite of common sense.

To Daphne, faith was more than putting forth a good effort and hoping for the best: Faith was knowing, being sure, even when individual effort wasn't good enough, could never be good enough. Jacquelyn had faith enough to believe in God, even to claim Jesus as Lord, but she'd mixed her faith with her own good sense, her own efforts — until she met something her own efforts couldn't control.

In a breathless burst of insight, Jacquelyn understood. She had been almost completely self-sufficient, glorying even in her loneliness, taking pride in her independence. She hadn't wanted help after her surgery; she hadn't wanted the other patients to know that she was fallible, that she was *like them,* diseased and in need of help.

No wonder she had felt no peace when she prayed! She'd been asking for God's help and yet pushing it away with both hands, trying to save her life on her own terms while using prayer as a sort of magical incantation. She'd been trying to convince herself that algae and shark cartilage and vegetables would save her life, and she'd closed her eyes and ears to the voices that spoke of God's wisdom.

Daphne's voice. And Jonah's. She had even pushed him away, not wanting to admit that she needed him. Oh, she had been thrilled to think she could add him into her life like a charming accessory for a new outfit, but the truth was, she *needed* him like a plant needs water, and God had brought him into her life for a purpose.

"Faith," Jacquelyn whispered, closing her eyes, "is the opposite of common sense. And for so long, God, I've been trying to do the logical thing, helping You out, being good, being efficient, responsible and smart. And I've been getting nowhere with either my personal life or my work, while Daphne had faith . . . and peace." She let her head fall forward into her hands. "If I surrender, can You give me that peace? Because I'm tired of doing things my way. I'm tired of worrying and making a mess of things. And so, God, I'm giving my life back to You."

She sat silent for a moment, her eyes

closed, her head resting on her palms. And then, like one of the perennials from Daphne's flower garden, tendrils of peace began to wend their way up through the broken surfaces of her weary heart.

She smiled, imagining Daphne sitting in some heavenly grandstand, clothed in a robe of glowing white, a thick and luxurious head of strawberry-blond hair spilling over her elegant shoulders. Daphne was smiling, too, and Jacquelyn felt a warm glow flow through her as Daphne's wide eyes met hers. "Stop trying so hard, Jackie," she whispered in a voice as soft as the brush of angels' wings. "Don't do so much. Just be a child of God and stay near our Father. Then you will find the answers you're seeking."

Jacquelyn felt herself nodding. Wrapped in a silken cocoon of euphoria, she lowered her head to her pillow and fell into a deep, restful sleep.

The clock showed that no more than half an hour had passed when she awoke, but she felt as if she'd slept for days, so deep and restful had been her slumber. Jacquelyn rose and stretched luxuriously, startling Bailey, who lay sprawled on the floor beside her.

"Is Jonah still here, boy?" she asked,

lowering her hand to rub his wrinkled forehead. As if he understood, the dog lifted his head and looked toward the foyer. Jacquelyn slipped from the couch and padded toward the door in her socks. Peering through the broken window pane, she saw Jonah sitting on the front porch steps, his bowed head resting in his hands.

Thank you, God. He hasn't left.

"Be a good boy and wait for me in here," Jacquelyn whispered to Bailey. The dog sat, an expectant look on his face, while Jacquelyn slipped out the door and approached Jonah.

Funny, the way her knees knocked. She felt as nervous as a schoolgirl at her first dance, and yet her heart was lighter than it had been in days. She couldn't explain how or why, but her soul brimmed with the simple joy of knowing that she could rest in God, and she wanted to share Daphne's secret with Jonah. He had grown up in church. The truth could not be far from him, she'd only have to remind him of what he had learned long ago.

"Jonah."

He didn't lift his head, but jerked slightly, as if she'd disturbed him from slumber or deep thought.

"You're awake, then?" His voice was flat.

"Good. I wanted to say goodbye."

"I want to talk to you before you go." A strange confidence filled her as she moved to sit by his side. Her tears and grief of the night before were no more than a distant memory, gone as completely as if they had been evaporated by an onrushing wind.

His face lifted, and he regarded her with exhausted, impassive eyes.

Jacquelyn hesitated, then with pulse-pounding certainty knew what she had to say. She wouldn't make things complicated. This morning there were no shadows across her heart.

Her eyes moved into his. "Jonah, I love you."

"Don't." The glitter in his half-closed eyes was both thrilling and frightening.

She felt herself blushing at her own boldness. "You can't tell a person not to love you. You can't stop what I feel for you." She looked away and laughed softly. "Heaven knows I've tried."

"You'll have to try harder." His brows drew together in a frown. "I wanted to say goodbye because I'm leaving the hospital and moving to California. I'm supposed to hear the final details from a friend of mine today."

Jacquelyn took a quick, sharp breath. *Leav-*

ing? How could he leave when she'd finally found the courage to surrender to the feelings she *knew* were right?

"How can you go? And why would you?"

His mouth tightened under her questioning gaze. "It has nothing to do with you."

"Then what?" She swiped her hand through her thinning hair, distracted, wanting to put the pieces together. He loved her, Daphne had said so. And his work was good; his patients adored him. So why would he go unless —

Her face burned as the memories came flooding back. Lauren and Stacy, whispering behind the nurses' station, the ugly rumors too horrible to be believed . . .

She wouldn't believe them. Love never gave up, never lost faith, was always hopeful, endured through every circumstance. . . .

"Don't go." She could hear fear in her voice. Fear, her old enemy, the reason she'd never found peace before.

"Jonah," she pressed on, "I can't lose you. Whatever it is, whatever they're saying, you've got to stand and face them."

Defiance poured from his heated blue eyes. "You don't know anything about it."

"Then tell me and I'll listen. And I'll

believe you."

He snorted and looked away. "Why should you? No one else ever has."

"I'll believe you," she repeated, reaching out to place her hand on his knee. "Because I *know* you. I've heard the rumors and I know they can't be true. You've never been anything but a gentleman with me, even here in my house."

Disbelief and frustration filled his expression as his eyes raked her face. Was he questioning her motives? Surely he was wondering why she'd had such a change of heart.

"Remember the letter you gave me?" she asked, searching his eyes. "Daphne knew both of us all too well. She said that I was too self-sufficient and that you had — how'd she put it? — she said that you had somehow 'lost the joy of your faith.' "

He didn't answer, but his eyes left her face as he considered her words.

"Daphne was right about me," Jacquelyn went on. "I have been so busy trying to do all the right things. You told me the same thing yourself. I was trying to eat the right foods, be the perfect nurse, be the perfect patient. And when the cancer came I even tried to impress God by being the perfect Christian. But he doesn't want *my* perfection . . . I suppose he wants me to rely on His."

"Now look who's spouting religious gobbledygook," Jonah answered, his eyes softening. "A week ago, you'd have fussed at me if I said something like that."

"A week ago I was in a different place," Jacquelyn admitted. "I thought I had the power to fix things. But I don't. I see that now. And faith is more than believing with my head or even with my heart. Faith is trusting with my life. Like Daphne did."

He tented his hands and lowered his head, knocking his knuckles against his forehead. For an eternal moment he said nothing, then he gave her a humorless smile. "It happened right after medical school and my residency," he said, his voice as faint as if he had moved a great distance away. "There was a nurse in the hospital where I was working. She liked me, I could tell, and so I took her out once. But she wanted more . . . *attention,* if you know what I mean, and I just couldn't do what she expected. I suppose my strict religious upbringing came through after all."

"Maybe those convictions were honestly your own and not your father's," Jacquelyn added.

Jonah shrugged. "Whatever. Anyway, this

woman freaked when I told her I wouldn't see her again. First she said she'd tell everyone that I was gay, then she said she had come up with something even better than that. The next thing I knew, she'd gone to the hospital authorities and said I'd tried to assault her. She said I'd made improper advances in the office and that she'd been trying to get rid of me for weeks."

A warm breeze blew by them with soft moans. Jacquelyn listened to the following silence, waiting for him to continue. When he didn't, she prodded him gently. "Wasn't there anything you could do?"

"No." His voice sounded tired. "Unfortunately, a few people in the office knew we'd dated. And they knew something was going on because she was on the verge of tears every day and I was my usual charming self — too charming, as you always say. But in those days I was nice to everyone. I hadn't yet learned that friendship and work don't mix."

"So they thought you'd been leading her on?"

"Something like that. It came down to a case of my word against hers. And since she'd been at the hospital for years, I knew people would believe her rather than me. For some reason people think that, because

I'm young and single, I must be some kind of playboy. In the end, she agreed to drop her complaint if I left the hospital. I got out of there with good references from my colleagues, but the rumor won't go away."

Jacquelyn pressed her lips together, remembering the many entries on his bio. "So you've been running ever since."

He tipped his head back and exhaled a long sigh. "What else can I do? They say it's a man's world, but whenever anyone says the words *sexual harassment,* it's the woman who automatically gets the benefit of the doubt. That rumor follows me like a shadow, and now Dr. Kastner's heard it. We're supposed to have some kind of meeting later today, and I know he's going to suggest that I move on. So I've already made plans."

He turned to her and Jacquelyn felt her cheeks color under the heat of his gaze. "I never meant to hurt you. I never wanted to care for you. I suppose it's only fair that you should know I did. But I can't stay here, and you don't need this kind of grief in your life. I would cause problems for you at work and I might complicate your recovery and treatment. You need to concentrate on getting better — you don't need to worry about me."

"Jonah, I *want* to worry about you." Her

heart hammered against her ribs as she turned and placed her hands on his shoulders. "You're always giving to your patients. Can't one of them give something back to you?"

He gave her a dry, one-sided smile. "You said I give too much."

"You should have pointed out that I gave too little." She tightened her grip on his shoulders, unwilling to let him go. "Go see Dr. Kastner today, and explain your story just as you explained it to me. I'll speak on your behalf. I'll tell him that you've been in my house and you have never, ever been anything less than a gentleman. And Mrs. Baldovino, and Joseph Redfield, and Lauren, and Stacy will testify, too —"

"It's not a trial." The grooves beside his mouth deepened into a sorrowful smile. "Jacquelyn, I can't expect you to do this for me. A man should be able to take care of himself."

"Sometimes," Jacquelyn answered, choosing her words carefully, "a man has to stop being self-sufficient and start being grateful for the help he's offered. Stop running, Jonah Martin, and be true to yourself. You didn't do anything wrong, and you shouldn't spend the rest of your life trying to outscramble that horrible rumor. Think of the patients who are counting on you! And . . . think of me."

His smile faded and he regarded her for a moment in thoughtful silence. "Jacquelyn, right now I'm too tired to think."

Her heart sank with swift disappointment. "Oh." Reluctantly, she released him. "I suppose I'll see you later at the office. And I'll be praying for you this afternoon when you meet with Dr. Kastner." Her hand reached up to touch his cheek. "If you want me to say something, please let me know. I want to help."

"Thanks." He said the word as lightly as if she'd just offered him a drink of water and not her heart. Then he stood and walked down the sidewalk, his hands in his pockets, his shoulders hunched.

Why wouldn't he stand and fight? She wanted him to stay; she wanted him to feel that he had found something here worth fighting for. But apparently his feelings weren't that strong.

Feeling the chasm between them like an open wound, Jacquelyn silently watched him go.

CHAPTER TWENTY

"God, heal the hurts of Jonah's heart." The refrain repeated itself endlessly in Jacquelyn's mind as she hiked to the place where they had left her car in the night. Fortunately it was less than half a mile from her house, and the walk gave her something to think about other than the terrible fact that Jonah knew she loved him . . . and was still intent on leaving.

What would it take to make him stay? She'd done everything but throw herself at his feet. She had begged him to stand before Dr. Kastner and fight to clear his name and she'd reminded him that his patients had placed their trust in him.

Why wouldn't he stay? He wasn't a defeated man, the flash of anger in his eye and the strength of resolve in his voice told her his fighting spirit was alive and well. So, if he loved her and he loved his work, why wouldn't he fight? There had to be another reason, something he had not shared, some motivation that made running more comfortable than remaining to confront his past.

What had Daphne written? *God bless Dr. Jonah . . . he is a comfort and a friend, though I fear he has lost the joy of his faith somewhere along life's way. Help him find it again, if you can.*

How could she help him go back to that place? She knew very little about his past. He did not talk much about anything but his carefree days as a preacher's kid in Oak Woods, Virginia. If Jonah hadn't lost the joy of his faith during the episode in which he was accused of sexual harassment, then when had he?

She reached her car, and her thoughts raced as she automatically unlocked the door. Such a trial would certainly be enough to test *her* faith, if she had found herself in a similar situation. Jonah had said that the situation eventually became his accuser's word against his, so that meant none of his friends were willing to speak up for him. She would be emotionally shattered if none of her coworkers or friends rose to her defense.

She slid into the driver's seat and rested her hands on the steering wheel, thinking. Jonah must have felt like a leper. If no friends or coworkers would support him, that left only his family back in Oak Woods.

Suddenly her mind blew open. *His family!* Through her conversations with him she knew his ideas of faith and family were firmly entwined. Was it possible — could his family have doubted him? Why not? She herself had doubted him when she first heard the rumor. And Jonah had been on his own for several years by the time he worked at UVA, an eaglet well out of the nest, perhaps a near-stranger to his parents. If not even his family had defended him during that troubling time, no wonder he had lost the joy of his faith!

She felt her heart rate increase as she checked and double-checked her memory. In all the time she had known him, Jonah had never once mentioned talking to his parents, receiving a letter from his folks, or visiting them. He had often mentioned his father, but always in the past tense, almost as if the man were dead.

Oak Woods, Virginia. How big could the city be? And how many Reverend Martins lived there? If Jonah's father still lived . . .

Feeling aggressive and alive for the first time in weeks, Jacquelyn started the car and shoved it into gear. She pulled onto the road and headed toward her house, not the office. She had a few phone calls to make, an urgent mission to accomplish. And if God was good, He'd do all the work involved. She only had to be obedient.

"Reverend Martin?"

As she'd hoped, there was only one pastor named Martin in the tiny community of Oak Woods. The Jonathan Martin who answered the phone had a strong, powerful, dynamic voice, one she could easily imagine booming over a pulpit every Sunday.

"Yes?"

"You don't know me, sir, but my name is Jacquelyn Wilkes. I'm a friend of Jonah's."

Her proclamation was met with silence. Jacquelyn waited a moment — was the man having a heart attack, or had he dropped the phone? But then the voice spoke again in careful, measured tones. "We haven't heard from Jonah in years. You'll have to forgive me for not knowing you."

"That's quite all right, sir." She tried not to let her relief show in her voice. At least the man was still talking.

"You're a friend of Jonah's, you say?"

"Yes, sir. I live in Winter Haven, Florida."

"Ah. Pretty state, Florida. Is he still a doctor?"

"Yes. And a very fine one. I'm —" she was

about to say *one of his patients,* but decided it might not be wise to say too much. "I'm a friend," she said again simply. "And I believe Jonah needs you."

The sound of another whisper, a woman's voice, buzzed over the telephone line. "Who is it? What's she saying? Where's Jonah now?"

Muffled sounds clotted the transmission, then the line cleared. "Miss, I really don't know what we can do for you. Jonah disgraced this community years ago, and he's never been repentant. He knows he's welcome here anytime he wants to come back, but until he confesses his sin, I'm afraid we can't welcome him home."

"What do you mean, he disgraced the community?" The words slipped from Jacquelyn's tongue before she had a chance to find a more diplomatic phrase.

"Oak Woods paid half the bill for Jonah's medical schooling," the preacher explained. "He was supposed to come back here and practice medicine in our town. But then he got into that trouble at the University Hospital, and the town decided they didn't want him."

"But, Pastor Martin," Jacquelyn protested, "no one ever proved Jonah guilty. When he left, the girl let the matter drop."

"She was probably eager to put things behind her," the minister went on. "I asked Jonah point-blank if he did anything to that girl, and he wouldn't answer me. Now if you hadn't done anything, wouldn't you rise up to defend yourself?"

Not if I was stunned that my loved ones didn't trust me. Not if my own parents questioned me, and the entire town was eager to cast me off.

An odd coldness settled upon Jacquelyn, a sickening and darkly textured sensation like a gust of foul wind from a Dumpster. *This* is where Jonah had lost the joy of his faith. Not in some big city hospital where strangers pointed and gossiped behind his back, but at home, within his own family. She had felt alienated when her father couldn't face her illness, but Jonah had been ostracized from an entire community.

"Reverend Martin," she said, speaking slowly and distinctly into the telephone. "Your son is innocent of those charges, I'd bet my life on it. And you have the power, today, to help him stop running from what has been the single most destructive event of his life. It was difficult when that woman accused him of sexual harassment, I know, but you and your people turned your backs on him and — well, I don't think he'll ever be the man God wants him to be unless you do something to help."

She gripped the phone tighter in her hand and turned to stare at her own reflection in the mirror. Her eyes were like searchlights; she only wished she could shine them into the souls of Reverend and Mrs. Jonathan Martin to expose the wrong they'd committed, intentionally or not.

"If you love your son, Reverend Martin," she said, her voice echoing with entreaty, "you need to call him this afternoon at the number I will give you. Please, pray about this, and take down the number. If you care for your son at all, you must call."

The minister's voice, when he spoke again, was stifled and unnatural — he probably wasn't used to strange women calling from out of the blue and telling him how to handle his son. "Well, ma'am, thank you for your concern, but I can't see that I can do anything —"

The woman's insistent whisper interrupted, the telephone was muffled again, and then a moment later the preacher came back on the line. "Give me the number," he said, his voice soft and clear. "We'll pray about this."

By noon, Jonah had taken a two-hour nap,

showered, driven to the office, seen three patients, checked the charts of a half-dozen others and noted that on his calendar Dr. Kastner had penciled in a meeting between two and three o'clock. "For your information," the sticky note on his calendar said, "Dr. Ivan Pressman, Assistant to the Hospital Administrator, will be sitting in."

Of course. If you're going to ask an associate to leave, you have to have a member of the hospital brass on hand. One doctor didn't peremptorily ask another to resign unless there was reasonable cause and that cause was attested to by someone in authority.

Jonah lowered his head to his hands and rubbed his throbbing temples. Like an old wound that ached on a rainy day, his head pounded whenever he realized he had to move on. Neither his excellent work nor the well-being of his patients mattered in this politically-correct climate. Just the shadow of sexual harassment was enough to send most hospital bigwigs scrambling to cover their hides. Well, enough was enough. At that two o'clock meeting today, he'd announce his intention to resign before they could fling those ancient charges in his face.

"Jonah?"

He looked up, startled by the sound of

Jacquelyn's voice. He hadn't expected her to even come in, and yet there she stood in her uniform, a patient's chart in her hand. He looked away, trying to hide his inner misery from her probing stare. This morning her honesty had warmed his heart, but it would take more than a woman's love to set things right in his life. He would only bring her pain if he stayed. He had brought nothing but dashed dreams and disillusionment to everyone who had ever loved him.

"Can I help you?" he asked, feeling guilty and selfish. Torment was eating at him from the inside, and yet he faced her with the most detached and professional expression he could muster.

"Yes," she whispered, her eyes full of life, pain and unquenchable warmth. "Irene Gordon — do you want her to follow the AC times four or the CMF times six? There's no note on the chart."

He raked his hand through his hair. "Let's get her through it quickly," he answered, trying to focus his scattered thoughts on the practice of medicine. "We'll go with the Adriamycin and Cytoxan every three weeks for four doses. Tell her we'll begin next week."

Jacquelyn nodded. "Thank you. I'll make a note of it, and you can sign the chart later." *Because you'll still be here.*

He heard her unspoken thought as clearly as if she'd said it, and he had to look away again. How could he deny the faith of this loving woman? By heaven above, God knew he loved her, too, but because he cared he couldn't stay.

He glanced at his watch. One-fifty. In ten minutes he'd receive his marching orders from Kastner and Company, and nothing had yet come through from Eric Elrod in California. It would be nice to tell the Chambers-Wyatt folks that he'd already found a place. *You don't have to ask me to resign. I was planning to, anyway. I'm beginning a new job in Los Angeles next month. . . .*

He picked up the phone and punched in Eric's number.

Jacquelyn paused at the reception desk, ready to call the next patient, but Gaynel's voice stopped her cold. "I'm sorry, sir, but Dr. Martin is on another line. Can I take a message and have him return your call?"

"Gaynel!" Jacquelyn hissed, leaning over the desk. "No! Don't let him hang up!"

"What?" The receptionist's face crinkled in confusion.

"Keep him on the line! I'll explain later!"

Without pausing, Jacquelyn tossed the chart on the desk and raced down the hall, pausing outside Jonah's office. The door stood open; she could see him sitting in his office chair, the telephone to his ear, one foot propped on the desk. The clock behind him said one fifty-three.

"Jonah." Jacquelyn made a slashing gesture across her throat. "Hang up. You have an important call on hold."

Surprisingly, he did as she ordered. "It's okay, I was on hold anyway," he said, offering her a tentative smile. "But maybe that incoming call is the one I'm expecting."

She waited a moment to see if Gaynel would forward the call, then sighed in relief when the phone rang. One fifty-four.

Jonah picked up the phone. "Dr. Martin."

She slipped around the corner and leaned against the wall, then closed her eyes and whispered a prayer. She wasn't absolutely sure that the call was the one *she* expected, but she certainly hoped so. If God was going to work things out, He didn't have to wait until the last minute.

During the next half hour, Jacquelyn joined Lauren and Stacy in tending to patients while doctors Kastner and Pressman fretted aloud in Kastner's office. Apparently Jonah

Martin had closed and locked his office door shortly after receiving a phone call just before two, and though the nursing staff could hear his muffled voice through the door, no one had any idea what was going on.

"Jacquelyn," Dr. Kastner called, his face bright with exasperation, "can't you get him in here? This is highly irregular, not to mention rude. He knew about this meeting, and he shouldn't keep us waiting."

"I'm sure his reasons are important," Jacquelyn said, giving Dr. Pressman a careful smile. But he showed no sign of understanding, and her stomach knotted under his withering glare.

At two thirty-five, Gaynel buzzed the nurses' station and told Lauren that the phone call to Jonah Martin's office had disconnected. His mysterious conversation had terminated, though she had no idea whom he'd been talking to. The caller had not been willing to leave a message, nor had he identified himself.

Lauren whispered Gaynel's message to Stacy and Jacquelyn, and Jacquelyn felt her spark of hope grow dim when Jonah's door remained closed. That caller had either been his father or his friend from California. Jonah was still inside, either further hardening his heart . . . or finalizing his plans to move to the west coast.

She turned back to her work at the nurses' station, telling herself that she'd be okay. If Jonah left she would face the harsh realities of loneliness, but she had faced them before and survived. Daphne had written that God wanted Jacquelyn to be His child, and she could be that. Simple. Dependent. Trusting. It would be wonderful to share her life with Jonah Martin, but perhaps God had only meant for him to touch her life in this short season.

In the silence of the hallway, the sudden click of a latch snapped like a gunshot. All three nurses stopped in their tracks and turned to face Jonah's office. Jacquelyn leaned against the wall, suddenly drained of will and thought.

The door opened and Jonah stepped out into the hall, his eyes snapping with — what? His eyes sought and found her, raking her with a fiercely possessive and accusing look, then suddenly he stood a breath away.

He touched her cheek in a wistful gesture. "My smart Jacquelyn," he whispered, the ragged words for her ears alone. "How could you have known? I didn't even understand."

Shock caused her words to wedge in her throat. "Was that your father? On the phone?"

He nodded as his reddened eyes smiled down into hers. "All is forgiven. And understood. And I'm going to go in there and tell Dr. Kastner and Dr. Pressman and anyone else who cares to know that I have done nothing wrong. And if they don't believe me, they can contact the UVA Hospital. They can even call the woman who started it all. I don't care. Because I know — I believe — things are going to work out. I'm done with running."

Jacquelyn felt her heart turn over the way it always did when he looked at her. "But how — what happened?"

"My father," he said, ignoring the other nurses as he took her hand and pulled her into his office, "called me today for the first time in years. And he begged my forgiveness, Jackie. He said that he'd been wrong to doubt me. At first I couldn't believe it. I thought someone was playing some kind of crazy joke. But he was sincere, and he was broken. He and Mother were both crying."

Despite the tears in his eyes, his mood seemed buoyant. "Suddenly, I felt the walls around my own heart fall down. Just like the old Bible story, you know, the walls of

Jericho. Seven times they walked around before the walls fell, and for seven years I'd harbored bitterness because my own folks didn't believe in me."

"Oh, thank God! I was praying for you!" Tears of relief came in a rush so strong they shook Jacquelyn's body, but Jonah held her hands so she couldn't wipe them away. She stood there, tears streaming down her face, as Jonah explained how he and his parents prayed, and wept, and laughed together.

"Before he hung up, Dad said that a friend of mine had called him this morning," Jonah said, a gentle softness in his voice. "And I know only you could have believed in me so much. Though I'll never understand how you knew I needed to talk to him."

"I know you love him," Jacquelyn answered, her heart reacting to his gaze. "You talk about him all the time, and yet you never seem to talk *to* him." She released a short laugh. "That's just how I used to treat God. But Daphne showed me how much I needed him . . . and then I knew what you were missing, and where you lost the joy of your faith. You left it in your father's house."

"Lucky me, to find a woman who is wise as well as beautiful." Jonah swept her into the circle of his arms. "I don't deserve you,

Jacquelyn Wilkes, but I thank God I found you."

She could feel his uneven breathing on her cheek as he held her close, then Dr. Kastner's voice rang out and interrupted the magic moment.

"Doctor Martin! We have been waiting for over half an hour!"

Jonah did not let her go. "Then you can wait a moment more," he called, his lips brushing Jacquelyn's cheek. He looked down at her and grinned. "I never have been one to stick to a schedule. And I'd like to take a moment to properly kiss you, but first I really should say something to these gentlemen in the hall."

"By all means," Jacquelyn said, laughing.

Keeping his arm around her, Jonah turned toward the startled doctors and nurses in the hallway. "Gentlemen, I apologize for my tardiness, but I hope you'll understand that something of an urgent nature has come up. And, by the way, if you are concerned with rumors regarding my past, I suggest you contact two parties — first, the administrator at the University of Virginia Hospital. You'll see that I was never formally charged with anything and I suspect that a certain nurse there has managed to cause trouble for more than one physician. And second, my lawyer. If you're going to seriously entertain old gossip, he'll be interested in discussing the ramifications of a libel suit against this hospital. Because I assure you, gentlemen, the rumors are *not* true."

The dumbfounded doctors stared at each other as Stacy's eyes widened.

Content to ignore the others, Jacquelyn looked up into her doctor's eyes. "You know," she said, twining her arms around his neck, "I think your reputation is quite safe. I can think of several patients who would sooner give up their wigs and anti-nausea medications than their beloved Dr. Martin."

"What about you?" He swallowed tightly as his gaze dropped into hers. "What would it take to make you give up on me?"

She paused, knowing his meaning went far beyond those simple words. "I'll never give up on you. Whether we have ten years or fifty, whether they are good times or sad. I don't think I could ever be complete without you."

"As I could never be home," he answered, "anywhere but here." He paused for a moment, his eyes alight with hope, love and a hint of mischief. "How can I be so blessed? I have a great job and I'm about to gain a wife with a dog —"

"Who'll give you unlimited hugs and snuggles," she finished. She lowered her voice to an intimate whisper. "Best of all, I don't even chew shoes."

And then, while Stacy, Lauren and Gaynel applauded, Jacquelyn quivered at the sweet tenderness of Jonah's lips. Dr. Baked Alaska, indeed, she thought, returning his slow and thoughtful kisses with all the love in her heart.

DISCUSSION QUESTIONS

1. Have you known anyone with breast cancer? How did her experience compare with Jacquelyn's?
2. If you were undergoing treatment for cancer, would you want Jacquelyn to be your nurse? Why or why not?
3. What do you look for in a doctor? Is Jonah Wilkes the sort of doctor you'd like to have, or would you prefer someone more detached and professional?
4. In most romances, the prospect of true love must be tested before it is affirmed. What are the issues and situations that test the budding emotion between Jacquelyn and Jonah?
5. Jonah tries to outrun rumors that could destroy his career. Is it possible to run away from such rumors? What should you do instead?
6. Daphne Redfield is an encouragement for Jacquelyn. How did she glorify God

through her death?

7. Do you believe it is always God's will for His children to be healed from illness? Why or why not?

8. Neither Jonah's nor Jacquelyn's parents are terribly supportive in their children's struggles, but it's often difficult for parents to know how to deal with the problems of adult children. What could those parents have done to help Jacquelyn through her cancer treatment and Jonah through his career crisis? Why did they hold back?

9. Who was your favorite character and why? Which character did you relate to the most?

10. Did this novel change your outlook on life in any way? Will you be different for having read it? How?

11. If the author were sitting across from you now, what question would you like to ask her?

AN INTERVIEW WITH ANGELA HUNT

Q: Some of the situations in this book are so detailed, I have to ask: Have you had breast cancer?

A: You're not the first to ask. While I haven't had breast cancer, I have had a suspicious lump cut out, so I'm acquainted with that anxious uncertainty and the coldness of the operating table.

Breast cancer has touched my life — my husband lost his mother to the disease, and my mother lost her best friend. At this moment, one of my friends has been given six months to live because her cancer has spread from her breast to her bones. But you know what? She's living her life to the fullest, making preparation for her heavenly home-going and telling people about Jesus. When I look at her, I am filled with admiration and I think, *You know . . . maybe time is the silver lining of cancer.* We are all terminal in a sense, but cancer forces us to look at life from an eternal perspective.

Q: Are the protocols described in this book in common use?

A: Breast cancer treatment is an ever-changing field, but I owe tremendous thanks to Beth Delassandro, R.N., and Dr. Robert H. McCreary, professionals at the Florida Community Cancer Center in Clearwater, Florida. Not only did they allow me to come to the center, observe and ask questions, but they also reviewed the most recent edition of this book to make certain our treatments were as up-to-date as possible.

Q: What advice do you have for women who might be at high risk for breast cancer?

A: There are several situations that place women at higher risk for breast cancer: a family history, for instance, and never having given birth. The best advice for all of us in those categories (as well as for those who aren't) is to perform monthly breast self-examinations and have an annual mammogram after age forty. The good news is that the breast cancer mortality rate is dropping. It is lower in 2006 than it was when I wrote this book in 1996.

If you find a breast lump in your monthly BSE, see your physician as soon as possible. The lump may be benign (mine was), but if it isn't, the best weapon against breast cancer is early detection and treatment.

Q: Do you have any advice for the woman who is currently in treatment for breast cancer?

A: First, I'd urge her not to panic if her doctor's treatment doesn't conform to what she's read in this book. Breast cancer treatment is an ever-changing field and protocols are personalized for each patient.

Second, I'd urge her to live life as fully as possible. None of us has a guarantee of tomorrow; all of us depend upon the Lord's grace for each breath we inhale.

Finally, with every atom of my being I know this is true: God is sovereign over everything and everyone. The challenges you face are not bigger or stronger than God. He has brought you to this time, place and situation for reasons you may not understand, but He does. You can rest in that. You can trust Him with your past, present and future.

Q: And if your readers would like to reach you?

A: They can contact me through my Web page: www.angelahuntbooks.com. I'd love to hear from them.

ABOUT THE AUTHOR

Christy Award winner **Angela Hunt** writes books for readers who have learned to expect the unexpected. With over three million copies of her books sold worldwide, she is the best-selling author of *The Tale of Three Trees, The Note, Unspoken,* and more than 100 other titles.

She and her husband make their home in Florida with mastiffs. One of their dogs was featured on *Live with Regis and Kelly* as the second-largest canine in America.

Readers may visit her Web site at www.angelahuntbooks.com.